THE CHAMELEON KILLER MYSTERY

SEEMS DETECTIVE SERIES
BOOK 4

GINA CHEYNE

First Published in 2023 by Fly Fizzi Ltd
Pyers Croft
Compton, Chichester
West Sussex PO18 9EX
www.ginacheyne.com

Cover design by Kari Brownlie

ISBN 978-1-915138-12-5 The Chameleon Killer Mystery ebook

ISBN 978-1-915138-13-2 The Chameleon Killer Mystery paperback

ISBN 978-1-915138-14-9 The Chameleon Killer Mystery hardback

❋ Created with Vellum

This book is dedicated to Andrew Healey
Wheelchair warrior

I must have liberty, with as large a charter
as I please

Virginia Hall, WW2 spy, in her 1924 school yearbook at the
age of eighteen

THE CHAMELEON KILLER MYSTERY

A SeeMs Detective Agency Mystery

By Gina Cheyne

CHAPTER 1
PRIOR PLANNING PREVENTS PISS-UPS

As the car stopped, Victoria looked up at the sky. It was clear with a light wind: a perfectly lovely afternoon for flying the Tiger Moth. A perfect evening for dying? Perhaps. She glanced at Stevie, who stared back emotionless.

'So,' said Victoria, 'now you know why I told you everything?'

Stevie was silent, her eyes moving restlessly around the car and stopping on the gun in Victoria's hand. Was she scared? Or planning? Looking for something in the car to hit her with? Victoria wasn't sure. But a Triumph Spitfire is such a small car it seemed unlikely there was a weapon hidden here.

'I think you do!' Victoria allowed her voice to be triumphant. 'And we are going down as one. Tonight we will be together ... where, do you think? Cosy in Hell? Greeted by Neil perhaps. I doubt Heaven has room for people like us. By the way, don't think of staying alive by tripping me over, hoping the gun will kill me by mistake. I've left all the information on my phone. The police will enjoy reading it all, I imagine.'

She licked her lips, her gun hand completely steady.

Victoria watched Stevie's gaze flicker over the weapon and back to her face. 'Pretty pistol,' Stevie said, her voice little more than a whisper. Victoria smiled. She manoeuvred her legs out of the small car and picked up the cushion she'd been sitting on. She tucked it under the arm leaning on the walking stick.

Stevie's eyebrows shot up. 'You won't need that. Although the Tiger has bucket seats, I have cushions in the parachute bays.'

Victoria snorted. Stevie was such an out-and-out pilot—even her terminology was that of an aviator. Obscure to anyone else, a secret language for them, letting everyone know they were as unified as the Masons. Anyone else would have said, *there already is a cushion.*

'Very thoughtful, darling. Thank you. But this is for my back. With my withered legs it helps to be pushed forward so I can use my muscles more effectively on the pedals, like a taut spring.'

Stevie put her hand across her mouth. Victoria could see Stevie's mechanical mind working through the details. Transferring her knowledge of machines to the human body and understanding its movements.

Victoria leant on her stick and slowly moved down the path to the Owly Vale flying strip, dragging her withered legs, the gun still steady in her hand. She motioned Stevie to walk slightly ahead of her.

As the path weaved past the house, Victoria saw a woman's shape framed in the long Georgian window. The woman waved a wrinkled hand.

Victoria's stomach made a nervous leap. 'Who's that?'

'My mother. She has dementia.'

'OK.'

At the bottom of the garden, they reached the hangar, and Victoria collapsed onto a low wall. This was the furthest she'd walked for a long time.

Stevie opened the electric doors, dived into the hangar to fetch the plane and angled the trolley under the Tiger's skid, lifting the machine with the other hand. She pushed the whole thing out onto the concrete apron as though it weighed no more than a bicycle, instead of half a ton.

Victoria watched, hunched on the wall. Regaining her strength. Stevie looked about twelve years old, Victoria thought, with her pixie haircut and her wiry frame. Hard to believe she was a first officer at British Airways and an important member of the SeeMs Detective team. Victoria herself was slim, but compared to Stevie she was a giant.

She gave a low whistle. 'Woohoo. Did you put this all down yourself? Build the hangar? All the concreting? Even the electric doors?'

'Yes.'

'You really will be a loss to society, won't you? Shame.'

Stevie put the trolley neatly back into the hangar by the wall and indicated the way to climb into the biplane along the reinforced portions of the linen-covered wings.

'You'd better sit in the front seat,' she said gruffly.

Victoria spat. 'Pah! You must think I'm green. I'm sitting where I can see what you are up to. I know there's only a radio in the back, not in the front. You won't be able to call for help, and I'm certainly not going to. Now I'm going to show you how brilliantly Victoria flies. Even after all this time.'

Stevie said nothing.

Victoria clambered into the back cockpit of the Tiger Moth, keeping her gun trained on the younger woman.

'Switches on.'

Stevie pulled the propellor and the obedient little craft started immediately. She pulled out the chocks, storing them by the trolley, then climbed into the front cockpit with a single lithe movement.

Victoria stored the gun in her flying suit, then, smiling slightly, she pulled out a second, a toy gun, and placed it in the map pouch. When Stevie saw that she had been fooled by a toy gun, she was going to be so embarrassed. Victoria chuckled quietly, thinking how angry and upset Stevie would feel. How she wished she was there to see her pain.

Victoria taxied away from the hangar and along a neat grass alleyway to where Stevie had mown a long wide strip with an orange windsock on one side. She turned the Tiger Moth to face into the wind.

Taking off, Victoria climbed to a thousand feet. Although her damaged legs vibrated on the pedals, unused to the pressure, she was surprised how quickly her 'flying muscles' returned. However, she knew they would not last very long, but then it wasn't going to be very long before they died.

She began circling, getting used to the feel of the light machine, so different from the airliners she used to fly. Laughing, she pulled back the power and dived down to the level of the trees sinuously. Propelling the machine low over the grass, rising for the bumps in the field, pulling straight up to avoid the trees, nipping over the branches, hearing the leaves tickling the underside of the canvas as she straightened up.

'Yay! Yay! Yay!' She whooped ecstatically down the

elderly speaking tube. 'I'd forgotten how much fun it was to fly.'

Once again she made a low fast pass over the fields, using the speed to climb straight up into the sky with an Immelmann turn at the top. 'Wee hee! To think we could have done this every day.'

Stevie said nothing.

Victoria adjusted the pitch of the nose and began climbing to height. One thousand. Two thousand. She levelled at three thousand feet and smiled at the country-side spread out like toys in the sunshine.

'I've always wondered,' she purred into the intercom. 'How long can you stay upside down before the fuel runs out of the engine? Haven't you?'

'No,' said Stevie.

Of course, Stevie knew the answer—she knew abso-lutely everything about all the machines she flew. She could have told Victoria that as there were no fuel pumps, the Tiger could only fly upside down for seven to ten seconds before the engine stopped. She could also have told Victoria that the seat belts in the back were frayed and about to break, but she remained silent.

'Now,' said Victoria, 'which way to enter? I think I'll do a loop or two first.'

Stevie said nothing.

Victoria dived the Tiger Moth to increase the speed, pulled up a little too sharply and then eased off too early. The G-forces pressed them into their seats as the machine fell out of the loop and slipped to the left, stuttering slightly.

'Oh! Lost my touch! One side stronger than the other,' she muttered to herself. 'Didn't compensate enough. Better do it again.'

This time she entered too gently, and the willing Tiger

only just staggered over the top and collapsed down the other side.

'Oh dear!' she said. 'No prizes for that one.'

She dived again.

'Right,' she muttered to herself, 'now, somewhere between the two.'

This time, she gave just the right amount of back pressure on the stick, kept it central, despite her aching legs, and the little Moth danced over the top of the loop and came smoothly out into level flight.

'Perfect,' she crowed. 'What a way to go!'

To think she hadn't lost her touch after all this time. She was such a loss to the flying world. If only! If only!

'Right, and now, the denouement. Thank you, Stevie, for being my friend. Had life been kinder to me, we would have got to know each other, probably spent happy lives together. All I ever wanted to do was fly on silver wings and doing it with you would have been perfect. Isn't it sad that one drunken evening, one drunken man, took that all away from us?'

Stevie said nothing.

Victoria undid her seat belt, letting the two pieces fall to the side. She rolled the Tiger Moth upside down and counted, holding herself in the machine with her hands.

'One, two, three, four, five, six, seven ...'

The engine stopped.

The world was silent.

For a moment Victoria held herself, suspended between life and death.

Then she let go.

Screaming. She fell.

Looking up, she watched the plane disappear above her. One. Two. Three.

Victoria pulled the rip cord. Her parachute blossomed above her.

She laughed.

In the sky Stevie was righting the machine, too busy to see what Victoria was doing, fighting to land a plane with a dead engine in an area of small fields intersected by trees and avoiding the village of Owly Vale.

Victoria laughed again. Let them imagine she was dead. Let them believe what they liked.

They wouldn't recognise her when they saw her again. They had no idea of her genius. Her ability with disguise. Not even Stevie understood she was a chameleon amongst humans.

Prior Planning Prevents Piss-Poor Performance! And her planning was perfect.

CHAPTER 2
SPINNERS, A NIGHTCLUB
FOR ALL COMERS

In Owly Vale, blackberries might be withering on the branches and hawthorn berries glowing red, but in London there were few indications of the arrival of autumn.

Caroline sat in her office, scanning the nightclub floor below her through the two-way mirror. Below her, at the bar, Stevie sat silently drinking lime juice. A regular, an airline pilot and one of the SeeMs detectives, Stevie came here before every long flight and always sat alone.

Today, though, was different. Stevie was edgy, glancing around, playing with her glass. She seemed, Caroline thought, to be expecting something to happen.

As Caroline watched, the basement car park door opened, and a woman walked in. She stopped and looked around like someone visiting a new place.

Stevie stood up. The woman gave a little wave, and for a moment Caroline thought it looked a little like Victoria, former owner of the bar and Stevie's girlfriend. But that was impossible; she was dead.

Caroline's phone rang and she turned away from the

mirror. When she again concentrated on the scene below, the unknown woman had joined Stevie at the bar. Caroline, who had spent many years observing people, decided they were strangers with something in common. Possibly flying. Possibly something deeper. But watching them gave no extra clues and her eyes slowly crept around the room.

The floor was filling up and the barmen were getting busy. As usual there were a sprinkling of wheelchairs, some folded, some left open. It had never occurred to Caroline when she first heard about the nightclub that people in wheelchairs would come to a place like this, but now she wondered why she ever had such thoughts. There were other people too. People who would normally be refused entry: oddballs, troublemakers. Here they were encouraged. Victoria had been totally sympathetic to anyone slightly different from the norm. She also employed very good staff.

Caroline's two favourite barmen, Tom and Oscar, were working tonight and both were running to keep up. Tom glanced up briefly and Caroline smiled, even though she knew the nature of the two-way window meant he could not see her. The glass had been put in by Victoria, who had left Caroline the nightclub—and a large amount of debt—in her will, even though they had only met once. A surprise that delighted Caroline but did nothing for her failing marriage.

Caroline looked down at the bar again. Oscar, the largest barman, was serving Stevie and the unknown woman. She had a particular affection for him, perhaps because he was a head shorter than her—not surprising as Caroline was six foot tall—but at least twice as wide, completely bald and loved to laugh. A huge, belly-filling laugh that filled the whole club. He was doing it now, talking to Stevie and the unknown woman. The woman, Caroline thought, judging from the top of her head, seemed amused and even Stevie's shoulders were shaking slightly. Oscar was good for people.

A sudden noise at the other end of the bar startled her and she looked away from Oscar. Her stomach tightened.

It was Rupert, and he was causing trouble, again. What was he doing here?

She heard his voice flying around the bar and up to the roof.

'Whatja mean I've sad se'nuf?'

Anywhere else his loud, slurred voice would have turned heads, but here no one even glanced his way. 'I's sardly started.'

As Caroline watched, Tom approached him, his manner clearly appeasing. Tom had a natural tact which Victoria had honed and improved. But even though Caroline trusted Tom, she shouldn't use him like this. This was her problem, not his. She forced herself out of the office and walked down the spiral staircase, approaching the man quietly as though he was a nervous animal.

'Rupert,' she said gently, 'how nice to see you.'

He turned towards her so fast she could feel the wind of his movement. More, she could smell it! Alcohol fumes blasted from his body.

'Roo-pet! Sow nice to see you!' he imitated her voice. 'Bitch! You could see me every day if you hadn't taken our daughter and run. Look what you've done. You've turned me into a drunk.'

Her body shivered, but she pinched her thumb, a trick her therapist, Anthony, had given her for stressful moments.

'Come into my office, Rupert. Let's talk about what is bothering you.'

She thought he might refuse, but, now flipping into the

more maudlin stage of his inebriation, he turned and followed her lethargically up the winding stairs.

As he clumped up behind her, Caroline thought it was like a repeat of history. Once before, Victoria had taken a drunk up to this same office. However, Caroline was not planning to kill her ex.

'I got the decree nisi today,' he said as they reached the office and he flopped onto the nearest chair. 'Let's get rid of it. Get married again. I need you, darling, and Lagertha. You are my family.'

Tears dripped down Rupert's face and he slumped, misery in human form. 'I can't live without you, darling. I can't.'

Caroline felt a wave of anxiety stream through her veins. She did sympathise. His parents had been unfair to him, just as hers had to her, and having to go back to live with them must be wearing for him.

Her shoulders sagged. Perhaps she could give him one more chance. He did love having her and Lagertha to lean on. They were his support system, just like Anthony, her therapist, had been hers.

She moved towards him, one hand outstretched. He flinched. He jumped up and his hands came up in fists, his face in a sneer.

She gasped and fell back. 'What?'

'Don't you try your tricks on me, little missy, oh so sweet. Everyone thinks you're so lovely, but I know the truth!'

She felt the hard surface of the desk behind her and looked away from Rupert to refocus. In desperation, she dropped her gaze over into the nightclub. Two big-footed women were dancing together like rival tom cats sizing each other up: strong, spitting women. She and Rupert were like that: dancers, fighters. Love and hate. Hate and love. But she had to think of Lagertha, to protect her too.

She pulled herself back into the present. The aggressive stage had died, and Rupert was now softly logical.

'Look, Caroline, I'm trying. I've moved out of my parents' and got myself a flat. I'm looking for a job. I'm going to change. It will be different. Come and see my new flat. Bring Lagertha round. She'd like to see where her poor old dad is living now, miserable without her.'

She pinched her thumb. Rupert had promised fifty, a hundred times, to get a job and then, the one time he got an interview, he turned up late and drunk. He wasn't short listed.

'I'm sorry, Rupert, I tried. I tried for ten years to be the wife you wanted. After Lagertha was born I tried even harder, but nothing worked ... Well, that's not true. I worked, endlessly, while you did nothing except write that bestseller that never happened, drink and shoot pheasants with your mates. You certainly managed to do that.'

His face infused with red as though a wave of fury was passing through him. When he spoke, his voice was harsh and ragged.

'Nag, nag, nag,' he said. 'You ruined my life. If you hadn't nagged me so endlessly, if you'd been a real wife who loved me and looked after me, I'd not've been forced back to the bottle. You silly bitch! You ruined everything with your middle-class work ethic. Your duty! Dooty pooty! Tooty frooty!'

He roared with laughter, his mood flipping again. 'My wife's an old frooty full of pooty dooty!'

She tried to talk, to be heard above his mockery, but he was shouting too loud. Even the drinkers below looked up, briefly.

When he took a gulp of air, she spoke, quietly, trying not to rival his shouts. 'There you are. Proof you are better without me! But I will let you have access to Lagertha ... I ...'

'Oh ho!' His voice whipped like a flick knife. 'You'll *let* me have access indeed. Listen to her!'

He turned away from her and addressed an unseen crowd.

'Listen to that fool, that conniving two-timing whore. Watch my lips. Many have underestimated me, none of them made that mistake twice. I'm going to get custody and never let you see your daughter. Never! You are a bad influence. And I will win!'

Again he addressed his assembled admirers:

'You know why? Because this woman, this wife, this mother is a freak. A mad woman. Ask me ...'

He swung his arms out to his devotees like a Trumpista.

'Ask me how long the imbecilic has been in therapy ... What? Do I hear five or six years? No, this half-wit has been in therapy for twenty-four years ... Or so she told me, although really it was just an excuse to shag lover boy, wasn't it!'

He turned back to his ex-wife.

'I know you followed him home ... you went into his flat and then all the sex started ... At least I know Lagertha is mine. I've seen the DNA tests ...'

Caroline stared at him, her body quivering unexpectedly.

'You've what? You've done DNA tests on her? And yourself? Why? How? I'm sure that is illegal.'

He ignored her and stormed on, his voice getting louder.

'Yes, bitch, and on you too, and your frigging mother ... seems we are all just one big happy family ... and we're staying that way with or without you ...'

He jumped up from the chair and stepped towards her, and she shrank back. But he turned and made his way towards the door. Then stopped. Still facing the door he yelled, 'I'll see you in court and your lover boy ... he sure as hell isn't Lagertha's father. That I knew already. She didn't get her beautiful blonde hair from that ...!'

He didn't say the word, but Caroline knew it was flying silently through his lips like a spray of spit.

He stormed out, slamming the door like a teenager in a strop.

Caroline stared at the door. Was it really shuddering, or was that her imagination? What did this all mean? Had he threatened her? And he'd been doing DNA tests. Why? When she first asked for a divorce, he didn't really seem to care. He'd already been seeing other women, he said. She was a frigid cow, he said. And they'd hardly had sex since Lagertha was born.

He was serious. He wanted to take Lagertha away from her. Why? He'd never spent any time with Lagertha even while Caroline was trying to pretend they were a family. Was it because he wanted revenge on his wife?

She looked down at the club floor and saw Rupert leaving. He stopped briefly to talk to someone, and for a moment Caroline's hands tightened, but he just said some words and moved on. The bouncers monitored him, but he left quietly by the street door.

Stevie and the unknown woman, Caroline noted absently, had already left.

Eventually, Caroline went back to her desk. She tried to read the insurance documents, but the words spun aimlessly around the page. Her body felt as though she had eaten something heavy and it was sitting unrelentingly on her stomach. Her head collapsed onto her arms, and she burst into tears.

All she had ever wanted was a happy family and even when she made compromises to get it, it was taken away from her. How could Rupert do this to her?

Her hand itched to call Anthony. She pulled her phone out of her pocket. Got up his number. She breathed deeply and then she deleted the number.

No!

She would do this alone. No one could help her. She would do it herself.

She got up and went into the little bathroom complex that Victoria had built next to the office.

She washed her face, redid her makeup and stared at herself in the mirror, gritting her teeth at her image to make herself feel braver. She would not let Rupert take Lagertha. She would do whatever she could to stop him.

CHAPTER 3
PERFECT SHADOWS

Leaving the nightclub, Rupert danced a few elated steps. He'd shown Caroline he was someone to be reckoned with. He'd shown that two-faced weasel wife the truth and she hadn't like his side of the coin. He danced down the street with joy, then stopped.

'Rupert, wait.'

It sounded like a request, but he knew it was a command. He turned and saw the woman in the wheelchair he had just talked to in the club had followed him out. His shoulders drooped.

'Drina?'

'How did it go? Did she see you were serious?'

'Of course. It doesn't take a lot to get Caroline into a tail spin. She has the confidence of a mouse on speed. I know how to put her in her place, silly blonde who never had an original thought. If she hadn't listened to that Big Dick, she'd still be my nice little wife.'

'Ah, yes, Anthony,' said Drina. 'Everybody's favourite therapist.'

Rupert laughed. 'Yup, Chekov was right. It is just a play on words. Therapist is only The Rapist in another form!'

'Nabokov.'

'Whatever, some foreigner. Together we will take them down. I think we might even suggest Cat was involved too. Do you know her? Caroline's mother, tall bossy whore, thinks she's God's gift to the world of detection just because she speaks a few of those dago parlances.'

'I do and she's half French.'

Rupert stopped speaking suddenly and stared at Drina. 'So, you know my esteemed ex-mother-in-law? How?'

Drina sneered. 'Yes. I know her. We are old ... *friends.*'

He waited hopefully, but Drina said nothing more.

'OK. Whatever ... anyway, I think we might suggest she was in collusion, that she was Anthony's lover too. A right little family throuple. We are going to sing in court. We will get alimony from Caroline as well as her child. We might even suggest that there was some child abuse. Perhaps we can get her locked up. Great!'

Drina frowned. 'I think it would be more sensible to stick to the facts. Judges probably don't have much imagination. I would just stick to the fact that Caroline was seen going into Anthony's apartment, and that Lagertha was home alone. That and the twenty-plus years of therapy will give you a strong case against her.'

'As long as she suffers as much as I have. She took away my manhood. She turned me into a drunk. She should be punished. I am the avenging wolf!'

He bared his teeth. Opening his eyes wide, he gave a long howl of triumph.

'What will you do when you get Lagertha?' asked Drina softly. 'How will you look after her if you are going to get a job? And you *will* have to get a job to support her.'

Rupert shrugged. 'My parents will look after her.'

'Oh yes?' said Drina, driving her wheelchair forward with a sharp thrust. 'Your lovely supportive parents. Who already have sister Angela's brood to look after.'

He turned angrily towards her. 'Shut up, Drina.'

'Umm, I wonder what other little secrets they didn't tell you!' said Drina, tilting her smiling face and looking up at him. 'What else they knew but didn't think to share!'

His face flared red, and he hit his fist on his hand. 'The bastards! But you can shut up or you'll feel this knuckle sandwich too, crippy. So then, darling Caroline will have to give me alimony. She's got that club now. Bet it makes loads of money.'

Drina wheeled her chair silently along the uneven pavement beside Rupert, manoeuvring dexterously through the bumps.

When they reached Drina's converted car, she transferred herself into the driver's seat, folding and storing her wheelchair in the back with practised arms. Rupert lit a cigarette and watched her, leaning on the side of the car and brooding about his ex-wife.

'OK,' she said, leaning out the window, 'you'll come to my house tomorrow at nine thirty? We need to be at the lawyer's at ten a.m.'

'Yeah, sure.'

Rupert shrugged and walked off down the road. Drina watched him briefly, then, getting her hooked stick, she reached out and shut the car door. She drove off towards Chelsea. Rupert walked on to King's Cross.

Even though King's Cross was now insanely smart, there was one small corner of crumbling architecture still left from the days when it was the base for homeless drug takers. Here Rupert climbed up the six floors to his flat. Wonderful view, the estate agent had said. Incredible price for such a lovely place. So central. Just perfect for a young, newly single man.

The price was undeniably good value. Perhaps not everyone would have classed a railway line as a lovely view, but, the estate agent had emphasised, the address was good. The house had once been one of the largest, most elegant houses in London—before it was divided into flats. There was even a large room on the roof for storage. True, it was no longer used, not even as the outside lavatory it subsequently became, but it was a wonderful protection from excessive heat or even rain if you were using the elegant rooftop terrace.

Rupert kicked the threshold of his flat, which stuck slightly, and forced the door to open with a judder. He had told the landlord about the many problems with the flat, but so far there had been no response.

He walked over to a cluster of bottles sitting on a shelf and poured himself a dram of whisky. He was surprised to see the bottle was almost empty. Someone must have slipped in when he was away and had a drink. The only person with a key was Drina, but there was no chance of her getting up here—six flights and no lift. Even Drina would be defeated by that one.

He slumped back on the sofa bed and slipped sideways. Bloody sofa, the springs were coming out the bottom and the landlord did nothing. Not a single response to any of his twenty emails. Not one. He should be struck off.

Since the whisky was finished, Rupert moved on to the vodka. He didn't like vodka and only bought it in case he could persuade one of those nice girls who moved in and out downstairs to come upstairs. He'd been so attractive when he was married and living in a big house, but now, when he was free, suddenly all those nice girls had faded away. She-devils.

Having finished the vodka, Rupert moved on to the gin. He gagged. Filthy rubbish. Tonic, that was what he needed. He got up and staggered to the fridge. To his disgust, someone had eaten all the food. The only thing left in the fridge was tonic water. He pulled one out and spun around looking for his glass. As he did so, it fell on the floor and broke.

'Cheap rubbish,' he screamed, kicking at the broken pieces.

One small sliver of glass flew up and cut his hand. Bah! Angrily he pulled out a hanky and wound it round the wound. He was going to get that landlord. Nothing but rubbish in this flat. He picked up a dripping plate from the sink and threw it at the wall. It shattered and the pieces clattered onto the floor, leaving the watery ketchup slowly sliding down the white paint, where it clung in globules like theatrical blood.

'There, keep your bloody rubbish!' he yelled. 'Fucking landlord. Can't even buy a decent plate.'

There was a knock on the door. Rupert staggered over, the bottle still in his hand.

'What do you want?' he yelled through the locked door.

'Rupert! It's Diego from downstairs. Are you OK? I hear a lot of shouting.'

Reluctantly Rupert slid the bolt and opened up. Diego glanced in at the bottle in Rupert's hand, the bloody handkerchief, the chaos, and he sighed sadly.

'Are you alone?' he asked, unnecessarily since the one-room flat had no hiding places big enough for a human being.

'Fuck you,' said Rupert. 'What do you want?'

Diego shook his head. 'I was checking you are OK. Please keep the noise down, Mr Rupert. My wife is trying to get some sleep. She is having a baby.'

Rupert laughed. He waggled his bottom. 'What sort of bloody man are you, keeping a pregnant woman in this sort of accommodation? Jesus wept.'

Diego turned pale and his fists clenched, but he moved away, saying stiffly, 'Keep the noise down, Mr Rupert, or I call the police.'

'Fucking DAGO!' yelled Rupert, slamming the door, hoping it might hit him.

'Ha,' he said to his invisible audience, 'that told him.'

Since he had broken the glass, Rupert now tried to put the tonic directly into the gin bottle. It escaped down the side of the neck in a stream of fizzy bubbles and dripped off the end, wetting his bloody handkerchief and diluting the blood which ran onto the threadbare carpet.

'Bastards!' he yelled at the bubbles. 'Get in there and stay there!'

He slipped down onto the floor and burst into tears. *Nothing loves me. Even the bubbles mock me. Nobody loves me. It's so unfair.*

His phone rang. Rupert stared at it. He could see from the legend it was Drina. What the hell did she want now? She was always wanting him to do something. She said it was for his own good, but he knew better than that. That sneaky tart was up to something. He threw the phone across the room, yelling at it.

'Come up and get me, you legless gimp. If you want me, come here.'

But then he stopped. Lying still in the middle of the chaos, a slow smirk filled his face.

'But I know something you don't know I know,' he said loudly. 'Knowledge is power. Power is respect. And respect means money. Ha! You'll all fear my power. Because I know your secret.'

He rolled onto his side and threw up.

CHAPTER 4
INDEPENDENT EYES
WORKING TOGETHER TO
MAKE A CAPTURE

At the same time Rupert was destroying his phone, Cat, one of Stevie's business partners, was staring at the office computer in Owly Vale and wishing Stevie was not flying long haul to South America.

'Bother,' she said as, yet again, the information on the screen sped upwards, leaving her with something completely irrelevant in front of her. 'What did I do that time? Come back, Stevie,' she muttered. 'Give up your job with BA and work here full time. I need you.'

Unfortunately, neither the screen nor Stevie reappeared, and Cat wondered if she should restart the machine. Sometimes that worked. Other times it just gave her a long wait. She started to fiddle with the mouse.

Finally, she got back to the screen detailing her latest case.

The SeeMs Detective Agency had been employed to discover why a pilot called Amy Earhardt had been kidnapped and, after being humiliated, released. The perpetrator, Victoria Bell, who was also wanted in connection with the death of a homeless man, had now disappeared and might be dead. It was Stevie, thought Cat, somewhat petulantly owing to the rebellious computer, who saved Amy, so why wasn't she here finishing the case? But, of course, she knew the answer. SeeMs Detective Agency didn't have enough money for full-time staff, and Stevie was an airline pilot, which allowed her to sleuth part time.

Cat looked again at the connections between Amy and the missing Victoria. 'Why did Victoria kidnap you, Amy?' she muttered out loud. 'Was it just because you were a successful pilot and she was a has-been? And yet Victoria Bell was the CEO of the Bella Chantry Trust—why should she care? Was it just because you both once loved Neil?'

As she started to work on that angle, her phone rang, the legend showing it was Amy's husband.

'Graham?'

'Cat. How's it going? Any news on Victoria yet?'

'No. But I meant to say ... don't tell anyone she is still alive. She may not know we know.'

'OK, sounds complicated. That you know that she knows that she doesn't know that you know ...'

Cat wrinkled her nose. He might be light-hearted about it, but she could see this was already a trying case.

'Yes. I'm working on finding her car too.'

'Her car?'

'Yes, if you remember, Victoria drove a car licensed in the name of Rebecca Finlater. I'm trying to discover who Rebecca Finlater is.'

Graham laughed. 'OK. Tell me about Victoria's possible disguises, so I can look out for her too. Perhaps I'll spot her in the supermarket—perhaps with Elvis.'

'Ha, ha. If only we knew them all. Truth is, Graham, the more I learn about her, the more I discover she's a master of taking on new personalities. She's like a chameleon who can blend in with her background and remain invisible in plain sight.'

Graham's laugh echoed down the phone. He really didn't seem to be taking his wife's kidnapping very seriously. 'Plane sight! Very funny. Now I'll be suspicious of everyone I meet. Did you get the payment OK?'

'Yes, thanks. And don't worry too much about Victoria. One thing I'm sure is that she will find us. She hasn't finished with us yet. She still wants her revenge for something … although we haven't yet figured out what.'

Graham made a strange noise. 'OK. Stay safe, Cat. Victoria is not worth dying for.'

'Thanks.'

CHAPTER 5
FIRING UP THE COLOURS
CAN BE A SIGN OF
AGGRESSION OR FEAR

The next morning, Rupert made his way to Drina's flat in Chelsea. He hated travelling by underground with a hangover, so he took the bus, dragging himself to the upstairs level. Someone had left a *Telegraph* on the seat, which he picked up and pretended to read.

By the time they got to the British Library, the bus was very crowded, but every time someone got on and started to go for the empty seat next to him, they stopped, sniffed, and moved elsewhere. Each time it happened, Rupert put down the *Telegraph* and watched them walk away, swaying with the movement of the bus.

Halfway to Chelsea, a man sneered at him as he passed, muttering '*loser*.' Rupert stood up furiously. He was not letting an insult like that pass.

'You are a load of wankers,' he yelled down the bus. 'I'd put good money on the fact your parents only met once! Ha! That was enough. You bunch of misfits and gits!'

He sat down again, laughing. 'There,' he told his invisible supporters, 'that told 'em, load of cranks and thieves.'

The bus stopped and the driver spoke into his microphone, his voice echoing around the upper floor of the bus.

'Out!' he said. 'You! The yelling man. Out! I won't have my passengers abused. Out. Or I'm calling the police.'

Rupert sat down determinedly, pulled the *Telegraph* over his head and made snoring noises. The bus stayed still. Rupert whistled under the newspaper. The passengers muttered angrily.

A shy female voice behind Rupert whispered, 'He will, too. I've seen him do it before. Last man got a right kicking, poor devil. Couldn't walk off the bus unaided.'

Rupert threw off the paper and jumped up.

'Wankers!' he yelled.

He ran down the stairs and out of the open door.

'Ha!' he yelled at the driver, shaking his fist as he backed away. 'Got yer! You'll never catch me.'

And he ran down the road before stopping exhaustedly, gagging, and almost collapsing in a heap. The bus chugged slowly past him.

An hour and a half later, Rupert arrived at Drina's place, streams of sweat intensifying his general odour of decay. She opened the door with her hands-off gadget and her hand flew to her mouth. Holding her nose, she beckoned him in.

'I've told the lawyer we'll be late,' she said, turning her chair expertly. 'I told him you had a quick job to do before leaving home.' She looked back at him over her shoulder and half-smiled. 'I may have given him the impression you were fixing things the landlord had failed to do.'

Rupert burped.

She wheeled away, gesturing him into a spare bedroom on the ground floor.

'In there. There's a shower and a bath. I put a set of

clothes in the cupboard. They'll fit you. I'm good at sizes, used to do it for a living.'

Rupert stared gormlessly. What was she babbling about?

An hour later, the pair left for the lawyer's office. Rupert sat in the back of Drina's adapted car and stared out of the window feeling sick. His head ached, even though Drina had given him several aspirins and cups of milky coffee. He hated milk in coffee, but she sat there and watched him drink it like a school mistress.

The entrance hall to the office block was small and a sign pointed to the lawyer's room up a twisty flight of stairs. A second, handwritten, sign lay on the floor, half in and out of the open doors of the lift:

Broken. Donut Use.

For a moment Rupert wondered what it meant, then he smirked. Honestly! Could no one spell these days? Drina would have to stay behind. No lift, no Drina—ha! However, she looked at him and smiled. Slightly raising one eyebrow, she pressed a bell at the base of the stairs. To Rupert's surprise, two young men came out of a neighbouring office.

'Ma'am,' said the younger man. 'Are you ready?

She nodded. He bent down and lifted her out of the chair and up the stairs, while the second man folded the chair and carried it up to the next floor.

'Prior Planning Prevents Piss-Ups,' said Drina over her shoulder to Rupert, her eyes glinting slightly. 'If you prepared as well as me, you wouldn't have any problems!'

Rupert burped again and stuck out his tongue behind her back. 'La di da,' he muttered.

Once upstairs, the young men put Drina back in her chair and melted away, murmuring, 'Call us when you need us.'

A door was open, opposite the defunct lift, across the

narrow landing, its jams only just wide enough for the wheelchair. Rupert chuckled, happily imagining Drina would get sore knuckles. But Drina, moving her hands skillfully along her wheels, entered the room unscathed.

The reception was empty apart from a couple of chairs, their stuffing sprouting out. Rupert gazed absently at the random bits of horsehair that decorated the floor. A plaque on the door next to the chairs announced: *Paul Falstaff LLB.*

Drina lifted her stick and rapped on the door. After a long pause it was opened by an old man who seemed slightly bent to one side. He stared at Rupert blankly before lowering his gaze to Drina and nodding his head in recognition.

'Ah, yes, come in,' he wheezed. 'Father denied access, isn't it?'

The office they entered was so cluttered it was difficult for Drina to move her chair without driving over some piece of documentation, but she pushed on forward over several books and parked in front of the desk. Rupert took the only chair, sniggering when he noticed it was difficult for Drina to see over the piles of papers on the desk to the man behind.

'So,' said Paul Falstaff to Rupert, 'you are Rupert Fletcher, denied access to your daughter Lagertha by youɪ ex-wife Caroline Harrington. Ha, keeps her name, does she? What name does Lagertha take?'

Rupert had no idea what he was talking about, but Drina answered. 'She is currently Lagertha Katherine Fletcher.'

The lawyer stared at her for a moment, then said, 'And may I verify who you are, my dear?'

'I'm Corinna Regis, always known as Drina,' she said. 'Rupert and I are very good friends and I'm planning to help him by looking after Lagertha while he is working. It is so difficult for fathers to both work and look after their children, as I'm sure you understand, so I'll always be there for him and darling Lagertha.' Her voice took on a soft lyrical tone.

'Oh good,' said Paul, his voice coming out in a wheezy cough. 'It was a question I needed to ask. And you, my dear, will you be able to show me some ID before we go to court? Modern restrictions make fools of us all, so it is as well to be up to speed.'

Smiling slightly stiffly, Drina brought out her driving licence from her pouch. He noted down the details.

'Nice address,' he wheezed again. 'In my youth all my friends lived in Chelsea, but now young lawyers are forced out to places like Battersea, which no one had heard of when I was young. Yes,' he said, rubbing his eyes, 'since I retired from full-time practice, the law has changed and not for the better, I'm afraid. Fathers had much more say in those days,' he sneered. 'Now it seems that the mother's word is the law. Women rule!'

Rupert hadn't a clue what the old fool was talking about, but for some reason Drina had chosen him to be his lawyer and she was usually foolproof.

'So,' he interrupted, 'can we get the bitch in jail for child abuse too?'

Paul stopped, looked down at his papers and back at Rupert with a puzzled look on his face. 'Are you suggesting ...?'

'Well, she's got some pretty odd notions, you know. She stopped me giving her red wine when everyone knows it is good for you, builds protein. Caroline doesn't drink, eats chocolate instead, which, of course, explains everything.' He spread his hands and simultaneously rolled his eyes.

The lawyer glanced from him to Drina and back again, his brow furrowed. 'I think we might leave the finer details of the case until later,' he murmured. 'For now we'll just concentrate on getting you unrestricted access.'

'And alimony,' slurred Rupert. 'Rich cow with a night-club can afford ...'

'Ah,' said Paul, perking up, 'she owns a nightclub?'

'Yes,' said Drina, her polite smile turning into a beam, 'given to her by an *unknown admirer*, I believe.'

'And, no doubt, if she has problems with childcare, she takes the child there?'

'Almost inevitably, I would think,' said Drina, looking meaningfully at Rupert.

'Lucky girl,' said Rupert. 'Wish my mother had taken me to a nightclub when I was five years old. No chance! I had to wait until they were out and I could sneak up and get the booze.'

As they waited for the men to take Drina down to street level, Rupert crowed in triumph. 'Ha, that will get her! I was great in there. Did you see how the lawyer bent to my will? He wasn't that convinced before I spoke. You did your best, but he needed a man to explain it right. But once I told him, he was like a ferret on a hare. We'll get that devil, Caroline. She'll be a wreck ten minutes after she gets the summons.'

'Yes,' Drina said, 'but you'll need to stay off the booze until we get Lagertha. The other side will have a detective following you, as sure as eggs, and it won't be those idiots from the Agency.' Her voice took on a mocking tone. 'The agency that sees that things are not always what they seem. Ha! As if they ever were. And as if they ever did. More likely the agency that never sees what is plainly in front of their stupid fat noses. Dullards.'

'Oooh,' said Rupert, 'what fun! I wonder what the dicky likes to drink. I could offer him something and then slip him a bit of Rohypnol.'

Drina ignored him and continued with her theme of injustice. 'Which SeeMs dicky would they choose? Stevie the dim pilot, Miranda the barstool bore or The Cat!'

At that moment the two men appeared from downstairs to help her back to the ground floor and she stopped talking.

Once in the street she wheeled her chair fast, heading for her car which was parked in a disabled bay in a side street. As they passed a supermarket, she stopped so suddenly that Rupert almost ran into the back of her and had to put out his arms to prevent himself collapsing on top of her.

'Have you got any food in the flat?'

Rupert's eyes flashed. 'No, and no booze either. I'll need some if I'm going to entertain detectives and the like.'

Drina stared at the pavement. 'I think we'll stick with food for the moment. OK, get a trolley and we'll stock up for the weekend. You can keep the clothes too. Makes you *look* like a gent anyroad.'

As they went around the shop, Drina picking healthy fruit and cheese that made Rupert sneer, she said, 'You will need to get a job if you want custody of Lagertha. The fact I'm supporting you won't go down well in court.'

Rupert sniggered. 'You can employ me, as a handler. Anyway, what else is a cripple to do with insurance pay-out money? You should be thanking me for giving you something to do.'

Drina rolled her eyes. 'I almost feel sorry for Caroline.'

Rupert laughed and spun the trolley on its axis, nearly hitting a couple of shoppers nearby.

'Ooh, this is fun. Caroline never let me go shopping. Didn't trust me!'

Once the car boot was full of bags of food, Drina drove Rupert round to his flat. As she dropped him outside, she repeated, 'OK, so stay off the booze and get some sleep. And start looking for a job.'

Rupert inclined his head politely. He watched her drive off round the corner, making sure she was well out of sight before he picked up the bags of food. Grinning impishly, he headed for a flat on the ground floor at the back of his block. He knocked and yelled loudly through the door.

'Hello. Mrs Cartwright. How are you today?'

After a long wait he heard a dragging sound in the flat, as though someone was heaving a heavy parcel. Eventually, after extensive clunking, the door opened a slit, and an old woman peered out, her face looking anxious.

'Who is it?'

'Hello, Mrs Cartwright. It's me, Rupert. I brought you the shopping you wanted.'

He lifted the bags and waved them so she could see them through the slit.

The old woman smiled and opened the door. 'Thank you, Mr Rupert, you are so kind. I'd quite forgotten I asked you. Come in and I'll get my purse.'

She limped away and Rupert carried the food into the kitchen at the back of the flat. The fridge was already stuffed with food from his last delivery two days ago. He pulled it out and put it in a black bag in the bin out on the back steps, replacing it with some of the new stuff but leaving the majority on the kitchen table. Pulling off the price labels, he hastily stuffed them in his pocket. When she returned to the kitchen, she slumped down on a chair exhaustedly, plopping her open purse on the table.

Rupert glanced briefly at the many twenty- and fifty-pound notes in it.

'So, how much is that, dear?' she said. 'Would twenty pounds cover it?'

He put his hand on his breast and smiled sympathetically. 'I'm so sorry,' he said, 'it is a bit more, but a hundred and fifty pounds will be enough.'

The old woman tutted. 'Everything is getting so expensive nowadays. The social hardly covers it.'

She passed him a hundred pounds in twenties plus another fifty.

'Happy to do it for you,' he said, smiling brightly. 'Would you like the same again on Monday? It's always nice to have food in, isn't it?'

Her hand waved vaguely. 'It is, love. And I'm so lucky to have you upstairs. Don't worry about putting it away. I'll do that. Give me something to do.'

'Not at all,' said Rupert, 'always happy to help a neighbour. Talking of which, shall I take your rubbish out?'

Mrs Cartwright wrinkled her eyes in confusion. 'Have I got some, dear?'

Rupert lifted out the black bag he had just stuffed and waved it. There was a lurid smell of rotting food.

Smiling, he lifted the bag onto his shoulders. As they walked to the door, Rupert looked at the table covered with knick-knacks.

'Oh! Very pretty,' he said. 'What a lovely crochet hook. My girlfriend loves crocheting.'

'Oh, does she, dear?' said Mrs Cartwright. 'Well, you'd better give it to her. My hands are too arthritic for crochet now and I don't have any relations left. She might as well have it.'

'Wow. Mrs C, that is so kind,' said Rupert, 'thank you.'

And he gave her a big hug before opening the door.

'Now, take care, Mrs C, not everyone in the neighbourhood is so nice. Bolt your door firmly and stay safe.'

'Thank you, dear. I am so lucky to have you upstairs.'

Puffing after climbing the stairs, Rupert reached the fifth floor. He dropped the stinking black bag outside Diego's door. Then rapping loudly on the wood, he yelled, 'Hey, Dago, you hungry? Come 'n' get it!'

He leapt up the last flight of stairs to his own room and shoved open the door.

As he placed the crochet hook on a pile of presents from Mrs Cartwright, he stopped and stared at the accumulated hoard. He lifted a child's baptism spoon on the pile, rubbing it between his fingers. It was silver plate with a decoration of crossed swords. He dropped it back on the pile and hugged his body. Tears filled his eyes.

For a moment he stared blankly. Then he hummed a bar of U2. 'You gave me nothing, Mother, and now it's all I got.'

The door banged in the wind and Rupert shot round, staring. He breathed deeply and, with a sudden movement, kicked the sofa.

'Women! Harpies! Bleeding me dry and saying "It's for your own good, Roopert. Be good, Roopert!" Pah!'

He stuck out his tongue, looking around at the ketchup mess, the chaos, and kicked the sofa again.

'Where's my daughter? Clean this up, woman! Girls are born cleaning, aren't they?'

And he roared with laughter, basking in the cheers of his friends.

'I need a drink.'

He searched the room, but there was no booze left. He ran down the stairs, pausing at the last flight to check Mrs C didn't look out, and headed for the street.

Pubs were open. He had been banned from all the nearest ones, but he knew one in Eltham where the publicans weren't so fussy. He headed for the station.

CHAPTER 6
PANTHER CHAMELEONS
GLOW IN THE DARK

Anthony said goodbye to his last client and leant back in his chair. Although he tried not to think about her, Caroline lived on the periphery of his mind, always drifting in and out like a cloud on a sunny day. How was she? Was she OK? She hadn't had therapy for more than three months, the longest since she ran away from her repressive boarding school at fourteen. Shutting her out of his thoughts, he started sorting through his notes for the following day.

Glancing at his watch, he noticed it was after eight o'clock. He ought to go home. It took an hour from the office to his house, sometimes more. He had an early start next morning—one of his long-term clients wanted to meet before going away for the weekend. He wondered vaguely if he had any food in the house or if he should buy some on the way home.

As he started locking up the office, his phone pinged.

He opened the WhatsApp.

Caroline!

Tant, Meet me at Black Scabbard Eltham. Urgent. Half an hour! Caro.

He frowned. Was it Caroline?

On the one hand, that gasping manner was how she wrote, and she had called him Tant—a corruption of his name and Aunt in French—since he had been her social worker back in the late nineties.

On the other hand, the Black Scabbard in Eltham was in a rough area where the meeting of a mixed-race couple would receive more than a little attention. And although Caroline might have suggested such a thing when she was fourteen, she had become much more streetwise since then. Moreover, when she stopped therapy, she said, 'I never want to see you again.' Would she go back on that?

The WhatsApp had her number and her picture. There were also two other participants, him and one called Mr Berthalot, with an unknown phone number, and an avatar of Vishnu. Who was the 'Third Man'?

So, he thought, spinning the phone around on his hand, if it wasn't her, who would send him a message like that? A message to lure him into the lion's den.

It wasn't the first time Anthony had been threatened or tested by clients, but it was unlikely any of his clients would know either Caroline's name, or that she called him Tant.

Only one former client could know those things, and she was dead, having fallen out of a Tiger Moth biplane some months before.

He reckoned he ought to go to the meeting. But he would need backup. He pulled up his address book and called a number. There was no reply, so he sent a text instead.

Locking his desk, his hand hovered briefly over a knife he kept in the top drawer, before rejecting the idea. A large

Black man with a knife ... well, it didn't take a huge feat of imagination to see where that would lead in today's London.

Should he take the car? That would mean going home to get it, then he would be so late that whoever sent the message would have gone by the time he got there. It would be difficult enough to get to Eltham from Pimlico in half an hour. He'd take the bike. He'd recently converted his push bike to an e-bike—something that made his DIY-obsessed dad proud, and possibly a bit incredulous. Anthony smiled. DIY was not usually his forte.

By the time Anthony reached Eltham, it was nearly nine o'clock. The street lights were on and dropping eerie shadows on the pavement. He occasionally biked past men and women on the pavement, but most of the shops were shut and the streets were empty apart from a couple of homeless people huddled in doorways, wrapped in blankets and boxes. A few men passed him muttering things he decided not to hear. A child of Black parents growing up in a rough area, Anthony had quickly learnt that even though he was a large man, his brain was going to defend him better than his fists, and avoidance was often preferrable to pride.

He opened the door of the Black Scabbard pub, and there was a sudden hush. Even though he had expected it, he paused, shocked by the flow of malice drifting towards him. For a moment he felt as though they were in a silent film and the caption read: *Sheriff, lend me your gun. I'm about to do a little missionary work.*

Before anyone else could move, an older man got up from one of the bar stools. Anthony tensed. Although the man was bald and had wrinkles, his shoulders bulged and he had a certain lightness on his feet, which made Anthony think of pugilists. There was a thin scar running under his left eye. But his voice was gentle when he said, 'Hi, take a pew, sit with me a moment.'

Anthony watched him, still unmoving. The man sat down on the nearest stool and smiled, tilting his head, the gesture beckoning rather than demanding. Anthony considered the stool; it was close to the door, and it would keep him away from the bulk of the room and their freezing eyes. He moved slowly towards it, his legs stiff, his muscles on alert.

'Beer?'

The man signalled to the barman before Anthony could reply. 'Two Courage Best,' he said, sliding some notes across the bar.

'I'm curious,' he said as their drinks were put in front of them. 'Why you come in here?'

Anthony looked at him, frowning slightly but also noticing the man had a slight Irish lilt, as though he had lived there long, long ago. As Anthony didn't speak, the man went on.

'You from here? New boy?'

Anthony rubbed his nose. It was interesting that such a simple query could both hold menace and innocent curiosity. He decided it was best to stay with the truth. 'I was sent a message, by a friend, asking me to meet ...'

He stopped, realising he had lost his companion's attention. A sudden loud noise at the far end of the bar had caused the man to swivel around to see what was happening.

Someone had just been denied more alcohol and he didn't agree with the verdict.

'You fucking wanker,' he yelled, 'whaj fucking mean I've had enough? E-nuff. I haven't had e-nuff of anything, mate. You are just like all your other fucking lot ... you from

Europe, aren't you? Bet you are Russian. Wimpy, eh? Escaping the fighting ... scaredy cat ...'

The shouter threw himself across the bar, trying to get to the bottles behind.

'Whajese for if not for drinking? Gimmie.'

The barman pushed him off the bar and the man fell back heavily, landing on the floor with a flump. For a moment it seemed as though he might stay there, then he stood up, waving his empty glass, which surprisingly hadn't been broken by the fall. 'Who's going give me what I need ...?'

As he spoke he turned slightly towards them.

'Oh,' said Anthony reflexively.

His companion swivelled back to him, aware and curious. 'You know him?'

'I do,' said Anthony slowly.

'Ah,' said the man, 'is that who ...?'

Whatever he was planning to say was cut off as Rupert spotted Anthony at the far end of the bar.

'What ho!' he yelled, almost running in their direction. 'Tantivy! It's my cuckold! My wife's best friend!'

Before either Anthony or the man knew what was happening, Rupert was upon them, his empty glass still in his hand. He waved it close to Anthony's face, almost hitting his nose in the sweep of his arm.

'Well, fuck me, it's the whoremaster!' Rupert turned to the men in the pub. 'This man seduced my wife, the fucking ni—'

Whatever Rupert might have been going to say stopped as the man's fist shot out and knocked him to the ground. Around them there was a swell of noise as men sitting around the bar and on the tables started muttering. Some looked keen to join a fight.

Anthony jumped up. He was about to go to Rupert's aid when the man said in a hoarse whisper, 'Go, now! If you go, I can stop things. If you stay, I won't be responsible. Go.'

Anthony glanced at the surge of moving people and gauged their number. Some twenty men. Rising, crouching poses, still undecided but starting to straighten up. He slipped back through the door and out of the pub, even while every instinct in his body screamed at him to stay. Something had happened there, and he wasn't quite sure what.

In the pub, the man leapt off the bar stool and down to Rupert's prone form with surprising agility. He signalled to the barman for a wet cloth and, having placed it on Rupert's head, he waved off the spectators who were starting to collect around the body. One or two were even looking at the door, which was still swinging after Anthony's fast exit.

The man stood up, effectively blocking their gaze.

'OK, folks, entertainment over.'

A couple of men moved from foot to foot restlessly, but there was something in the old man's aura of command that caught them, and they paused, muttering and still ready, but they didn't follow Anthony out of the pub.

It was only a few minutes later when Rupert opened his eyes. He stared up at the man, the rafters of the pub and a couple of drinkers who were still above him, looking down with cold stares.

'Oh fuck!' Rupert said as his memory slowly returned. 'Where's the Big Dick? The King of the Jungle?'

The man leant over and gripped his shoulder so tightly Rupert barked, 'Wha ...?'

'Up,' said the man roughly. 'On your feet, boy.'

Rupert was thin, but he was over six foot tall, and he was amazed to be pulled onto his feet by the man, who, although considerably smaller in height, was apparently built of solid muscle.

'Sit!' said the man, forcing him onto a bar stool.

Rupert collapsed onto the stool, sagging weakly like an enormous half-stuffed teddy bear. He burped.

'Coffee,' the man ordered the barman. 'And a glass of water.'

Growing bored, the audience melted away.

'Now,' the man said to Rupert, 'talk and keep talking until I tell you to stop.'

Rupert started to giggle, but the man put his hand on his knee and squeezed hard. Rupert's eyes filled with tears. 'Stop!' he gasped, trying to punch the man's hand away and finding it hard and unresponsive. 'Stop!'

The man took his hand away and clicked his fingers. 'OK, talk.'

'S'what do you want?'

'Who are you? Who is the Black man? And why were you both in this pub in Eltham where we don't like strangers?'

Rupert raised his head and stared at the man for a brief minute. He felt a flush of relief. A light bulb of brilliance. He could get rid of Anthony forever, and his wife would come back pleading.

'That man,' he said, 'is an undercover cop ... Ow!'

The clamp on his leg returned swiftly and the pain was worse than before.

'Don't fuck with my head,' said the man in the same gentle voice. 'Rozzers are pretty thick, but even those idiots are not going to send a Black man undercover in a completely white area. Now start again and tell me the truth.'

'OK,' said Rupert, 'but I need a whisky ... double ...'

The man shrugged and nodded to the barman. 'So, who is he?'

Rupert knocked back the whisky in one slug. 'His name is Anthony, and he is a therapist in Pimlico, a social worker, and he slept with my wife ... He seduced her, and he turned her against me ... She used to do what I wanted until ...'

The man shrugged again. 'Where do you live?'

'King's Cross, Mansionetta Flats.'

'OK, let's go.'

'How about one more for the road ...?'

The man turned to the barman, pushing a couple of fifties across the bar. 'Give me the bottle,' he said, then he lifted Rupert with one arm, steered him outside and pushed him into an elderly Mercedes which was parked a few yards back from the entrance.

'Don't be sick,' he said, 'or I'll throw you on the street. Headfirst.'

Rupert waved a lordly hand, but although he tried to speak, his voice came out in an incomprehensible slur.

The man drove gently, watching Rupert swaying on the back seat through the mirror. He stopped outside Mansionetta Flats and turned to look at Rupert, who had fallen asleep. He rubbed his nose thoughtfully.

'OK, this it?'

Rupert opened his eyes and burped. He shut them again and collapsed against the door.

The old man looked at him. He pulled him out and draped the boy's body over his shoulders and tramped up a couple of steps into the hall.

Mrs Cartwright limped over. She leant on her stick,

watering the dried flowers from a kettle. 'Oh dear, the poor young man,' she said. 'Is he all right? Has he had a turn?'

'Hummph,' said the old man, 'nothing he can't sleep off. Where does he go?'

'At the top, dear. Sixth floor at the end. Green door.'

'You haven't a lift then?'

'Ah, deary me, no, love, that would be grand, but no.' She smiled. 'Cold for the time of year,' she added.

The man frowned. With a swift movement he turned and crouched, dragging Rupert's arms around his neck and lifting him onto his shoulders. With one more twitch of his shoulders, he got the boy supported on his back and began the long climb skywards, Rupert's long legs banging against the steps as they went. Mrs Cartwright watched them for a while and then turned and dusted the now wet plants.

The old man was panting by the time he reached the green door on the sixth floor. He kicked at the door, which was already ajar, and dropped Rupert on the bed, his bottle still clutched tightly in his hand.

For a moment the man looked at the bottle, then he shrugged, turned and made his way downstairs. As he passed the fifth floor, a door opened and a young man with a flop of dark hair looked out.

'Mr Rupert?' he asked.

'Yeah.'

'Is he OK?'

'Alive, if that's what you mean.'

Diego nodded. 'Maybe tonight he won't sing, or shout?'

The man lifted his shoulders, testing their movement separately. 'Maybe.'

He walked on down the stairs. Passing Mrs Cartwright, who was still dusting although her feathers were now soaking wet, he stopped.

'That door, the front. Is it always open?'

She looked at him blankly, her eyes wide open. Eventually, she said, 'All welcome here. We have an open house for all.' She giggled. 'Would you like a plant? I could pick you one from the bunch. Good flowers for the time of year.'

He stared at her, his lips pursed, then said, 'Who owns the block? Any idea?'

She stared blankly again and smiled. 'Cold for the time of year.'

He looked back up the stairs. Shrugging, he went outside and climbed into his car.

Upstairs Rupert rolled off the bed onto the floor and took the top off the whisky.

'Fantastic!' he yelled at the top of his voice. 'I showed 'em. Beat that Big Dick to a pulp. He'll be sore in the morning.'

Rupert took another swig of whisky and began to sing.

Down one flight Diego and his wife put in their ear plugs.

CHAPTER 7
CHAMELEONS CHANGE COLOUR TO FIGHT AN OPPOSING MALE

Anthony walked tensely towards his bike, his heart beating hard. Rationally, he knew he'd have been crazy to stay, but the instinctive part of him felt it was less strategic withdrawal and more cowardly flight.

He took off the security chain, wondering whether to call Caroline's number. No, they had decided she was doing things alone. He must leave her be.

He would go to Pimlico and sleep in the office. The ride would take an hour or so, but the exercise would calm his pulsing emotions. He pulled on his hoodie and shot into the road, biking fast.

He deviated his route to pass by King's College. There he stopped and looked in through the glass window, examining the porter. Perhaps this was someone he knew, someone to whom he might say 'hi'. He was always grateful to King's for the bursary it gave him, for the education and the harmony of the place. One of the best times of his life. But the porter was young, wouldn't have been there in his day. The man looked up, but he didn't smile or even seem to register his presence. Anthony's phone rang and he dragged his eyes away from his alma mater. It was Cat.

'Anthony, are you OK?' Her voice came out in a rush.

'Yes, I'm fine, Cat, thanks,' he said, now relaxed enough to laugh. 'Is this in response to my text for urgent backup?'

Cat made an embarrassed sound. 'I'm so sorry, Anthony, I went to one of Frank's gigs and we've only just got out. I just saw your text. I hope it wasn't really urgent.'

'Nah, Cat,' Anthony said, 'it's fine. Nothing.'

He considered asking about Caroline, but he knew the mother and daughter relationship had been strained at times. He left it. 'Thanks, Cat. See you soon.'

However, as he closed the phone, his brow furrowed. So, if the old man hadn't been sent to the Black Scabbard by the Agency to protect him, then who? It was unlikely that he was there by coincidence—all Anthony's instincts rebelled against such a conclusion.

So, who? Why? Was it the same person who sent the text?

CHAPTER 8

CHAMELEONS ARE SOLITARY
AND TERRITORIAL

Drina wheeled her chair up the ramp to the front door, which swung open and automatically fixed itself next to the wall, giving plenty of room for her chair to roll in. She laughed. It was so nice visiting these modern places, fully adapted for wheelchair use—and so rare. She wheeled herself over to the lower part of the reception desk, unattended as usual, and pressed the button.

A harried-looking woman came out of the nearest room. She smiled when she saw Drina.

'Oh, it's you, dear, no need to ring in future, just go right in. I'm afraid she's not her best this evening. Good and bad. Good and bad. We are so short staffed it's a joke, but ...' She left the sentence unfinished and rushed back into the room she came from.

There was a scuffling noise coming from the room and Drina could hear the carer saying to someone, 'Wait, Petal, I'm there, take your time.'

Drina turned left and headed up the hall until she found the room she was looking for. Again there was a big flat pad for disabled entrance, which she pushed. The door swung open, revealing a dishevelled bed containing an old woman whose body shape hardly lifted the covers. The woman's head was turned towards the door and her eyes were shut.

'Hello, Mum,' said Drina, 'how are you today?'

The woman's eyes opened with a flash of blue and she put a wrinkled hand out from under the sheets. Drina gave the hand a gentle kiss.

'We're doing well for you, my darling,' said Drina, picking some flowers out of the pouch in her chair, 'one down, one to go! You'd be pleased if you knew what I was doing for you.' Drina laughed softly. She moved forward until she could reach a vase next to the bed, picked out the flowers already there and examined them before throwing them into the bin with a sneer. She replaced them with her own.

'You can send me dead flowers every morning,' she sang quietly to the old woman, whose eyes flashed in apparent understanding.

'Yes,' said Drina, 'all that glitters is not gold and all the stories can be wrongly told.'

She stroked the old woman's hand. 'I'm so sorry for all the pain you suffered. Your children gone, your heart broken. The world is too, too cruel, but we are righting your wrongs. Righting your wrongs! I'm only so sorry most of the guilty ones are already dead. But not all, not all.'

The old woman moved the sheets slightly. 'I had a farm in Africa,' she rasped, humming a little tune.

Drina's eyes filled with tears, and she took the woman's hand and squeezed it. 'You will again, my darling, you will.'

CHAPTER 9
IF A FEMALE CHAMELEON CANNOT LAY EGGS, SHE WILL DIE

Caroline was cleaning the house with furious energy when the doorbell rang. Since Rupert had left, Caroline seemed tireless and was always cleaning and cooking. It was only when she was at work, or helping Lagertha with her homework, that she relaxed.

Turning off the hoover, she walked to the door and, as she did so, noticed a police car out the window. Her stomach did a dance. *Mum!* What had Mum been doing? Why did she cause her daughter so much trouble? What could she have done this time? Surely, she couldn't be misbehaving now she had Frank. After Dad died, Mum had gone wild. Dressing in short skirts. Going to pubs alone. Vanessa said she was making up for not having a proper teenage life, but why did she need one? She was already nearly fifty. Odd time to grow up, surely!

Opening the door, she saw it was two policewomen. Unusual. *Don't they usually have one of each?* she thought. Or was that only in movies?

'Hello,' said the taller of the two women. 'Are you Mrs Fletcher? Wife of Rupert Fletcher?'

'Oh God,' said Caroline, pulling nervously at her right ear, 'what has Rupert done? Was he drunk? Say he didn't go to the school. Is Lagertha OK? She's not involved, is she?'

The two women exchanged glances.

'Can we come in, Mrs Fletcher?'

Caroline stared at them wildly for a minute. Then she pinched her thumb. Anthony's trick was supposed to calm her in moments of stress, but sometimes it just gave her a sore thumb.

'Oh, yes, of course.'

The two women came in and put their hats on the table. Caroline stared at the hats. She felt as though she was in a film. Did they wear those hats in the car, or did they keep them in the back, lift them out and then put them on, in order to arrive with hats in hand and put them on the table. Why?

The two women glanced at each other again.

'Is anyone else here?'

'No,' said Caroline, automatically looking at her watch. 'But my mother is picking Lagertha up from school and taking her to her house. I was going to join her after work this evening.'

'Oh, yes,' said the smaller woman. Caroline realised they still hadn't given her their names. 'You own a nightclub, is that right?'

Caroline frowned. The woman was making it sound like an accusation. She sat down and the women did the same, dropping down on the sofa opposite her.

The PC continued. 'Could you ring your mum and ask her to come here first?'

Caroline frowned. 'I could, but why? Oh, and what are your names?'

The smaller one blushed. Clearly she should have said her name at the beginning. 'I'm PC Mates,' she said, belatedly getting out some ID and gesturing it in Caroline's direction, 'family liaison officer. This is PC Brave. Please ring your mother. We have some news to tell you and we think ...'

She didn't get any further because a little girl came in through the front door at full speed, throwing herself on her mother and thrusting a picture in her lap.

'Leggy, darling.'

'Mummy! Look. I painted a camel at school. So nice! Grandma says it should be in an art gallery.'

She suddenly noticed the two women on the sofa and stared at them, taking hold of her mother's hand and putting it in her mouth.

A few seconds later, Cat followed her granddaughter. There could be no doubt she was Caroline's mother. Both women were thin with strikingly symmetrical faces, almost to the edge of beauty, and their resemblance was uncanny. However, their dress sense was at opposite ends of the fashion world. Caroline in long black skirts, and baggy shape-disguising shirts, while Cat was wearing a bright red mini-skirt over red and black striped leggings and Christian Louboutin boots, taking her height to about six foot three. Caroline's blonde hair lay straight down her back while Cat's was primped into curls.

'Darling,' Cat started, followed by 'oh' as she noticed the policewomen, 'you are here already.'

PC Mates looked up at her, surprised.

'Yes, one of your colleagues was at the school when I picked up Leggy. She said I was needed over here. She told me. Have you told Caroline yet?'

PC Mates shook her head. 'No, not yet.'

'What? What?' said Caroline, her blood shooting through her body in an anxiety fest. 'What's happened?'

She pulled her daughter to her, gave her a kiss and then, glancing at her mother, said, 'Leggy, why don't you go upstairs and get that painting you were working on yesterday? We can show it to Grandma and the nice women.'

Giving the policewomen another nervous look, the little girl ran upstairs.

'OK,' said Caroline, 'what?'

'I'm sorry to tell you, Mrs Fletcher, that your husband, Rupert Fletcher, was found dead this morning in his flat in King's Cross,' said PC Mates.

'King's Cross,' said Caroline interestedly. 'He got a flat there? I wonder why he chose that area. It is awfully close to my sister and her family, but he always said he hated them.'

Again the two women exchanged glances. Caroline wondered if she was getting paranoid or if there was something they hadn't told her.

'How did Rupert die?' asked Cat.

'We don't have the full details as yet. Our forensic team are there now.'

Caroline blinked. 'Your forensic team? Why? He drank like a fish; I expect he just kept drinking until he died. Does that need a forensic team?'

The women looked as though they were going to say, 'beyond our pay grade,' but they didn't speak.

Caroline felt a cold thread creeping into her stomach. She looked at the two policewomen in front of her and nibbled at her tongue. 'Are you suggesting it was ...' She wasn't sure how to put it. 'Foul play?'

'He was shot,' said PC Brave.

Caroline looked at her mother and back at the policewomen. Her mind went blank. *Who would shoot Rupert?*

Cat said, 'Shot? Are you saying he shot himself? Or that it was a burglary gone wrong? Who on earth would want to shoot Rupert?'

Caroline, hearing her mother echoing her thoughts, came back to life. 'Pah,' she said, 'one of his creditors maybe. How could Rupert have anything worth stealing? Anything he did have he sold for alcohol, even when he was living with me. No self-respecting burglar would bother with him.'

'Maybe,' said Cat, shaking her curls, 'but a thief wouldn't know that.' She turned her attention to the policewomen. 'What are you suggesting?'

PC Mates turned towards Cat, a quizzical look on her face. 'We are the family liaison team. We just inform the relatives. You will be contacted further. Mrs Harrington, we believe it is important your daughter isn't left alone. Can you ensure ...'

'Hang on,' said Caroline, 'I'm not a child. Talk to me, not my mother. I see no reason for changing our plans just because Rupert is dead. I'll go to work tonight and then go down to Owly Vale to be with my mother and Lagertha this evening. OK?'

The women picked up their hats. 'As long as you are OK,' said PC Mates, her voice soft, 'but if you do need anyone from the family office, just let us know.'

She passed Caroline a card and smiled gently.

'Honestly,' said Caroline, after they'd gone. 'What a lot of fuss over Rupert. Frankly I'm glad he's dead. Did you know he came to the club a few days ago and threatened me?'

'No? What with? I mean, how could he threaten you? You haven't done anything, have you?'

Caroline wrinkled her nose. 'Thanks for the vote of

support, Mother! No, of course I haven't, but he'd gone completely barking, said he'd done DNA tests on Leggy and himself and you and me.'

'On me?!' Cat's eyes flared. 'That's illegal. You can't go doing DNA tests on all and sundry without their permission. How did he manage that? I'm sure the laboratories are pretty hot on that kind of behaviour.'

Cat frowned. 'Why would someone murder Rupert? People usually murder for money, or fear. He had no money. And who would be scared of Rupert?'

She stared at her daughter. 'Odd thought, but could Rupert have known something about someone and blackmailed them?'

'Hardly. The only thing he cared about was where to find the booze.'

Cat nibbled her underlip. She needed to discuss this with her colleagues in the Agency. Miranda had great instincts and Stevie had her computer. Unfortunately, they were both away.

'OK,' Cat said, 'are you going to the club? If so, Leggy and I will set off for Owly Vale.'

'Yes ...'

They were disturbed by a knock on the door and the postman looking in through the window.

'Postie. Recorded delivery!' he shouted.

Caroline went and got it. She signed his computer terminal and slit open the envelope. She pulled out a thin document and laughed.

'Huh! Look at that, Mum. It's like a ghost from the grave.'

She threw the papers on the sofa and went to make some tea for her mother and Leggy.

Cat picked up the papers and scanned them. It was from a lawyer employed by Rupert. A couple of typewritten pages full of legalese announced that Rupert was going to go for custody of Lagertha.

Cat frowned. She'd known Rupert for twenty years and he'd never shown any interest in children. Why did a man who clearly did not like children insist on getting custody?

CHAPTER 10
MALE CHAMELEONS ARE HARDIER THAN FEMALES

After Cat and Lagertha had left, Caroline went round with the hoover. She packed herself a suitcase so she could drive straight from Spinners to Owly Vale, and she changed into her nightclub wear. It soothed her to have different clothes for everything she did. She kept nightclub wear in one part of the cupboard, school mother clothes in another, while everyday wear graced a third part. Each section was clearly labelled—such a relief after the chaos of life with Rupert where everything was thrown on the floor.

She stopped and briefly thought about Rupert's death. Then she shook herself. No. That way madness lies. He must have shot himself. How would he get a gun? He used to have a shotgun, but that, like everything else that wasn't nailed down, had been sold to pay for his boozing habit.

So, perhaps he was shot by someone else, but who on earth would bother to shoot the losing no-hoper Rupert? Besides, as she knew from the occasions when she'd been forced to watch Rupert shooting pheasants, a gun makes a lot of noise. There must be loads of people who heard the bang. At least that meant the whole thing would soon be over.

What should she tell Leggy? Rupert hadn't spent much time with his daughter, but then, Caroline thought, nor had her own father and yet she had loved him, had been devastated by his death. For a long time she blamed her mother, although it wasn't Cat's fault she hadn't noticed he had MND. Victor was the only one that clocked their father's head sticking out, and that was only because he so seldom saw his dad that when he did, it was obvious. She shook herself. She would tell Leggy soon. The girl ought to know. But it might be better if they knew how Rupert died. Easier to explain.

Caroline drove to Spinners and parked in the basement garage. Victoria had thought of everything when she created the club and access was simple. Although Caroline usually took the lift straight to her office, tonight she stopped one floor earlier going into the club itself. She liked the atmosphere of the place, and seeing the number of people around gave her an indication of her success or otherwise.

To her delight, the place was packed, and she could hardly get in through the door. She pushed through the crowd and slipped in behind the bar where Tom was serving, aided by Paul, Karen and Methuen.

'Heaving tonight,' she said into Tom's ear as he pulled a pint of Guinness for a tall woman in blue silk. 'Looks good.'

Tom partially turned with a rueful smile. 'They all want a glimpse of the action,' he said quietly, his lips hardly moving. 'The place is full of people I've never seen before.'

Caroline stared, pouting her lower lip. 'What you mean?'

'Someone spread it around that Rupert was killed shortly after coming in here to threaten you. He was screaming he was going to take away your daughter.' Tom snorted. 'They didn't get the name right though, so she's been anything from Lager to Chinty.'

'Chinty! Where did that one come from?'

Tom shrugged. 'You should hear the rumours that are drifting around.'

He finished serving the customer and turned to her.

'Why don't you go up to the office and listen in? I went up there earlier and I was gobsmacked at what's being said. Someone has been starting the rumourmongers early and some of it is honestly laughable.'

Caroline felt very cold and wished she had gone home with her mother. Would she find it laughable?

'Oh, by the way, your sister's here,' said Tom. 'She's in the office.'

'Vanessa?' Caroline asked, although she only had one sister.

She swallowed her desire to ask him why and just muttered thanks before taking the spiral staircase up to the office.

Vanessa was sitting at the table, surrounded by papers. As Caroline opened the door, she was setting aside the nightclub licence and moving on to another document, which Caroline could see had an embossed heading. Vanessa looked up and once again it struck Caroline that they must be the most unlikely twin sisters in existence. Caroline was tall with long fair hair and very white skin. She had the sylph-like appearance of her mother, while Vanessa, although still tall, had a stocky look, dark skin with reddish-brown curls cut into a short, mannish style and a much greater resemblance to their sporty father. It was as though Vanessa had been born to work, while Caroline had been born to decorate a room. She smiled at the thought.

Vanessa would hate that description, even if she agreed with it.

'It's good,' Vanessa said, seeing Caroline hovering on the threshold. 'Everything in the paperwork looks fine. You can't imagine how important that is in a case like this.'

Her sister gasped. 'What? What? What case? And what are you doing here?'

Caroline tried hard not to panic, but she could feel the sense of insecurity that Vanessa always engendered in her rising in her veins. She pinched her thumb hard.

'Why is the paperwork so important? Is this to do with Rupert's death? His ... his ... suicide.'

Vanessa frowned and swivelled her chair so she could see her sister better. 'Suicide? Who said anything about suicide?'

Caroline went over to the cupboard and got out some chocolate. She took a bite before replying.

'Why would anyone want to shoot Rupert? He didn't do anything. Literally! Who even knew him? All he did when he was at home was drink, so presumably that was all he did in his flat too. Most of his friends had dropped him. He was a complete wuss.'

Vanessa snorted. 'You.'

Caroline had crammed the whole chocolate bar into her mouth, so it took a moment to reply.

'Me? Me what?'

Her sister sat stolidly, watching the chocolate being gulped down before saying sternly, 'Yup. You. You have plenty of motivation. For a start, Rupert was trying to get custody of Lagertha. He threatened you in front of witnesses. And he suggested that Anthony was Lagertha's father. Or, even if not, that you had been having an affair with him before and after. He went and got DNA tests for heaven's sake.'

The chocolate dripped down her chin, but Caroline ignored it. 'How do you know about that?'

'The whole of London knows about it,' said Vanessa rather excessively. 'He yelled it up and down this nightclub, and who knows where else he went. Nothing was private with Rupert.'

'But ...' said Caroline, wiping her chin with a hanky, 'but ... I've never so much as kissed Anthony ... He was my therapist, not my lover. He wouldn't have broken whatever medical code that depends on, even if he wanted to.'

Her sister shrugged. 'Not what the gossip is ...' She grinned maliciously. 'And you know what people say about smoke and fire.'

Caroline pouted properly this time. 'Thanks. You're a great help. So, you've looked at all the paperwork, what now? Anyway, how are your much better halves?'

'Funny for you,' said her sister, 'but your brother and my lover are fine, thanks for asking. Gloria sent her love. Victor probably would have done too, but he's away somewhere frightfully important on business, so no use asking him anything.'

Caroline frowned. 'So, are you telling me that people are seriously suggesting I killed Rupert last night? Was it last night?'

Vanessa nodded.

'How was I supposed to do that? I had a night off from the club last night. I picked up Leggy from school. Took her home. She and I had supper together, then played chess until bedtime.'

'Chess? You play chess with Leggy?'

'Yes, and backgammon, the banana game, loads of

games. Last night was chess. Don't you play board games with your kids?'

Vanessa rubbed her nose. 'Victor and Gloria do. I'm busy most evenings. I scarcely get home before ten, sometimes later. But we're off the point. You don't have an alibi for last night, at least not after Leggy went to bed.'

Caroline's eyes widened. 'Are you suggesting I'd leave her alo—'

'No, of course not,' snapped her sister. 'But I'm not the one you have to fear.'

Caroline laughed. 'And where am I supposed to have got a gun from? The liaison PC told us he was shot. I don't even know how to shoot.'

'Prove it! Your husband—'

'Ex-husband.'

'Your ex-husband had a gun licence. There were guns locked in the cabinet in your house. Presumably you have a key.'

'Ha!' said Caroline. 'Shows what you know. Rupert took them away and sold them, but even when they were there, I didn't have access to them. Because I don't have a licence, I can't even have a key to a gun safe in my own house. If I wanted to get those shotguns out, I had to ask Rupert's friend Percy and he had to come round, open it up and take them out, never letting them out of his sight. It, my legal eagle sister, is the law!'

Vanessa stuck her tongue out. 'Good. Then you're OK on that angle. But believe me, sis, it may be the law, but not every gun owner sticks to it. You'd be surprised how many shotguns just get left under the bed or behind the sofa. Did you ever have a go at shooting?'

Caroline screwed up her nose. 'Course not. I hate any kind of blood sports and I don't eat meat. Why would I?'

Vanessa snorted. 'You and Rupert really were a marriage made in Heaven, weren't you? Why on earth did you—'

'You are starting to sound just like Mum,' said Caroline, her voice taking a low warning tone.

Vanessa took a slow intake of breath. 'Thanks. I have started to see that Mum has some good points. Now that I'm not dependent on her.'

'What does that mean? It's not my fault my husband couldn't earn a penny.'

'Yes, and I suppose it's not your fault that you ran away from school at fourteen and refused to do any work, while I studied non-stop day and night, determined to make something of my life without parental input.'

'Oh, eff off, I thought you came here to help me.'

'I did. I think you are OK. You'll convince anyone. But, of course, that leaves someone else open to accusation.'

Caroline frowned. 'Who? Are you suggesting Mum might have done something? It is true she was annoyed he had her DNA checked ...'

'Did he? He got a DNA check on Mum? Why? And, actually, how? The labs are usually pretty hot on making sure you aren't doing someone else's ... unless you are police, of course. Did Rupert have any friends in the police?'

Caroline shook her head. 'Not that I know of. His friends were usually drunken reprobates like him and only interested in money and sex. Most of them didn't even have proper jobs.'

Vanessa moved on her seat. 'But no. To be honest I doubt that the police are going to jump to the conclusion that Mother got a gun and went and shot Rupert. She may have a detective hobby, but that doesn't make her Annie Oakley.'

'No, but she might have gone shooting with Dad. When he was still alive.'

Vanessa rubbed her nose. 'Yes, although I don't think wives were encouraged to shoot in her day. She might be able to shoot, but I doubt if she did much.'

'Was Rupert shot with a shotgun?' Caroline asked suddenly. 'Surely that must be suicide. People don't go wandering around London with shotguns, do they?'

'Why not? As long as you're also carrying the certificate, it's legal, and King's Cross is a big station up to the north where a lot of grouse and pheasant shooting is done. But as for the first part of the question, I don't know. The police haven't talked to me. I only came in here to make sure everything in your set-up is legal. We don't want Rupert's death to spiral off into other areas.'

Caroline said nothing. Why did Vanessa always make her feel nervous, as though they were on the edge of a precipice?

'No, it wasn't Mum I was thinking of,' said Vanessa, starting to clear up the papers, 'but Anthony.'

'Anthony?' Caroline had only just sat down, but she jumped onto her feet again. 'Anthony? What has Anthony got to do with this?'

Vanessa put out her hands placatingly. 'Nothing as far as we know, but remember Rupert was shouting he was your lover, and even though we know he wasn't, it still gives him a potential motivation. And, I hate saying this, but one must be realistic. He isn't well protected.'

Caroline started sweating. 'Well protected? What do you mean?'

Vanessa looked into the middle distance for a while. 'Look, Caroline, I'm a lawyer. I've been in the law since I was twenty-one. There's no getting away from the fact that some people are more likely to be prosecuted than others. It's the way of the world.'

Caroline began to shake. 'I don't like this,' she said. 'Are you saying outright that because Anthony is Black and working class, he is more likely to be a suspect than someone who is white and rich? Is that really what you are saying? We are not in the USA. This is the UK, where you can believe in your police and your law courts, can't you?'

Vanessa put her hands over her lower face and sat for a while, her eyes dull, before she said, 'Let's hope so.'

CHAPTER 11

A CHAMELEON'S GENDER DIFFERENCES DEPEND ON ANCESTRY AND HERITAGE

Cat had put Leggy to bed and was settling down to wait for Frank, who was at a gig, when a phone rang somewhere in the kitchen. Cursing Frank, who never put the phone back on its charger, she searched the kitchen, following the noise. Finding it under the dogs' bowls, she flicked the green switch just before the caller rang off.

'Cat?'

'Yes.'

'Jane Fletcher here. Oh Cat, such awful news. Honestly, I really thought Rupert was going to get better and now this happens. He told me he was getting a job.'

Cat heard the woman's voice break.

Cat snuffled sympathetically. 'Oh, my darling, isn't it awful. Do you want to talk through things for a bit?'

'Actually, Cat, if it's OK, I'd like to come over. I was down staying with Angela—you remember Rupert's sister, the one with the twins and the three other children, one every three years. Quite a little family it is, and so noisy you wouldn't believe. Ted's not here. He stayed at home. He identified the body and after that he decided to stay in London, at his club. But I'm not far away at all and I really wanted to come over and chat. Would that be OK?'

Cat smiled cynically but kept her voice sweet. 'Of course. I've got Leggy here too and ...' She paused a moment before going on, but she had to warn Rupert's mother that her ex-daughter-in-law would also be around soon. 'Caroline's coming here after work, but that won't be until two or three in the morning.'

Jane sighed deeply. 'Oh dear, I did wish they would manage to stay together. Your daughter was such a lovely girl. I thought she did wonders for my boy.'

Cat heard a slight sob, then Jane said brusquely, 'I'll be there in ten minutes.'

Cat went upstairs to check the spare room bed was made. There was a good chance that Jane would want a drink or two and then want to stay the night. By the time she got back to the kitchen, Jane had arrived and was tapping on the door, before pushing it open.

'There you are, sweetheart. So lovely to see you but in what terrible circumstances. But I really had to see you. The thing is, you see ... Well, what it is ... The thing is ... I need to tell you various things, things that I'm afraid you don't know ... before they all come out.'

Cat lifted a bottle of wine and waved it invitingly.

Jane shook her head. 'Do you have any whisky? I'm afraid wine rather goes to my head.'

While Cat got the whisky, Jane settled herself on the sofa, pushing off the dogs, who shuffled off unwillingly, wrinkling their noses. 'Do they always take over the best places?' she asked, sniffing and lifting the dog rug to find a clean spot.

Cat smiled. 'Yeah, well, they are Frank's dearest companions and the only ones that don't jeer at his jokes, so what can I do?'

'Ah!'

Jane accepted the whisky, refusing water and asking for ice. Cat left the ice and the bottle by her side.

Once she was settled, Jane began again. 'Look, I don't know if Caroline told you this, and, to be honest, she probably doesn't know the whole story ... but the thing is, Rupert did a DNA test.'

Cat stared at her. She'd expected Jane to be full of stories about Rupert as a child, curious about how he died and wondering how her granddaughter was managing the death of her father, but instead she seemed only interested in some DNA tests. It seemed an odd reaction, but perhaps she'd already discussed Rupert's death so much with his sister she didn't want to go over it again. Cat didn't really believe it, but she tried to suppress her detective cynicism.

'Yes,' said Cat, 'I did know, and he seems to have done ones for Caroline, Leggy and me too, which I feel is illegal.'

Jane spread her hands, saying, 'Doesn't really make much difference now, does it, dear? But there is something that is very important, and I feel I must tell you because it really affects Leggy.'

'Leggy?' said Cat. *What could that be?* She looked appraisingly at Jane over her glasses. What diseases might she have that she could pass genetically to Leggy? How would that come out in her DNA? She realised Jane was still talking and wrenched her mind back into listening mode.

'Yes, you see, it isn't really our fault. I mean, Rupert was born in the seventies, and we didn't really know about the effect of genetics and certainly not that someone, or was it some people, were going to de-sanctify that whole genome string thing. I mean, how could we?'

Cat stared at her, torn between mystified and horrified. Jane had always looked so healthy, although she did tend to knock back a lot of whisky. Perhaps she had a liver problem. Would that be genetic? Or perhaps a propensity towards drinking?

'Are you telling me you have some terrible diseases that Leggy will inherit?'

It was Jane's turn to look mystified. 'No. What on earth gave you that idea? Do I look like someone with a disease? Completely healthy, me and my whole family. In fact we don't really believe in doctors. I think it just gives children a chance to skip off school pretending to be ill and supported by the doctor. And, of course, Ted totally agrees.'

She gave an odd laugh.

'So, what exactly are you telling me?'

Jane looked at her sadly. 'Well, you see ... I mean, you may have noticed that Ted and I were slow to have kids.'

Cat smiled politely. She was nineteen when she married and had kids immediately, so most people seemed slow to have children in comparison. However, as she hadn't met Jane until Caroline married Rupert, she had never held a view on this subject. She didn't interrupt, hoping Jane would get to the point shortly.

'And of course there was no IVF in those days, or if there was, we'd never heard of it. And then Charlotte fell pregnant.'

'Charlotte?' asked Cat, confused. This Charlotte seemed to appear from nowhere. 'Who is Charlotte?'

'Oh, she was the daughter of my best friend, Maggy, lovely girl, gorgeous really but no sense of responsibility, not like her sister who was oh so responsible!' Jane wriggled in her seat, throwing out her arms theatrically. 'Horrible woman, no heart. A doctor too. Who'd want a doctor without a heart? Cut her sister off when it happened and yet the parents were so loving and so then she cut the whole family off. She could afford to, of course, great job and a rich husband. Honestly!'

Cat felt like rolling her eyes. What was she talking about?

'Well, we said we'd take it, and he was such a lovely little boy, deep blue eyes like his mother and such a cheeky little face. And you know in the seventies, well, they weren't so hung up on paperwork in those days. And we thought, well, just go for it, you know? Later, when she did it again, well, we would have liked another baby, but we couldn't. I mean, you do understand, don't you? We were living in a village, and it wouldn't have been kind to the child. That sort of thing ought to happen in towns, don't you think?'

Jane turned sad, weeping eyes towards Cat.

Cat bit her lower lip. Her detective powers were being challenged. 'Are you telling me someone called Charlotte got pregnant, had a baby who you adopted as Rupert, and no one knew anything about it because it was all done privately?'

'Well, yes,' said Jane. 'We thought it was for the best. You know, Charlotte was only sixteen, and her parents were old. It all happened on some cruise somewhere. When they told me about it, I started fatting up—you know, pillows and the like—so that everyone was expecting it when Rupert was born.'

'What about the doctor? The hospital?'

Jane laughed. 'Dear Doctor Thos, such a nice man. He'd been treating us all for so long, played golf with Ted, and you know, doctors' salaries weren't then what they are now. He was so funny, dear, he would come for a home visit and say "Looks bad! Better have a whisky. That'll clear it up." I don't think he thought much of doctors any more than I do, even though he was one himself!'

She gave a huge guffaw of laughter and took a gulp of whisky.

'Besides, he had known Charlotte since she was a baby, and her parents. He wouldn't let the side down. The only weak link was the sister, but when she cut the family off, that problem left with her.'

Cat's mind buzzed. A bribed doctor? Very old, about to retire? A disgusted sister flouncing off. A supportive family.

'So, you had a home birth?'

Jane giggled. 'It was lovely. Charlotte did all the hard work, and I got the baby. She lived with us a month before the birth. We told everyone it was to help me when the baby arrived as I was determined on a home birth. People weren't so nosy in those days, and there was certainly none of this social media rubbish that ruins everyone's lives.'

'What about Angela?' asked Cat curiously. 'Was she also adopted?'

Angela's mother laughed. 'Well, that was the funny thing. Once we'd got one baby, then suddenly I could get preggers, and I had another. Only a year later, but no one was counting, were they?'

'I see,' said Cat slowly, 'and Rupert discovered this for the first time when he did a DNA test to check Leggy was his daughter?'

Jane drank her whisky before replying. 'Well, yes. I mean, I never guessed he would. I mean ... why would he? We were the best parents. And ... look, to be honest he didn't seem too fussed at all about the divorce. Didn't seem to care if Caroline took Leggy ... until suddenly he changed.'

She took another gulp of whisky, emptying her glass.

Cat frowned. 'When was that? Was it when he got the decree nisi? Did it suddenly all become more real?'

Jane helped herself to another whisky before replying.

'I wonder,' said Cat thoughtfully, 'did his mother perhaps come looking for him? What happened to Charlotte and her family?'

'Well, thing was ... after the second one they felt they really couldn't stay in England, so they went off to America to start a new life. Shame because they were great friends, and you don't often find people that much on your wavelength.'

'A second one?' said Cat.

Jane gave her an 'I told you already' look and nodded. 'I still miss Maggy—she was a laugh in a way few friends are. She was generous too, but I guess that is often the way with rich people. Doesn't affect them, does it?' Her voice took on a cynical tone, but Cat ignored it. 'I did hope they'd settle a trust on Rupert, but they didn't. Such a shame.'

Wise people, thought Cat, not that they were to know he'd have drunk it away as soon as he got it.

'So, what happened to the second baby?' she asked. 'Did Charlotte keep her or was it a boy?'

Jane shrugged. 'No idea, only that it was ... well, you know ... as I say I'm very liberal, but you know ...'

Cat was about to ask more when they were interrupted by the noise of smashing outside.

'Oh my goodness,' said Jane, jumping up and hurrying to the window, 'what happened?'

Cat didn't even get up. She laughed. 'Caroline has arrived. That will be the noise of her scraping the side of her car on the gate or the wall. Often happens.'

Caroline came in at a run. She stopped on the threshold and stared.

'Oh, Jane, it's you. I saw the car and I thought ... I thought it was all a bad dream.'

And she burst into tears.

After Caroline had gone to bed with a hot chocolate, Cat and Jane sat down again. Jane poured herself another whisky. Cat felt very relieved she had made up the bed. Clearly Jane was in the mood for an all-night session. She poured herself a glass of wine.

'Caroline is looking very pretty,' said Jane, and Cat thought her voice sounded testy, as though Caroline wasn't looking upset enough. 'Does she have any idea who killed my boy?'

'No,' said Cat. 'Not a clue. Have you got any ideas?'

'No,' said Jane, and again her voice sounded raspy, 'but we haven't seen him much since that woman took him away.'

'Oh,' said Cat. 'Which woman? Caroline thought he was living with you, until he came to Spinners and told her otherwise.'

'Yes.' Jane took another gulp of whisky. 'He seemed quite happy living with us until he got that odd girlfriend.'

Cat frowned. Caroline hadn't mentioned a girlfriend. Jane might behave as though a girlfriend was virtually irrelevant, but for someone of Rupert's weak personality, any girlfriend was likely to be vitally important.

'Oh, I didn't know. Did she help him?'

Jane glanced towards the door, as though there might be spies outside. She lowered her voice. 'I doubt it. I don't really like to talk about her. She was odd.'

'Odd?'

'Well, you know me, I'm as liberal as the next gal ...'

Cat bit her lower lip. 'Did you meet her?'

'Yes, she came to pick him up in her car. He told me he gave his car to Caroline to help her with Lagertha. He was such a nice boy. So good to his old mother.' She wiped away a tear. 'Always bringing me presents.'

Cat sipped her wine. She bought that car for Caroline after Rupert sold the one his parents had given them.

'And?'

'Well, as I say, I'm not one who judges others, far from it, but she was telling him do this and do that and put everything in there. I bet she was the one who made him do those DNA tests. I'm sure he'd never heard of getting yourself tested until she came along with her suspicious mind.'

She looked in Cat's direction, although her eyes were glassy and distant.

'That was why he left. Said we weren't his parents. Had never treated him equal with Angela. He even tried to pretend we weren't interested in Lagertha, which simply isn't true. I treated all my grandchildren equally, didn't I?'

Cat said nothing. For once she agreed with Rupert. Jane had never shown any interest in Leggy and was perfectly happy that she should spend any time Caroline was busy with Cat and Frank.

'So,' said Cat, 'just tell me, why was she odd?'

Again Jane looked at the door, as though someone was listening and going to report her to the thought police. 'She was in a wheelchair!'

Cat moued. 'A wheelchair? So she couldn't walk. That's hardly odd, is it?'

Jane shrugged. 'Well, I don't believe in it,' she said obscurely.

'In what?' asked Cat, mystified once again.

'Look, there are too many people in the world already,

you know. It's better we keep the well ones, not prolong problems. You know, if they are born all wrong, well, then it's better they just have a quick injection. End it all. Parents get another one and ...'

Cat nibbled her lip. She had heard this kind of eugenic talk before. It wasn't uncommon when the children were young, but times had changed and now people were more humane. She wondered if it was this that drove Rupert to drink.

'Are you saying she was disabled from birth?'

'Yes. She told me it was a birth accident. Mother died, father remarried, and she was brought up by a series of aunts. Must have been difficult for the aunts. Poor things. Not even your own and such a burden.'

'I wonder, Jane,' said Cat, hoping to stem the flow of a conversation she was not enjoying, 'if you would allow us to visit Rupert's flat. I mean, when the police have finished exploring it.'

Jane shrugged. 'Yes, of course. I don't have a key or anything, but I expect Drina will have one ... if you want to ask her.'

'Drina?'

'The crip ... the woman in the chair.'

Cat nodded. 'Do you have an address for her?'

'No, although Rupert thought he might live there, but then it transpired she had found him something else. But I do have the address of his flat. I'll text it to you.'

'Thanks.'

CHAPTER 12

ROCKING, SPITTING, HIDING
AND CURLING THE TAIL ARE
SIGNS OF STRESS

This was PC Puddle's first solo interview. Up until now he'd been a probationer following a more experienced officer, so doing his first interview alone was both thrilling and intimidating. He stood for a moment outside the pub door, preparing what he should say and the way he should say it.

At the station they had given him the job in an almost dismissive manner.

'Victim was a drunk,' the sergeant said. 'Owner of one of the houses in Eltham thinks he recognised him on his CCTV as someone making a scene in the street, so go and check out all the pubs in Eltham. OK?'

He gave Puddle a map which covered a good twenty pubs and stretched several miles. Puddle had a nasty feeling he was trying to get rid of him, to let more experienced coppers do the real work.

He'd already been into two pubs in Eltham before he entered the Black Scabbard. Both pubs had been virtually empty, and the barman could hardly be bothered to give him the time of day. Puddle was feeling cross and bored.

He'd be sent on a fool's errand. Nobody went to the pub at ten a.m. in the morning.

The Black Scabbard was rammed.

He stopped and took a hasty breath. He hadn't expected so many faces to be looking at him as he entered. A quick scan of the pub showed a man standing behind the bar, and even though he wasn't smiling, he looked OK. Friendly. Puddle approached him, trying to walk casually, as though he'd interviewed thousands of people and always got the result he wanted.

'Hi,' he said, placing his shiny identity card on the bar proudly. 'I'm PC Puddle. We're investigating a death and I believe the victim was seen in this area on the day he died.'

He put away his card and pulled out a picture of Rupert. Donated by his mother and taken many years before, it showed a happy boy grinning at the camera.

'I'm looking for anyone who might have seen this man.'

He got out his pad and glanced at it even though he had already memorised all the details of the case. 'The night of the 26th, two weeks ago on Wednesday. Were you on that night?'

Before the barman could speak, a middle-aged man sitting by the window and covered with tattoos yelled, 'Was that the drunk who fought the jiggaboo?'

The young policeman looked over at him, frowning slightly. 'Jigga who?'

'Yeah, an effing Black man?'

The policeman turned to him, interested. His instinct told him there was something here. Perhaps he was about to get a lead before his colleagues—that would show the duty sergeant and his poncy attitude. 'Can you tell me a bit more? Was there an altercation between the deceased and another man?'

The man leant back against the table and looked the constable up and down. 'We talking about a tall thin bloke wearing a sharp suit?'

'Sounds possible,' said the PC. 'Dark hair. It says here he was tall, had blue eyes and a thin face with slightly protruding ears.'

The man made an obscene gesture and altered his voice to a higher pitch. 'Yeah. Noticed the eyes of course, darling!' He grinned at his mates and squirmed on the stool, before returning to his normal voice. 'Posh bloke. All wharr wharr, so you could hardly understand what he said. But give him his due, he was drinking quiet like until the other bloke came in.'

PC Puddle moved across the room to stand near the man. He opened another page of his notebook, letting his pen hover over the page in an official manner. 'Great. Could you describe the man who came in?'

'Yeah,' said the tattooed man, 'the new bloke was big. He was a ni ... He was Black.'

'Anything else?'

'Well ... you know ... curly hair ... white teeth ... oh yeah, and another posh suit. Spiv. You know the type.'

The policeman frowned. Was this man assuming he was racist like him? He tried to take back control of the interview. 'Could you tell me what happened? Can you perhaps give me a sequence of events?'

'Sure can,' said the man, rapping his hand on the table. 'In came this ni ... Black man, all aggressive like. You know. We was just sitting having a quiet pint, minding our own business like, and this guy barges in. He throws back the door like we're in a cowboy movie and strides in like he owns the place. Drug dealer! Had it written all over him. You could see he was trouble from the moment he entered the room, throwing his weight around like he thought he was back in the jungle.'

'And then?'

'Well, he ordered a pint ... and then this other guy saw him and yelled ... said that the fucking ni ... Black man had got his wife up the duff ... He stepped up peaceful like, you know, considering their history like, and the Black guy took a swing at him and knocked him cold. Then ran for his life. He could see we was not going to let that happen in our manor.'

'I see,' said the PC, turning to the two men seated behind the speaker. 'And is that how it looked to you?'

'Certainly did,' said the nearest man, 'looked like he was out for a fight. And he was big. Way more than six foot, nearer seven, and muscles what looked like a fighter. Evil eyes too.'

There was a general round of agreement from the other drinkers on nearby tables. Someone added he had a big nose, and it might have been broken.

'And did anyone follow him? Out on the street?'

The guys exchanged glances. 'No way,' said a smaller man with a tattoo of a snake on his wrist, 'we're peaceful like here. We don't fight, whatever the provocation, do we, boys?'

There were murmurs of agreement and one man added, 'We's veritable Gandhis, we is.'

The PC finished his notes and went over to the bar to talk to the bartender.

'Did you see it?' he asked. 'Were you on that night?'

The man looked at him for a moment. Then he looked back at the men at the tables.

'Sure,' he said, 'it was just like they said. Except one thing.'

The mood across the room suddenly stiffened.

'There was an old man here too. He took the boy away, the one who was hit.'

The mood of the men relaxed.

'That's right,' said the main speaker. 'He weren't from round here either.'

'So,' the policeman asked the barman, 'you don't know who he was?'

He shook his head. 'Never seen him before.'

'Or the other men?'

'Nope.'

CHAPTER 13
CHAMELEONS NEED UVB
LIGHT TO SURVIVE

After two weeks of staying in Owly Vale with her mother, Caroline was thoroughly bored. Every morning she did home schooling with Leggy, every afternoon they walked or played games. Leggy seemed to be taking her father's death quite calmly. Perhaps, Caroline thought, having seen so many fights between her mother and father, this seemed like just another episode in the child's life or perhaps she hadn't understood how terminal death was.

Caroline herself chaffed under her mother's well-meaning ministrations. She'd always preferred her father, although, as Vanessa pointed out rather vulgarly, he held their brother, Victor, in such high regard compared to them that they were able to see by the light that shone from his arse. At least he didn't fuss like Cat did. They were too alike, she and her mother, too many trigger points. Her mother was just annoying.

'Mum, we're going back to London. I need to get back to work.'

'Oh, darling, is that wise?' said Cat, quickly checking

Leggy was not within earshot. 'We still don't know who killed Rupert or why, or even how. If he was blackmailing someone, they might think you too knew the information and come after you.'

Caroline sneered. 'Blackmail? Yeah, right! What information could Rupert possibly have? Someone cheating on the price of booze perhaps?' She jumped up and got Leggy's work books for this morning's teaching. She knew she should probably end there, but she wasn't going to let this go. 'You think I'm so much safer here? In Owly Vale, Capital of Nowhere. How will you defend me? Swipe all marauders with a frying pan? Set Frank's elderly Labradors on them? I think I'll be safer in London with Tom and Oscar to protect me.'

'OK, in the club, yes, but what about when you are at home? I mean ... I know you have CCTV outside, but what if they're in already ...'

Cat's eyes were soft with worry and Caroline forced herself to be gentle and put her hand on her mother's shoulder. 'Yeah, Mum, OK. But I think we'll find Rupert killed himself. I bet they find the gun slid under a sofa or something. I'll be fine. Don't worry.'

Caroline had been away less than twenty-four hours when Cat received a telephone call from her.

'Mum,' she said, and Cat could hear her voice shaking. 'Vanessa was right.'

Cat went cold. It was very rare for the sisters to agree on anything, and she never ever remembered hearing Caroline say Vanessa was right before.

'About what?'

Cat could hear Caroline taking deep breaths and it was a

while before she spoke again. When she did her voice sounded heavy. 'They've arrested Anthony.'

'Oh my God,' said Cat, her mind whirring. She taught her children not to swear, but this was a special occasion. 'But are you sure? Arrested? On what grounds?'

Caroline made a noise. 'OK, they've taken him in for questioning. But it's the same as arresting if you ask me! They say he had a fight with Rupert in a pub. There are witnesses. They have him on CCTV leaving the pub and getting on his bike. He apparently pedalled off so fast it seemed like he was running away.'

'Anthony? I just don't believe it.'

'Apparently a lot of people saw it. They all say Anthony came into the pub like he was stalling for a fight. Rupert saw him and came over, the two fought and Anthony knocked Rupert down. Then he ran away.'

'Must have been someone else,' said Cat. 'I can't see Anthony getting aggressive and into a fight, even with Rupert.'

'They came for him,' said Caroline incoherently, 'in a Zulu Tango Two van. At work. Vanessa says those are only used for prisoners too aggressive to be in a car.'

Cat shook her head, although Caroline couldn't see her. She wished Vanessa wouldn't interfere. 'Are you sure, darling? How does Vanessa know these things? Are you sure she's not just winding you up?'

Caroline was crying on the phone and couldn't speak.

'But, darling,' Cat continued, 'why would they be in the same pub? Anthony works in Pimlico and lives in Maida Vale; Rupert lived in King's Cross. How could they have met in a pub? Where was it?'

'Eltham,' said Caroline, 'called the Black Scabbard, ghastly name and a scary area.'

'Oh,' said Cat. With all the hoo-ha over Rupert's death, she'd completely forgotten about Anthony's text. 'Oh!'

'What?'

'Well, Anthony sent me a text saying he was going to a pub in Eltham after getting a text from you. He didn't believe you sent it. He thought it might be a trap and although he was going to go, he needed backup. Unfortunately, I didn't get the text until too late. But when I talked to him, he didn't say anything about a scrap in a pub. Indeed, he just made it sound like he'd been getting nervous over a non-event. So, of course, I forgot all about it.'

She gave a light laugh, hoping her daughter would join her.

'My God!' said Caroline. 'He asked you for help and you let him down! If he's killed in prison, I'll never speak to you again. Never. Ever, ever.'

She rang off, and Cat imagined she wished it was possible to slam down modern phones.

Cat moved the phone around in her hand. This needed some deep discussion with her colleagues. She knew Stevie would still be away, but it was possible Miranda was back from her holiday in Morocco. It seemed like ages since she left.

She called Miranda on WhatsApp, hoping she was not in too much of a holiday mood to get back to work. Miranda answered after the first ring.

'Cat!'

'How are you? Good holiday?'

'Pah,' said Miranda, 'the first couple of days were brilliant. Phillip was relaxed, happy, much the man I knew before we married. Then, on day three, he got a call from the office. Out came his computer and from then on I was travelling with a zombie. He was in London at the office, and

I was in and out of souks, pools, hiking through the Atlas Mountains, visiting glorious Moroccan architecture, but all on my own.'

'Ah ... but ...' said Cat, hoping to stop the flow.

However, Miranda was just warming to the full tale of Phillip's inadequacies. 'And then, when I get back from a full day of touristing, what is he doing? Is he working? No! He is watching boxing on Moroccan TV. From twenty years ago. He said this scarred English boxer, Charles FitzRoy, who boxed for the police, was a superhero twenty years ago and how amazing that the Moroccans were still showing him. Not that I consider it amazing; there are police everywhere on the streets. My taxi driver said they were checking licences, but I reckoned they were looking for immigrants.'

'And ... yes ... but ...'

'So, after a while, I couldn't wait to get home and start investigating.'

'That's good,' said Cat. 'A lot has happened while you were away.'

'I know,' said Miranda, 'Agata picked me up from the airport.'

'Your sister? The one who's training to be a policewoman?'

'That's the one. She's lucky; she's been included in the police team investigating Rupert's death. OK, only as a gofer really, but she can listen. We need to talk. See you in the office in five?'

'You bet. Any chance Stevie is back yet?'

'In a few days. I've been talking to her. They fly out tomorrow, but they are going via Rio. She's dying to get back. Bit of FOMO, I think.'

'FOMO?'

'Fear of missing out.'

'Oh dear, more Orwellian inability to speak properly in the young,' said Cat, 'but I'll send her a WhatsApp to get her up to speed before she gets back. Then she can hit the computer running.'

Miranda laughed. 'See you in the office in five?'

CHAPTER 14
UNLIKE HUMANS,
CHAMELEONS DO NOT LIVE
IN FAMILY GROUPS

As Cat left home to walk around to the office, her mobile rang. It was Caroline. Perhaps she had already forgiven her.

'Mum,' said Caroline, 'I've just talked to Anthony's parents. They want to employ you to find Rupert's real killer. I said SeeMs was just a hobby and pretty useless really, but they seemed to think you'd done some good work. Anthony must have been kind when he told them about you. Anyway, Kaya wants to meet you. I'll text you her phone number, OK?'

'Yes, thanks,' said Cat, rather surprised, not just by her daughter's take on the job but that Anthony's parents would want to employ the SeeMs Agency when they so clearly were involved in the whole case and related to the victim. She wanted to point out to Caroline that Anthony had actually only been taken in for questioning and everyone was panicking, but her daughter had already ended the call.

As she arrived in the office, Blinkey, Stevie's mother, was standing by the door.

'Password!'

'Morning, Blinkey, lovely morning. Did you have a nice breakfast?'

'No, wrong.'

Blinkey, with surprising agility, leapt sideways, blocking Cat's attempt to circumvent her.

'Naughty, naughty! No password, no entry.'

Cat nibbled her lip. She wondered if it really was a good idea using Stevie's mother's house for their office. Having their constant input might help with Blinkey's dementia care and support her carers, but it did sometimes divert their attention from their work.

'Oh,' she said, looking over Blinkey's head, 'what's that up there?' She pointed into the house and Blinkey looked round. Cat nipped quickly past her and into the office, only to hear Miranda and her dog meeting the same treatment.

'Password.'

The dog barked.

'Well done,' said Blinkey, 'you may pass.'

Miranda and the dog charged into the office, Miranda heading for the coffee and her dog jumping ebulliently onto the sofa.

'Good morning,' said Miranda, 'lovely to see you, Cat. I bought you a rug—it's made of camel hair by Berber women —but I left it at home. I'll bring it round later.'

Cat laughed. 'OK, tell me about Agata and why she came to Gatwick to meet you. I can't remember when someone last met me at the airport.'

Miranda gave Cat a coffee and sat on the sofa, pushing her dog onto the floor.

'OK, but it doesn't make for easy listening.'

'Go on.'

Miranda stretched out her legs. 'When the family liaison officer reported back about giving Caroline the news of

Rupert's death, she said Caroline was cold, almost offhand and appeared to already know the news. She said, even allowing for shock, she thought the way Caroline received the news was very odd.'

Cat put down her coffee, undrunk. 'Did she take into account this was her ex-husband?'

'She certainly did, and they all seemed to know that Rupert had threatened to take Leggy away from her.'

Cat blew out sharply. 'Honestly! Everyone seems to know every word Rupert said to Caroline in Spinners. Anyone would think the nightclub had a direct line to the newspapers. Or is it that social media thing again? Either way it's weird. Any more on the cause of death?'

'Yes. He was shot by a .22 pistol. Entry at close range through the back of the head.'

'Have they found the pistol?'

'Nope. Not yet. They have the bullet, but not the gun.'

'Do the police have any other suspects?'

'Apart from Anthony, you mean?'

'Yes.'

'Well, presumably anyone in the flats Rupert was living in could have done it. Agata said it was an old block with lots of tiny flats.'

'Yes,' said Cat, 'they might have opportunity, certainly. But motive?'

'Rupert was a drunk,' said Miranda. 'Perhaps he annoyed one of the other residents so much they couldn't take any more. Think of living in a tiny flat with Rupert yelling and screaming all night. It would send you crazy.'

Cat nodded. 'Certainly possible. There was a case like that years ago. The perp was so angry he didn't even remember killing the victim and it was only when he had hypnosis that it all came out.'

Miranda stroked the dog. After a pause she said, 'Agata says the investigating team were keen to interview Caroline. The only reason they haven't done it yet is that they thought it would be better to tail her and see if anyone else was implicated.'

'Tail her? For heaven's sake. Like a spy film! Is she still being tailed? I wonder what they made of her meeting up with Rupert's mother in my house.'

'Agata wouldn't know anything like that. But anyway, meanwhile they had PCs asking questions in the flats where Rupert lived, and in the nightclub where he made the allegations. Then, having heard that he was in the Black Scabbard pub in Eltham, they sent a PC round there.'

'How?'

'What?'

'How did they hear that Rupert was in the Black Scabbard pub?'

'CCTV. Apparently Rupert was yelling in the street and although the owner of the house with the camera was away, his neighbours weren't. He came back a few days later and checked the footage. As it happened there was a picture of Rupert in the paper and he recognised it as the same man on the CCTV. So he called the local police, and they passed it on to the team.'

'A gold star for joined-up policing,' said Cat. 'I bet that doesn't happen often.'

'Cynical Cat! And then, after the police went to the pub and heard the story about Rupert's fight, they checked the pub CCTV.'

'Are you saying they identified Anthony from the footage? It must be pretty high quality. I thought the problem with CCTV was blurred imagery and that you could never work out who it was.'

'No idea, but all I can say is that if they were tailing Caroline, they'd also be looking into her background and they'd find she had a therapist. I guess they would say "oh look, a Black man leaving the pub and a Black therapist" and make twenty-five.'

Cat chewed a finger. 'Rather a leap, yes, but perhaps not for a policeman looking for a suspect. Anything else?'

'Not at present. Agata's gone back to taking notes for the team and doing as much gofer work as they need.'

Miranda got the dog lead. 'Look, I'll take the dog out for a bit. It always helps me think. You want to come?'

'No, I think I'll ring Stevie and give her an update. She might be able to use her magic computer to find out why Rupert's picture was already in the papers.'

'Yes,' said Miranda, halfway out the door. 'Good point. Think how many murders there must be every day. Why is this one so interesting?'

CHAPTER 15
THE VEILED CHAMELEON IS
THE MOST COMMON TYPE

Next day, when Leggy was at school, Caroline decided to go to the club to work through her finances, think about logistics and generally keep her mind away from potentially chocolate-needing problems for as long as she could. As she got ready, her telephone rang: an unknown number. She ignored it. It was almost certainly a reporter trying to get some inside angle. Both at home and at the club, she'd been besieged by them. Luckily, she had thought of getting someone else to drop Leggy at school, so there, at least, her daughter was free from aggravation.

As Caroline got into her car, she noticed the number of photographers had thinned. Did they know Anthony was in for questioning, or had another, more pressing story got their attention instead? She drove fast past the stragglers, hoping to hit one, but the photographers jumped clear.

As she arrived at the club, her phone bleeped again. This time with a text. It was short and said: *My name is Drina Regis. I was Rupert's girlfriend. Can you ring me on this number asap?*

Caroline stared at it, this strange, abrupt message. Was it just another reporter trying to be clever? She'd like to have some input from someone. Should she ring her mother? No, Cat would just interfere, insist on ringing the girlfriend herself.

She walked up the stairs into the bar. Only Oscar was there, polishing glasses. She was glad to see him. Perhaps he would tell her something funny to cheer her up. She tried to say a cheerful good morning, although her body felt so pained and miserable it was all she could do to talk at all.

'Oscar,' she said, 'you are early today.'

His eyes smiled reassuringly at her. 'Seems I'm not alone. You OK? It's a frightening time for you, and if you need someone to talk to, remember I'm here.'

He could read her thoughts. How wonderful. He was a nice man.

'Thank you, Oscar,' she said. 'Since you mention it, there is something I wanted to discuss with someone.'

He inclined his head.

She proffered her phone, saying, 'Look. I've had a text from someone saying she was Rupert's girlfriend and she'd like a chat. Do you think it's genuine?'

'Could be,' said Oscar, reading the message. 'As you know yourself, Rupert could be charming when he was sober. I'm not surprised he had a girlfriend. Do you want me to ring her for you, find out what she wants?'

Caroline rubbed her nose. Easier to let him do it, but it was a cowardly way out. 'No,' she said. 'I'll ring her now. See what she says.' She felt safer phoning with this big man's presence behind her.

Drina answered her phone on the second ring. She had a warm, friendly voice. 'Caroline, thank you so much for ringing back. I know it must sound strange to you, me contacting you like this out of the blue. But when Rupert did the DNA tests, he discovered more things than just his adoption and so, well, I wondered if you would like to come round to my house and chat about them. I think you'll find them interesting.'

Caroline frowned. 'Can you tell me on the phone?'

'No. Too personal.'

'Oh, OK. When were you thinking?'

'Now? If it suits you. I'm not doing anything. And there's no time like the present. If you're not too busy.' She gave a little, almost modest, laugh.

Caroline felt herself panicking. Now. Already? With no preparation? She grabbed her thumb and pinched, but still felt awful. Then she looked at Oscar. Why not take him with her? She'd told her mother she felt protected by Tom and Oscar.

She looked questioningly at him. He nodded. 'OK, but I'd like to bring a friend if that's OK.'

'That's fine,' said Drina. 'I'll text you the address.'

CHAPTER 16
CHAMELEONS ARE MASTERS OF CAMOUFLAGE

Oscar drove Caroline over to Drina's house in Chelsea, saying it was probably more relaxing for her, and if they got any press interference, he was good at avoiding trouble.

'Done speed driving in my time,' he said, winking at her.

She wondered what that meant, but really she had too much to think about without worrying why her barman had learnt to drive fast and defensively.

'Nice house,' said Oscar as they pulled up in the private drive outside the free-standing house. 'Must be worth a bomb. You don't get many places in London that have their own forecourt. When you think how people fight for simply a private garage miles away, how much more would they pay for a spread like this?'

'Yes,' said Caroline, her mind preoccupied, not really interested in the wealth or otherwise of Rupert's former girlfriend.

To their surprise the front door was open. Oscar pushed it and went in, saying loudly, 'Hello? Anyone there?'

'Hellooo,' replied a voice from the room on the right, 'come on in.'

They went into a beautifully furnished sitting room with pieces that looked as though someone paid a lot for them in an auction house. Drina was lying on the gold brocade sofa.

'Come in, come in,' she said rather magnificently. 'I'm afraid I've just had my bunions done, so I can't get up and help you, but my maid has left some coffee and biscuits on the side. Help yourself.'

Caroline blinked. The voice sounded the same as the woman's on the phone, but the attitude was completely different. Suddenly this woman seemed to be a lordly person, whereas before she had sounded normal. Caroline wondered if there would be any chocolate in the biscuits.

As they took their coffees, Caroline was relieved to see there were chocolate biscuits. They sat down on armchairs opposite the sofa. Caroline fidgeted in the chair. It was uncomfortable. Lumps. The cup was too frail. They were sitting too far away for any intimate things that Drina might be going to say. She felt hot. She glanced at Oscar, but he was relaxing back in his chair with his coffee, a happy smile on his face. She pinched her thumb and tried to fold into the chair.

'So,' said Drina, 'I've got some interesting news. It particularly affects your daughter.'

Caroline sat upright. She gobbled up the chocolate biscuits, then jumped up, went over to the plate and grabbed two more, her mind blank.

Drina smiled.

'Yes. As I said, Rupert and I were girlfriend and boyfriend, but, luckily, as I'm a very religious person ...' She put her head on one side and gave a sympathetic smile. 'Nothing carnal had happened between us.'

Caroline felt bile in her mouth.

'I say luckily,' Drina's smooth voice continued, 'because when we did the DNA tests, we discovered we were brother and sister.'

She gave a 'would you believe it' type smile towards Caroline. Caroline pinched her thumb. 'Why did you do DNA tests on yourself?' she asked sharply.

Drina stared at her, then said, her voice now harsh and speaking fast, 'Oh, how foolish of me. You, of course, are not adopted. You have always known your parents. You can take it for granted that your parents wanted you. You have no concept of the void that sits in your heart when you don't know your mother or your father. How could you possibly understand what it's like to be without a family. How silly of me to imagine you had the ability to sympathise.'

She stopped and gave an enormous sigh, which echoed through the large room. 'I, sadly, have no idea who my mother and father were. What terrible reason meant that they had to give their baby away? Was I pulled screaming from my mother's arms? Was she tricked into giving me up? Forced? Cajoled? And so here I am, searching. Forever searching.

'Of course I do DNA tests. I search the library. I contact people. I ask: who am I?

But how could I expect you, from your loving, supportive family, to understand.'

The room became tense, silent. Drina glared at Caroline. Caroline glared back. How could Rupert have subjected her to this woman?

Oscar gave a loud chuckle, which hovered in the strained atmosphere. 'Well,' he said, 'oh my goodness! How lucky you did the tests. You could have married, and then look what would have happened ... your children ...'

'Indeed!' said Drina, still looking at Caroline with open loathing.

Caroline felt a pulse beating in her throat. Her whole body felt sweaty. She pinched her thumb so hard she could feel a bruise starting.

The unbearable silence returned. Caroline felt a weight was pressing on her, holding her to the chair.

Then Drina's voice suddenly cut into the tension, giving Caroline a shock. 'Of course, Rupert had never really felt part of that family. He and his sister and even his mother ...' She sighed and again looked at Caroline. 'They didn't understand his pain.'

Caroline stared back.

Drina snorted. 'Suffice to say they had very different outlooks on life. He had always wondered, poor thing, how someone so kind and liberal as himself could have such terrible right-wing relations, with their strange, elitist and even, although I hesitate to say it, eugenic vision of life.'

Caroline shook her head. Rupert was not as described. He was a drunken bum. He hit his wife. He hit his daughter. He was not kind, sensitive. No!

Drina took a delicate sip of her coffee. 'He was such a kind, generous man with such a large heart, as, of course, you know yourself.'

Her smile was warm enough to include the whole world.

'And then, oh, the joy of discovery for us both. He had a sister as kind and generous as himself. As loving and as longing to share our benefits with the world. And I had a loving, intelligent brother. We had so much in common.'

She stopped, as though to allow the others to share in her joy. Oscar's face filled with a broad smile. Caroline was stuck to the chair.

'But then such sadness. Just as we discovered our beautiful, happy relationship, he died. Killed! Murdered. And now I have no more relations ... No more soulmates with whom to share my thoughts and aspirations.'

Drina allowed some tears to fall down her cheeks, which she mopped, carefully, with an elegant handkerchief.

'What a tragedy indeed. However, I must now tell you more about your daughter's new relation.' She gave a little laugh and had another sip of coffee.

'I was brought up in care. It wasn't brutal. Firm but hard. No real love. But lots of lessons.' She smiled, her eyes caressing them. 'Many of those were from the University of Life, a harsh but fair place. Luckily that spurred me on to make money. I never wanted to be poor again. You can see how well I did ...' She waved her hand magnificently. 'But always, always I longed for relations, for someone special to be related to me.'

She smiled sadly at Caroline.

'The only lucky thing is that I still have one wonderful young relation alive and how I long to see her and pamper her with all my wealth. When can I see young Leggy?'

Caroline felt sick, and she didn't think it was the chocolate. She looked at Oscar, but his benign face gave the impression that he thought Caroline should be pleased.

'So,' continued Drina, 'when can I meet the little girl, my lovely niece?'

'Never!' said Caroline, jumping up furiously, her body suddenly coming to life. 'Come, Oscar! We're going. You keep your greedy, vile hands and all your slutty money away from my daughter. I don't know who you are, and I don't believe a word of what you are saying. Oscar, we are off.'

Caroline ran out of the door and jumped into the car, which fortunately Oscar had left unlocked. He walked slowly after her, pausing only momentarily to say something to Drina.

As Oscar drove her home, he asked gently, 'Didn't you think there might be some truth in what Drina Regis was saying? She seemed like a genuine person to me. Sincere.'

Caroline breathed deeply and didn't speak. She pinched her bruised thumb and enjoyed the pain.

'And it would be nice for Leggy to have all the money that is clearly tied up in that house.'

Caroline looked at him. To her it seemed clear that Drina did not seem at all genuine, that the whole thing looked like a nasty gutter-press type of set-up. But she liked Oscar. He was a good man, cared about the clients. Made her laugh. She wavered.

'Stop here,' she said to Oscar. 'Just outside the newsagent.'

She jumped out. 'I won't be long.'

Caroline returned in a few moments laden with chocolate, tearing at the silver foil and cramming the contents into her mouth. 'Thank you,' she said. 'Back to the club, please. I need to think about this.'

She let the chocolate digest and then said slowly, 'You don't think she is an undercover press person trying to get a story?'

'No,' said Oscar, 'never crossed my mind. Where would anyone get such a house if they were just a tabloid journalist? But we can look it up. We'll easily find out who owns the house, and then you can make your own decision.'

Caroline ate more chocolate and stared through the window at the passing streets. She knew everyone would say she was crazy, but this did not feel right.

* * *

Back at the club they walked up the spiral stairs to Caroline's office. Oscar, it seemed, was good on the computer and quickly found sites about house ownership that Caroline had never heard of. She pinched her bruised thumb, wishing she had listened better when Stevie gave her computer lessons. She didn't find the internet interesting.

'Now,' he said, interrupting her thoughts, 'see here. We just put in her address and see who owns the house and for how long.' He fiddled a bit and then pointed to the screen.

'Wow. Look at that. The house has been owned by an Emily Corinna Regis for thirty years. She must be older than she looks.'

Caroline blew out. 'She looked about fifty to me, maybe older.'

Oscar glanced at her and then back at the screen. 'So, she does own the house. And what a house, eh? It would be a nice place for little Leggy to play.'

He got up and, leaving the site in place, went back to the bar to help Tom, who had just arrived.

Caroline felt sick and she still didn't believe a word of what the woman said. She stared at the website. Oscar seemed to know a lot about the internet for a man around sixty. But then she knew hardly anything, and she was much younger. It didn't always go with age or gender.

Could she trust him? There seemed no reason why not. He worked for her. He'd never even met this Drina Regis before. Why should he care about her? Perhaps he was right, and she was the owner of that house, but that still didn't mean there was any connection with Rupert and, by extension, Leggy.

The remaining chocolate sat untasted in her hands, its silver paper rustling as she rubbed her hands together.

She needed more input. She needed to do research, but she wasn't sure how.

Where should she start? And then an idea popped into her brain, and she sagged with relief. Someone far more computer savvy than her, and definitely on her side. She rang Stevie on WhatsApp video.

The phone rang a couple of times before it was answered and a sleepy-looking Stevie appeared on the screen. Caroline felt a spasm of guilt, which only lasted a nanosecond. Her need was greater than Stevie's desire for rest.

'Hello. Caroline? What's up?'

'You awake? Where are you?'

'I guess so. I'm in Rio. I was dozing, watching the TV, and wondering what it would be like to be trilingual like your mother.'

Caroline blew a raspberry. 'Stevie, listen,' she said. 'This is important. How easy is it to check someone's DNA?'

Even though she was miles away and watching Portuguese channels, Caroline could hear Stevie's surprise. 'I assume this is not your own DNA you are talking about. You haven't suddenly decided Cat is not your mother?'

'Ha, ha,' said Caroline. 'What a lovely idea. But no. A woman called Drina Regis. She says she is Leggy's aunt.'

Stevie made a noise. 'Leggy's aunt, eh? An unknown aunt who suddenly appeared? I guess you're not talking about Rupert's sister, Angela?'

'No. Angela's not really related to Rupert. He was adopted.'

Stevie looked sympathetically at Caroline. 'Yes, your mum did ring me about that. You OK? That's a lot of new things to take in at once.'

Caroline nodded. 'Yes. No. Not really. But I don't feel this woman is really who she says she is. I feel ...' She ploughed on even though ultra-rational Stevie was looking confused. She knew Stevie wouldn't judge until she'd heard the facts. 'There's something odd ... awful even about her ... Her speech is all theatrical ... sort of mad ... I wouldn't trust her in a film fantasy, let alone real life.'

'You could try ringing Jane,' suggested Stevie, 'Rupert's mother. Or maybe ask Cat to do it. Jane told her the first lot of information.'

'Yes,' said Caroline, 'but I need to find out about this Drina person ... Can you check if she really owns that house?'

'I'll try. I could get into the Land Registry.'

'Great,' said Caroline, 'and then how do we find out if she is telling the truth about her DNA?'

Stevie drew a zero on her cheek. 'So ... Can you get me anything of hers? Her spit would be good, hair, with a root, or fingernails. Perhaps you could have a drink with her and keep the cup? Or steal her toothbrush?'

Bother, thought Caroline. If only she had kept one of the chocolate biscuits, but perhaps you couldn't get DNA from chocolate. What was DNA anyway? People were always talking about it and how important it was, but what actually was it?

'Isn't there any other way?' she asked. 'I mean, if she wrote a letter and licked the stamp ...'

Stevie made a noise. 'Er, has she written you a letter? Aren't stamps all self-seal? Have you been watching eighties movies again?'

Caroline didn't think that was funny. 'Yes, no, OK,' she said. She breathed deeply. 'OK. So, I do need to get something from her fluids then? All right. I just hoped ...'

Caroline moved the remaining chocolate around in its

paper. She could do it, but it would need an amount of acting she wasn't sure she could accomplish. Could she send someone else as an intermediary?

'When are you back, Stevie? Could you …?'

Stevie stifled a yawn. 'I'll be back in a few days, but can't you or one of the others get something before then? It takes time to check DNA.'

'Who? Miranda? She'd probably just take a test tube over and ask her to spit in it. No, it's got to be more subtle than Miranda.'

Stevie said nothing.

Caroline fiddled with the chocolate paper. 'OK, OK. I know what you are thinking. All right! I'll ask Mum if she can do it. Besides,' she said, more to herself than Stevie, 'she is going to be the detective in charge of the case. Anthony's parents have asked her to find out who Rupert's real killer is.'

'Good,' said Stevie, her voice making Caroline jump, 'I think she was getting bogged down trying to find Victoria for the Amy case. This will give her something else to think about. I've got some ideas too, and I'll start researching now. Don't worry, Caro, we'll find out what's going on.'

CHAPTER 17
CHAMELEONS USE CHANGING COLOUR AS SOCIAL SIGNALLING

Caroline put down the phone and stared at the floor below. It was too early to have any clientele, but Oscar and Tom were tidying and cleaning. They really were the best barmen, and she was so lucky to have inherited them both from Victoria. The internal phone rang. 'Hello?'

'Hi, Caroline,' said Tom. 'I've got a PC Puddle on the line. He wants to talk to you about making an appointment for his boss to come and see you. Is it OK if I put him through?'

'Yes, fine. And when he's gone can you send Oscar up to me?'

'Sure,' he said.

PC Puddle came on the line to make an appointment for later that day.

A few moments later Tom came back on the line. 'Sorry, Caroline, but Oscar's had to go. Apparently something urgent came up, but he's called Methuen and asked him to cover tonight. I hope that's OK.'

'No problem,' said Caroline, although she was a bit disappointed. She had been going to ask Oscar to get a DNA sample from Drina. He was so tactful he was bound to find a way to do it. Now she'd have to ask her mother.

* * *

A couple of hours later, DI Worsted and DS Jones were brought up to the office by Tom. He offered them coffee, which they refused, magicked an extra chair from nowhere and left.

'Thank you for seeing us, Mrs Fletcher,' said DI Worsted, squeezing into the chair Tom had brought. Caroline couldn't help feeling that if he was called upon to run after a criminal, the bad guy would win. DS Jones was a small woman who looked as though she did fitness training. Perhaps, Caroline thought whimsically, she did the running for her boss.

'No problem,' said Caroline. 'Have you found out how my ex-husband died yet?'

DI Worsted looked steadily at her. 'Yes,' he said, 'he was shot with a .22 pistol. We have the bullet and we have recently found the gun that it came from.'

'Oh good,' she said, 'can you tell me where?'

'Yes, it was in the home of Anthony Dyer. The gun had been wiped of prints, as had the silencer, which, somewhat surprisingly, had been broken down into various elements and hidden around the room.'

There was a silence. Then Caroline screamed.

'No! I don't believe it. It's not true. You're lying. Someone put it there.'

DS Jones got up and came over to Caroline. She knelt in

front of her. 'Mrs Fletcher, that may be true. We only know what we have found. Please tell us about Anthony Dyer. He is your therapist, correct?'

Caroline stared at her. She got up, slightly knocking into the detective, and went to the cupboard. Got out the chocolate. Crammed some into her mouth. She went back to her seat, DS Jones having helpfully moved out of the way, and sat down.

'Anthony would not have killed Rupert,' Caroline said. 'He isn't a killer. If it had been the other way around, then it would be possible. Rupert might well have killed Anthony but not ...'

'Mrs Fletcher,' said DI Worsted, 'tell us why Rupert might have killed Anthony.'

Caroline blew out. 'Pah. He said I was having an affair with Anthony. Of course, I wasn't. He was my therapist. He wouldn't do that. He has huge morals.'

At that moment the spiral staircase creaked, and Cat appeared in the room.

'Sorry,' she said to Caroline. 'Tom called me. Said the police were here.' She turned to the detectives. 'I'm Cat Harrington, Caroline's mother. I hope you don't mind ...'

'It's entirely up to Mrs Fletcher,' said DI Worsted.

Caroline gave a sharp breath. 'I call myself Caroline Harrington. I kept my maiden name. Anyway, we are divorced. I wouldn't want his name.'

Cat put her hand gently on her daughter's shoulder before focusing on the detectives. 'Tell us what you found, and where, please.'

'Yes. I've told your daughter we found the gun and the silencer in Anthony Dyer's flat. And I was just asking her how well she knew Mr Dyer.'

Caroline just shook her head and pinched her thumb, so Cat answered. 'He's been her therapist for twenty years.'

The police detectives exchanged glances.

'Anthony doesn't know how to shoot,' said Caroline. 'Rupert was the one who loved massacring small birds and animals, not Anthony.'

There was a slight silence then DI Worsted said, 'We've found a shooting certificate from the Acu Pistol and Rifle Club. We still have to ascertain if it was his.'

Cat looked at Caroline, who shrugged.

'Do you know what time Rupert was shot?' Cat asked.

'Estimate is between ten p.m. and two a.m. The post mortem showed a lot of alcohol in the body, which can sometimes slightly slow the cooling period. We are awaiting updates, but the team said that was a good working diagnosis.'

'Thanks. Where is Anthony now?'

'He's in the custody suite.'

'So, he hasn't been charged?'

'No.'

'So,' said Cat, 'was there anything else?'

DI Worsted looked at her and back at his notes. 'There was clear evidence of fighting in the flat,' he said. 'Plates thrown against the wall, broken glasses, and we found blood on the floor, which has been sent for analysis.' He paused. 'Have either of you ladies been to his flat?'

'No,' said Caroline.

'Not yet,' said Cat. 'But I'd like to go over and look at it if you've finished. I'm a detective working for the family.'

Again, the detectives exchanged glances.

'I can't stop you,' said DI Worsted, but he didn't look happy. He rose slightly in his seat. 'Is there anything you'd like to ask us?'

Cat was about to ask if they had any suspects apart from Anthony when Caroline broke in. 'When is Anthony going to be released? He is innocent. If you knew him like I did …' She burst into tears.

CHAPTER 18

SOME CHAMELEONS ARE EXPERT AT SURVIVING OUTSIDE THEIR NATIVE HABITATS

Cat spent the night with Caroline and Leggy. Caroline had been so miserable she hardly spoke, spending most of the evening looking between the window and her phone. Cat did the cooking and played with Leggy. In the morning she left Caroline still staring out the sitting room window and took Leggy to school. After that she got the train to visit Kaya and George, who lived in Peckham.

Anthony's parents lived in a Victorian terraced house with three bedrooms near the railway line. The house had recently been painted and shone out against the others in their street, most of which, judging by the number of bells, had been converted into flats.

Cat rang the bell and Kaya answered the door so quickly Cat wondered if the old woman had been standing next to it.

'Come in,' she said, leading the way into a warm front room full of boxes of multiple offers from Aldi and Lidl, all carefully tucked away under the table. 'Would you like some cake with your tea?'

'Thank you,' said Cat, and she was surprised when Kaya immediately returned with the teapot and three cups. They *had* been waiting for her. 'George will join us in a minute, but he's just fixing a drain that has broken at the back. He loves doing DIY,' she added proudly. 'Would build his own house if he had the money.'

Kaya gave Cat a large piece of cake. 'You need feeding up! Young people don't eat properly anymore.'

Cat laughed. Kaya was about half Cat's height and very trim; she made Cat feel large and heavy. She smiled to herself. His father must be a big man like Anthony. 'Oh,' Cat said, 'I love you. Not many people call me young any more, but, luckily for me, my boyfriend cooks beautifully and loves it, so I'm able to spend my days sleuthing.'

Kaya smiled. 'Lucky for us too.'

There was a noise by the door and Kaya turned as George walked into the room. A compact man with greying hair, he smiled at his wife and put his hand out to Cat, before realising it was still a bit dirty and looking embarrassed. He laughed, hastily withdrawing it.

'Oh no,' he said, glancing at his wife, his voice lumpy with affection, 'Mum's going to send me away to wash my hands. I'll be back in a moment.'

Kaya smiled lovingly back at him and cut her husband some cake, while George went and washed his hands. When he returned George said, 'It's so nice of you to help us, Cat. We were going out of our minds not knowing what to do for our boy, when your daughter rang and suggested your agency.'

Cat blinked. 'Caroline suggested it?'

'Yes, indeed, she said she would pay for it, but we weren't having that. Anthony is our responsibility. We were so sorry when his wife left him and that they didn't have any children. Ant is so good with children. He's a credit to us. But then ...'

Kaya gave a discreet cough. Unspoken communication passed between them, and Cat wondered what he had been about to say. She felt a strange pang of jealousy. She didn't think she'd ever had such an ability to understand another person's thoughts with just a look. Her late husband, Charlie, gave her looks of command, which she understood and obeyed. And now, with Frank, it was a whole different relationship based on laughter and light, but they were so different in every way they couldn't share the unspoken thought and yet they loved each other.

'So,' said Cat, 'I need to ask a few things, and if some of my questions are invasive, I apologise. Is that OK?'

'Of course,' said George, while Kaya added, 'We have complete faith in you, Cat. And we know that Anthony is not guilty. Our son would never fight someone, let alone kill them. We know he wouldn't have done any of the things he is accused of because we know him and his personality.'

George smiled at her but added, his voice quavering slightly, 'I have no fear about his integrity, but I do fear he may not be judged well by people who don't know him.'

Cat looked at them and eventually she said, 'I know you don't want to say this, but are you frightened he will be judged first on the colour of his skin and secondly on the evidence?'

George and Kaya looked at each other and then back at Cat. Neither of them spoke for a while, then George said, 'We were brought up to trust the British legal system, we were brought up to respect the police and believe in their integrity, but recently there have been some alarming cases and we are bothered.'

'Did you know the police found a gun in Anthony's apartment when they searched it?' Cat asked.

Kaya's eyes opened wide and instinctively took George's hand. 'A gun? Whose?'

George squeezed her hand before saying, 'If he had a gun, I'd suggest he took it away from one of his wilder clients. I can't believe he would have bought one himself. Why would he?'

'Do you know if he knew how to shoot?'

Again they shook their heads. 'Anthony is a very gentle man,' said his mother, 'a kind man.'

George looked at his wife and then at Cat. 'A clever man,' he said, 'wise. At school, when he was insulted, he learned to stop and think about it, rather than immediately react. He said to me he would consider the insult for a long time, why the other person had insulted him, if they had some under-lying problem themselves or if there was something between them, and how he should react. Perhaps,' George said, shaking his head, 'this meant the other boys thought he was soft or didn't care, but I never heard of him being involved in a fight. Never.'

'Just one thing, though,' said Kaya, and Cat saw her eyes were dark with dread. 'He did sometimes take the blame for other, smaller boys to protect them. And he always stood up to bullies.'

CHAPTER 19
CHAMELEONS ARE HAPPIEST
WHEN UNOBSERVED

After leaving Kaya and George, Cat took the rail service to Chelsea. Unwillingly she had agreed to her daughter's request to go and meet Drina and get a DNA sample. Although she had no idea how to get one, she thought she would just appear on Drina's doorstep and find some excuse to pop into her bathroom. However, when Cat rang the bell, she saw the drawback of the surprise assault method: no one answered the door.

What happened to the maid? she wondered. The maid who, Drina claimed, put out the biscuits. Where was she? Perhaps she was out shopping, and Drina didn't want to get up and hurt her feet.

Cat looked around her and saw a camera pointing down from the eaves of the house towards her face. CCTV. Of course, a house like this was bound to have cameras. Odd, though, if they had CCTV and an automatic opening system that Drina wasn't opening the door. Cat was at the house less than a week after her daughter's visit. Could the bunion rehabilitation have ended already?

As Cat walked away something suddenly hit her. Jane

Fletcher had talked about Rupert's girlfriend. There were unlikely to be two girlfriends. Cat thought the name might well be Drina. But Jane said that Rupert's girlfriend was in a wheelchair owing to a birth accident. This woman, however, said the only reason she couldn't get off the sofa was bunions. She must ring Jane later and get some more details.

There was more to this, but what? And why would that be something to lie about? Stevie had checked out the house and it did indeed belong to a Miss Regis. Of course it was possible she had broken in and was pretending to be Miss Regis, but if so, where was the real one? And given all the CCTV around, wouldn't the real one soon pop up and demand an explanation? It seemed more likely this woman was really Drina, but why not admit to being in a wheelchair? Unless she wasn't and that was done simply to deceive Rupert and expose his mother's prejudices. But then again, why? Stevie was right. They needed to check that DNA.

Cat walked down to Kensington High Street and went into a café where she had a coffee and a doughnut. She called her daughter.

'How are you, darling?'

'Fine. Don't fuss. I nearly didn't hear the phone. I'm hoovering.'

Cat felt relieved. 'Caroline, you are going to have to agree to let Drina come and meet Leggy, then you can get a sample from her.'

Caroline tutted. 'So you failed then,' she said, irritated. 'She saw it was you and pulled down the shutters.'

Cat returned to the matter in hand. 'Whatever. We need to get her DNA so we can find out if she really is related to Rupert and therefore Leggy. You'll need to win her trust.'

'Err, how? I can't force her to spit on something. Or are you suggesting I jump on her and pull out one of her hairs? Or do you think I should puncture her skin and get some blood? She'd probably call the police and accuse me of GBH or something.

Besides, I don't want to tell Leggy she's got an aunt if it's not true. No, we must verify it before I'm going to let Leggy meet her. My daughter is more important than anything.' She paused. 'Even Anthony.'

'Good point,' said her mother.

When you meet a brick wall, find another way. And, she thought, all her children were in line for the Brick Wall Society gold cup.

'All right. Perhaps I'll watch the house for a moment and see if she returns—and how, since she's supposed to be housebound.'

'OK,' said Caroline, sounding unenthusiastic. 'Enjoy it then.'

As Cat walked back towards the house, it occurred to her it was quite difficult to watch a house when there were no cafés or shops in the same street to sit in, whiling away time in an unsuspicious manner. A drone would be helpful, but then could you really have a drone flying down a London street without anyone noticing? In the Victorian era, you could pay small boys to hang around on the street and no one would notice. Nowadays they were more likely to be arrested as potential drug mules.

She could smoke a cigarette for a while, hanging about, but how long before that too attracted attention? Even a street sweeper, if such things still existed, was in perpetual motion. Was there anybody who could just stand on a street, watching a house, and get no attention?

Yes, there was, she thought suddenly. One group of

people could be on the streets and never be seen: the home-less. If she sat in a doorway opposite the house, wrapped herself in old clothes and put out a cap, she could sit there all day and no one would even remember her.

Cat went back to a charity shop in Kensington High Street. However, it seemed the charity shop was at the higher end and there was nothing in them a homeless woman could afford. Instead, she bought some unmatching accessories and dropped them in a puddle. Then, suitably draped, with a cap out in front of her for donations, she sat in the opposite doorway and watched. And watched. And watched.

This, Cat thought, getting bored, was one of the less interesting parts of being a private detective. She shuffled about, trying to get comfortable, then looked at her watch, which had stopped. She pulled out her phone. Only a few moments had gone by.

After a few hours it started to get colder and colder. Slowly darkness descended on Kensington and Chelsea. The same darkness, thought Cat, now getting irritable, as that in Owly Vale. She wished she was down there, with Frank cooking her supper. She got out her phone again. Odd, really, that no one walked down this street. If she had been a real beggar, she'd be wasting her time here.

Just as Cat was about to get up and go, a woman walked by and dropped a pound into her cap.

'Oh!' said Cat, not sure that earning a pound from some valiant woman wasn't a bit like stealing. 'Thank you, how kind, but I don't really think ...'

The woman stopped and looked back at her. 'What? If you beg, you must expect to get something.'

'Miranda! What the ...?'

Miranda laughed. 'Honestly, Cat, I didn't know you were in such dire straits. You could have asked for a loan.'

'Very funny. How did you know I was here?'

Her friend laughed again, this time rather derisively. 'Look all around you, my friend, and what do you see? Cameras! Did you really think you could sit here as a homeless woman and not be spotted? Especially as you keep pulling out your phone and checking the time!

'The man opposite called the police. He said you were probably a burglar checking out the houses. He wanted a Black Maria to arrest you.' Miranda giggled. 'Fantastic, eh? I like the idea of a black coach and horses picking you up in the street. Do you think the horses were black as well as the coach?' She stuck out her tongue thoughtfully.

'Anyway, you are lucky. Agata took the call and when she looked at the CCTV, she saw it was you. She rang me and, as I was at my mother's, I came over. Shall I take you home?'

Cat got up slowly, feeling her muscles. 'I was trying to watch the large house over there. The woman inside claims she is Leggy's aunt, Rupert's half-sister, and she wants input with the child.'

'Really? How odd. But if you're waiting for a car, there isn't any point sitting here—there is a garage out the other side. I doubt anyone ever drives in this side, at least not anyone from the house. Strangers probably come in here. And deliveries. Perhaps you should have set yourself up as a delivery girl. Either way, it's time to go or the police will be on you.'

Cat followed her friend to her car. At least she wouldn't have to try and get back to Owly Vale by train. She had forgotten to check the timetable and they were bound to be on strike again.

* * *

Next morning when Cat got into the office, Miranda was there working on the computer. Cat raised her eyebrows. 'You must be missing Stevie. I've never seen you even lift the mouse, let alone surf away like a snowboarder.'

'Ha, ha, Cat, needs must. Nice to see you awake for a change!'

Cat grimaced, but Miranda was right. As soon as she got into the car, she fell asleep and didn't wake up until they arrived at Owly Vale.

'To be honest I think it was pretty wise of me to sleep though your interesting driving.'

'Ha, ha. I'm looking for Anthony's alibi—you, that is, since he was talking to you at eleven p.m. Halfway through the call, Rupert was being shot. Stevie said your phone knows where you are all the time, so if we can get Anthony's phone records, then we can track where he was at the time Rupert was killed. I was googling how to do it.'

'And?'

'Well, it wasn't as easy as I thought. You can see where the phone is now, but not the history of where it has been.'

Cat shrugged. 'I bet Stevie can do it. Leave it to her.'

Miranda mirrored Cat's shrug. 'OK,' she said, 'so the gun was found in his flat and we currently don't know if he knows how to shoot.'

'No, we need to go down to the shooting range and find out if they remember him. OK, what else?'

'Well, we need to visit Rupert's flat. You said DI Worsted said it was OK.'

Cat bit her lower lip. 'Yes, although he didn't look happy about it. You know they have the right to keep it until the case is solved.'

'Lucky he said yes then.' Miranda winked. 'Even without their permission we can visit the other flats, the block. I saw there was a flat available for rent in the block, so, if necessary, we can visit that. And then just accidentally get the wrong flat ...'

'Ha, ha.'

'By and by, we could look at Rupert's former friends who might have thought his behaviour could reflect on them. If you think he knew something about someone and was blackmailing them, it could be one of them.'

'Maybe.'

'OK, but I'm brainstorming.'

'OK,' said Cat. 'Let's go and visit the Acu Shooting Range.'

CHAPTER 20
CHAMELEONS SHOOT
VISCOUS SALIVA AT
THEIR PREY

The Acu Pistol and Rifle Club was just south of London, between Biggin Hill and Kenley airfields. Considering how close it was to town, it was surprisingly green and rural. The detectives parked in a large gravel pit with ropes to show people the edges. All the cars were parked tidily next to one another.

'Look at that,' said Miranda, 'bank manager parking! I've always thought people who shoot were rebels. Punk parkers demonstrating their unique wildness.'

Cat shook her head. 'Really! Like Rupert and his friends?'

Miranda snorted. 'OK, point taken. Bankers all round ...' She roared with laughter and Cat sighed. Clearly Miranda was in one of her exhilarated moods.

The club had a small reception hut on the edge of the car park and a larger building over to the left with signs to offices and training rooms. In the hut a man with grey hair was cleaning a shotgun. He looked up as they entered the hut and smiled.

'Hello, can I help? Actually, I don't work here, but I can

probably push you in the right direction if you tell me which chappie you're after.'

Miranda looked lovingly at his shotgun. 'What's it like to shoot a gun? Do you feel powerful when you do it? Is there a sort of God-like feeling that you have the ability to take away life with one squeeze of the trigger?'

The man's eyes opened wide and, moving his body between Miranda and the gun, he placed it in the gun cabinet, locking it with an ostentatious flourish.

'I'll get an instructor,' he said, 'but no, since you ask, it isn't a feeling of power but a desire for accuracy. I'm just here shooting clays, practising so I shoot pheasants more cleanly. Better for them, better for me. Win-win as you lot would say!'

He went out and Miranda giggled. Cat pinched her. 'Behave!' she whispered in case he came back. 'People here take shooting seriously. They won't be any more amused by your jokes than Stevie would be if you laughed at using aeroplanes to fly into buildings. Some things aren't funny.'

'Actually, most things are,' said Miranda, wiggling her head.

She looked out the window. The man they had just talked to was leaning over a stocky man with a military haircut, gesturing and pointing towards the hut.

'We'd better run, Cat,' said Miranda, 'run while we are still ahead. Arggh, no chance! They've got so many guns here they'd get us before we got to the car. We'll have to tough it out. Man the barricades!'

'Stop it!' said Cat, frowning. 'Remember we've got serious work to do and try and behave like an adult.'

The stocky man came into the hut. He looked at the women warily. Cat wondered if he'd come across oddballs wanting to 'feel the power of guns' before.

'Hello,' he said, his voice a mixture of polite and guarded, 'you interested in learning to shoot?'

'No,' said Cat, looking sternly at Miranda and moving slightly to put herself between Miranda and the new man. 'We are detectives from the SeeMs Detective Agency and we're just trying to find out something for a client.'

She produced one of the rather official-looking cards that Stevie had made for them. The man glanced at it, then looked back at Cat. 'You'd better come into my office,' he said. 'I don't think I've ever been asked anything like this before.'

They followed him into an office lined with certificates. Miranda examined them admiringly. 'Wow! You've won a lot. The school too. Power! You must feel as though the world is your ... ow!'

'Stop it!' murmured Cat, her lips hardly moving. She looked at the man to discover he was staring at them. 'I'm sorry. Sometimes she gets overexcited.'

He stared from one of them to the other, his eyes narrowed.

'It does happen,' he said, his voice dry, 'but not usually with detectives. Usually with criminals looking for a new source of weapons. Or children.'

Cat assumed he was joking and laughed politely. She sat down in front of the desk.

'Our question is really very simple. We are trying to discover if a client of ours had a day's shooting here. He has one of your certificates in his flat and we wanted to see if he'd done a course, or a trial day, if you call it that. Or was just a spectator.'

The man blew out. 'We have a hundred or so trials a month. If he had a certificate, he almost certainly was here, but it might be hard to track that it was him and not someone taking his place. Do you have any idea when he did the day?'

Cat shook her head, and he made a despairing noise.

'OK. I'll check the computer list of clients. What was his name?'

He tapped the mouse and the computer sprang into life.

'Anthony Dyer,' said Cat.

As the man started searching down the 'D's, Miranda, who was still gliding around the walls, stopped, pointing excitedly at a picture behind glass.

'This is him,' she said, indicating a couple of people wearing ear defenders and holding pistols. A short distance away was a target. 'Look, Cat. Here he is! Even though he's wearing a headset, I'd spot him anywhere.'

'Ear defenders,' said the man automatically as he and Cat looked up.

'Oh, him!' said the man, looking at the picture. 'Yes, as you can see they were both here, both shooting. Unusual couple. We post pictures of anyone outside of the norm or else the winners. It's to encourage others. We may have used them in our advertising brochures, depending on when it was.'

His look was oddly lewd, and Cat shuddered. Why the salacious smile? Frowning, she got up and joined Miranda. There on the wall was a picture of Anthony and next to him, in a wheelchair, was Victoria Bell. It was an old picture and was starting to curl even under glass. She stared at it. What was Anthony doing on a day's shoot with Victoria? She rubbed her nose thoughtfully and went back to her seat.

Miranda was looking at the date. 'This picture says 2016. Is that right?'

Cat stared at the wall above and behind the man. Anthony was not Victoria's therapist in 2016; they'd stopped long before. So, it wasn't against their company rules, but he'd told Cat he hadn't been in touch with Victoria, or so Cat thought, her mind going back to the last time she'd talked to him. Did he actually avoid her question? What was happening here? They needed to talk to Anthony before they went any further. Miranda and the man were still talking.

'If that's what it says,' he was saying, his voice patiently bored, 'then that's when it was. I remember them. Odd couple. He was a rookie, but he got the hang of it PDQ.' He stopped, looked at the women and added, 'Pretty damn quick. She was good, clearly done it before. You don't get many in wheelchairs, and though there are some in the paras, there aren't many women. We've never had one down here before, let alone with a Black companion. Unusual that.'

'They're using pistols here. Is that what they would have shot?' asked Miranda, pointing at the photograph.

'Yeah,' he said, but he wasn't listening to the question. He stared out at the moving sky, his fingers performing a little dance on the desk. Eventually, he said, 'Yeah. She was kinda ... it's hard to put your finger on it, but I wouldn't have let her have a licence, if you know what I mean. We have to do a lot of on-the-hoof psychology here, get to know people, and she was a bit different. He was all right. I'd put him down as her carer or something. But ...' He shrugged. 'It was only a trial day and you do get a few weirdos at those anyway.' He laughed. 'Usually with the big corporations.'

* * *

On the way home Cat said, 'Why was Anthony with Victoria long after they stopped having therapy together?'

'Even if they were still having therapy, a shooting school is hardly the place for it,' said Miranda. 'More like a happy day out with friends.'

Cat felt her stomach rumbling. Bad thoughts often made her hungry. 'We need to talk to him. I don't like the way things are going. Have you talked to Agata recently? Is he still in the custody suite or have they charged him? Or, hope against hope, let him go?'

'Not sure. I'll find out. But if he's still in the custody suite, they don't allow visits.'

Cat shook her head. 'Odd that. So now we want him to be charged and remanded just so we can visit him and ask questions.'

CHAPTER 21

THE MEDITERRANEAN
CHAMELEON LIVES IN SPAIN

The next day, the SeeMs detectives took the Tube to King's Cross and walked to Rupert's flat. Agata had confirmed the address Cat had been given by Rupert's mother.

The streets around the Clerkenwell area were a mixture of old and new, of beautiful Georgian and Victorian houses, mostly restored, and some minimalist modern. As they got towards Rupert's area, however, the new buildings ran out and the quality of the housing degenerated.

Mansionetta Flats had once been an elegant Georgian townhouse, the sort to make you imagine bejewelled men and women arriving in golden carriages with ostrich feather plumes on their horses, laughing and joking. The former house was now divided into two and Rupert's flat was in the side that would once have housed the servants' quarters and the backstairs, giving smaller flats with lower ceilings. The other side of the house had an elegant sweeping staircase and, no doubt, stunning rooms, and had been turned into a hotel. The door of the former servants' quarters was open and blowing in the breeze. Cat looked at the flimsiness of the door and wondered if it would sustain a frontal attack if someone was determined to enter the block. She thought even if she gave it a good kick, it would fall inwards.

A hunched old woman, with a stick in one hand, was rearranging the plastic flowers in the hall as Cat and Miranda stepped through the door. The small space was dominated by little postal boxes with handwritten names jutting out from the left-hand wall. Under the boxes was a sturdy stool.

'Aren't they lovely?' said the old woman, waving a feather duster in the direction of the flowers. 'Not much scent though.'

She pulled out the stool and sat down, leaning on her stick.

'No,' said Miranda, smiling at her. 'But they are very pretty. Did you buy them?'

'Oh no, darling,' said the woman. 'They grow wild in the garden. There's not much earth there, but they pop up in the cracks.'

She continued dusting from her seat but then, finding she couldn't reach the flowers, stopped. 'Are you coming to look at the flat upstairs? It's recently become vacant.'

Cat swallowed. She was thinking of lying when Miranda interrupted.

'Is that Rupert Fletcher's old flat?' she asked.

Mrs Cartwright angled her head to one side and smiled. 'Nice boy. Lived on the sixth floor. Always bringing me food. So kind. He gave me these flowers, said they brightened up the house and they were very good value, less than fifty pounds.'

Standing up, she began to dust the tops of the flowers, her feather duster causing the dust to float into the air in a cloud before resettling.

'Nice,' murmured Miranda politely, and she turned for the stairs. She stared up the steep first flight. 'How many floors are there? Do you have a lift?'

Mrs Cartwright shook her head.

Regretfully, Miranda started climbing. She looked back to say something to the old woman and her foot twisted and slipped under her. She grabbed ineffectually for the bannister but missed it. She crashed back down the flight and landed on her ankle.

'Oh, bother!' she said, sitting on her bottom and stretching out her foot. She leant forward and massaged her ankle softly. 'Ouch! Sorry, Cat, I should have been paying attention. I'll have to sit down here while you go up. Bother. I won't be able to do all those stairs. Silly me.'

Cat smiled sympathetically at her and continued up the stairs. She had no idea if Miranda had really hurt her ankle or if she simply thought she would like to talk to Mrs Cartwright without appearing to do so. Miranda's modus operandi was always different to other people's and mostly seemed to rely on intuition, much to the annoyance of Stevie, who preferred a more rational approach.

It was a long hike to the top of Rupert's flats, and the stairs were particularly steep and uninviting. Cat stopped, panting, on the fifth-floor landing.

She saw there were two doors on this floor. One must be under Rupert's flat, she thought. Perhaps the occupants had met Rupert. Perhaps they knew him. Once she'd looked at Rupert's flat, she would know which door to knock on.

Breathing deeply, she dragged herself up the last flight, which seemed even more precipitous than the rest of the stairs.

There were two opposing doors on the sixth floor. One was open and there was no furniture inside. Possibly, she thought, that was the one ready for renting. A quick look showed Cat the ceiling was low and the room cramped. Perhaps Rupert's was better. She passed a couple of low steps and a door that looked like it might lead to the roof. She tried the door, but it was locked.

Rupert's flat had a piece of police tape hanging dejectedly across the opening, and the door itself was ajar. She pushed it open and stepped over the tape.

The room was a mess.

Some of the mess had clearly been caused before the police arrived: a ketchup stain on the wall, broken plate and broken glass and dried blood on the floor, all seemed unlikely to be caused by police searches. It could have been the result of a fight as DI Worsted suggested. Or, Cat thought, it was the sort of thing Rupert might have done himself. More than once Caroline and Leggy had escaped to Owly Vale when Rupert was destroying their house.

The police had attempted to fingerprint the broken pieces and their special dust lay everywhere.

The only things of even workable value was a pile of silver plate ornaments, including a crochet hook, sugar tongs, grape scissors and a child's baptism spoon. Cat picked up the spoon and turned it over. There was a date, but it was so worn she couldn't read it. Nineteen ... nineteen something. Too early for Leggy. Whose could this be? Surely not Rupert's. She dropped it back on the pile. If it was a burglar who killed Rupert, he clearly hadn't wanted any of his possessions.

In the corner of the room, there was a small fridge and a sofa bed. The room itself was tiny and Cat wondered where Rupert was hoping to put Lagertha if he got custody. If this was where he was intending to bring her, there was no chance he would have succeeded. She wondered why he even bothered to try. He didn't want a small child cramping his lifestyle, so why? The only possible reason must be money. Somehow, Rupert must have been convinced that if he took Lagertha, he would also get lots of money to look after her. She shook her head and thought about the night-club. Did he believe there was so much money in the night-club that it would make him a rich man? Or did he perhaps hope that Caroline would give him the nightclub and wander off to live in Owly Vale as a destitute divorcee? Or did he think she owned the freehold of the building in Clerkenwell? That certainly would be worth a packet, but the Bella Chantry Trust had retained that. Victoria's gift to Caroline had been debts and little more.

Musing, she went down the steep stairs to the next floor and tapped lightly at the door below Rupert's flat.

There was no reply. But, just as Cat was thinking of going away, she heard the door being unbolted and a chain applied. An eye in a small male head with a black flop of hair peeped out through the cavity.

'Yes?' he said. Cat heard a Spanish accent.

'*Buenos dias*,' she said, and then, continuing in Spanish. 'I'm sorry to alarm you. I wanted to ask a few questions about the man upstairs.'

He looked at her curiously. Then the door shut again, and she heard the noise of the chain slipping off, and he opened the door again. '*Mucho gusto*,' he said. 'You Castilian?'

'Thank you,' said Cat. It wasn't the first time she'd heard this response to her Spanish and she always reckoned it was a compliment. 'You are from South America? Maybe ... are you Columbian?'

His eyes lit up in alarm and she wondered if he'd had problems. She hurried on in Spanish. 'I recognise the accent and the phrase. When I learnt Spanish the speakers of Spain didn't use it the same way.' She paused. 'Of course, that might have changed. I learnt Spanish so long ago.'

He gave a strangely twisted smile. 'You speak good Spanish. That is unusual here, but you, you are not Spanish or even from South America?'

'No,' Cat said, 'but my mother was French, and she had a very great regard for languages. She thought it was important to be able to converse with people in their own tongue, if possible.'

The man laughed. 'A very tall blonde lady. I would not have judged French either. What was your father?'

She couldn't help thinking that her Spanish friends were always telling her how duplicitous the English were, with their polite words and behind-your-back comments. *We Spanish*, they told her, *are much more upfront.*

'English,' she said, also laughing, 'but again very tall. I think we were Vikings.'

He smiled. 'You want to come in? I'm Diego. Are you come from the police? Is this about Mr Rupert?'

'Please. It is about Mr Rupert, but I'm not from the police. I am a detective. I'm working for the family. My daughter was Mr Rupert's ex-wife.'

Diego's face dropped and he braced against the door as though he was going to shut it, but with apparent effort he held his nerve. '*Ex*-wife?' he said.

'Ex-wife,' she repeated, 'and I am the grandmother of his child.'

Diego put his hands to his cheeks. '*Guau!*' he said. 'A child! You can come in.' Whispering, as though afraid Rupert's ghost might jump out, he continued. 'I find it hard to imagine that Mr Rupert could have found a girl to marry him, but perhaps he was nicer before. I think you will not like what I tell you.'

As she was about to cross the threshold, Cat remembered a question she had when looking at Rupert's flat.

She glanced at the steep steps to the sixth floor. 'I wonder, er, do you know...? There are two little steps next to Rupert's door. Do you know where they lead?'

Diego sneered slightly. 'It goes to the roof,' he said. 'The estate agent, he told us there was an elegant roof garden. You want to see it?'

Cat nodded, intrigued, and he disappeared into his flat, returning with a key.

As they walked up to Rupert's floor, he said, 'We all have keys, but it makes no difference.'

Cat frowned. What did he mean?

The two little steps were almost vertical but had a solid bannister on one side. Cat walked up the precarious steps and onto the roof above and stopped, shocked. The whole area was covered with black bags. The biggest pile was near a metal block in the far corner, but, owing to their number, the bags had spread out across the roof. A couple were split, and their unappealing contents had fallen onto the asphalt.

'No one wants to take their rubbish all the way down, so they leave it here,' said Diego bitterly. 'Mr Rupert put all his rubbish here. Bottles mostly.'

Cat watched a couple of rats darting from one split bag to another, their lack of fear obvious. She gagged and breathed deeply. Rupert had been intending to bring Lagertha to live here. How would that have affected the girl?

'But ...' said Cat. 'But does anyone remove the bags? I mean ... this is a health hazard.'

Diego waved his hands expressively. 'Sometimes a man comes and puts them in the chute ... but it is closed at the top, so we cannot do it.' He gave a spurt of laughter. 'The man, he is muscles all over, so ...' Diego wound his thin body into the shape of a bigger man and Cat laughed. 'Yes, so I think maybe he started thin like me, but moving so many black bags he is now muscleman!'

He shook his head and turned to head downstairs. Cat, pinching her nose, walked over to the metal box. It had double doors, locked with a key. She pushed the doors, but they remained solidly shut.

Diego was waiting for her at the bottom of the roof stairs. 'Once,' he said, 'I asked the man moving the bags who owns this place and why they no keep it healthy, but he does no speak much English and he shrugged and said, "big company, very busy."'

Cat thought again about Lagertha running with the rats on a roof without railings and shuddered.

'Does the old lady downstairs ever come up here?' she asked as they went down the stairs to the fifth floor.

Diego looked back at her in surprise, nearly tripping over the remaining stairs. 'Mrs Cartwright, you mean. The caretaker. No. How would she? She has bad legs.'

Useful caretaker, thought Cat, who can't leave the ground floor. But perhaps there was a historic reason. 'Do you know how long she has been the caretaker?'

Diego shrugged. 'Since long time. When we arrived there was a Mr Cartwright. He goes up and down and everywhere. He likes young women. I tell my wife, no open the door unless I am here. Then one day he falls in kitchen, dead. He has bad heart, we are told. When he dies Mrs Cartwright is away, visiting her niece. When she come back she find him dead. Since then, just Mrs Cartwright and her bad legs.'

'So, apart from a man who sometimes moves the bags, no one else comes up to the sixth floor?'

Diego glanced back up the stairs before going into his flat. 'There was a man in the other flat a few weeks ago, but he left. A few times the estate agent has come up with a future tenant, but the tenant remains future.' He laughed.

Cat followed Diego into his flat.

'You like coffee?' Diego asked. He indicated a closed door next to the living room. 'My wife, she is asleep. She is about to have a baby and she needs much sleep.' He shook his head, wincing. 'Mr Rupert, he did not need any sleep.'

As Cat listened to Diego's recital of Rupert's behaviour, his drinking, his singing, and his swearing, she shuddered.

'Whenever Mr Rupert in the building, we wear ear plugs. I go up, I say, Mr Rupert, my wife having a baby, please keep noise down. And what happens? More noise. *Entonces*, now ear plugs. But they are not so good. We still hear.'

'Did you tell the police about this?'

Diego shrugged. 'The PC, I have his card. He came to ask questions. But he doesn't speak Spanish, so we speak in English. My English is no good. I tell him about the singing and swearing, but he only want to know if I hear anything on the night Mr Rupert died.'

'And did you?'

'Yes, there was an old man. He carried Mr Rupert up to his flat. He told me Mr Rupert was asleep and left. But he was not asleep and after the old man go, he started singing.'

'So, he was alive when the old man left?'

'For sure.'

'Did you know the old man? Had you seen him before? Was he a friend of Rupert's?'

Diego shook his head. 'He was a bald man with big

muscles,' he said, 'and a scar here.' He ran his finger under his eye.

'Did Rupert often go out at night?'

'In the beginning, yes. But then he began to stay in more and drink here. We put in ear plugs, but you can still hear. Every night, he would sing, break things, shout. Sometimes he go up on the roof and sing.

'Every night, I would go upstairs and ask him to be quiet. It made no difference. Then, after many hours, maybe two, three o'clock, we would hear *thump*.' Diego demonstrated with his hands. 'And Mr Rupert falls asleep. Then we are happy, we too can sleep. But not much. And I must work. The baby is coming.'

'Did that happen on the night he died?' Cat asked.

Diego nodded. 'Yes. And then we sleep.'

'Did you hear anyone come up later?'

Diego put a hand to his cheek. 'It is possible. I will ask my wife if she heard anything, but we are always so exhausted living under Mr Rupert that we sleep heavily once he stops singing and crying. But she sleeps less than me, not so deep.'

Cat thanked him and, leaving him her card, she walked back down the steep stairs.

CHAPTER 22
THE FLAP-NECK CHAMELEON IS MOST COMMON IN SOUTH AFRICA

After Cat padded safely up the stairs, Miranda turned hopefully to Mrs Cartwright. 'I wonder. Do you have a chair or something? I feel rather silly sitting here on the floor. Perhaps I could have some hot water and see if that helps.'

'Of course, darling,' said Mrs Cartwright. 'If I give you my shoulder, can you hop into my flat? You could sit on the sofa. I could treat you. I used to do some nursing a long time ago.'

'Oh, that is kind. Are you sure it wouldn't be any trouble?' said Miranda, standing up on one foot and leaning across Mrs Cartwright's shoulders, sharing her stick. Together they hobbled and dragged themselves into Mrs Cartwright's ground-floor flat.

'Not at all, darling,' wheezed the old woman, sitting on the sofa, exhausted. 'I'd like the company. Now that nice boy upstairs has gone, I don't have any more visitors. Such a shame. He was so kind to me.'

Miranda found it hard to believe she was talking about Rupert. She'd never heard anyone call him kind before, although his friends probably enjoyed his jokes. She collapsed onto a surprisingly comfortable sofa, took off her shoe and sock and put her leg up.

'So,' said Mrs Cartwright, 'you need ice.'

She dragged herself up from the sofa and, using her stick, swayed unevenly into the kitchen like someone learning to ride a bicycle. As she opened the fridge door, the smell of rotting food flooded into the living room, making Miranda gag.

'Ooh,' she said, uncertain if it would be rude to comment. Clearly Mrs Cartwright had a lot more food than she could eat.

While the old woman continued her search for ice, Miranda gazed around the small room. There were a few pictures, mostly cut from magazines and put into frames: celebrities, the queen and one of the royal family. Next to the sofa was a photo showing an elderly couple standing in front of red rocks. It didn't look like Britain and Miranda wondered where it was.

Mrs Cartwright came back from the kitchen pushing a trolley, on which balanced a bowl of ice and a dishcloth.

'Now, dearie, when I was nursing and someone had a nasty sprain, we used to put ice in a dishcloth and wrap it around the part for a few minutes, then take it off and put on hot water, and then apply the ice again. It always took down the swelling.'

She again collapsed onto the sofa beside Miranda's legs and breathed heavily for a moment. Then she filled the cloth with ice and placed it around Miranda's ankle. Miranda felt bemused. A minute ago she was writing her off as someone who thought plastic flowers grew in the garden, now Miranda was her patient and the nurse seemed extremely efficient. She wasn't sure that Stevie's demented mother Blinkey would be up to this level of nursing.

'Did you work in a hospital?' Miranda asked. 'As a nurse?'

'Sort of,' said Mrs Cartwright, smiling. 'I was sent to South Africa to help in a field hospital. It was an odd time.' She gave Miranda an enigmatic look and added, 'When one gets old, one looks back too much. Better not to.'

Miranda frowned, wondering. Mrs Cartwright looked about eighty years old. Would that mean she was in South Africa under apartheid? She inclined her head at the photograph of the older people. 'Was that in South Africa?'

Mrs Cartwright laughed lightly. 'No, dear, that is Arizona. Those are my parents, well, my mother and step-dad, lovely kind people. When I came back from South Africa, I was ill and to help me recover they took me to America. But then, a few years later, I met Mr Cartwright—my husband, God rest his soul—and I came back here, and we lived very happily here until he died a few years ago.' Her shoulders drooped slightly. 'Sadly, he couldn't have children. But the flats were different then, full of lovely young ones. He was so good with them. So good. Loved to spend time with them.'

Miranda saw there were tears in her eyes as she shook her head.

'He sounds nice. Your husband. Do you have any photos of him?'

A little flash crossed Mrs Cartwright's face, and her smile was hard. 'No. He didn't like photos of himself. Thought he looked ugly.' She snorted. 'And he really wasn't a bad man at all; it was just, well, you know, in one's youth, one can be foolish. But, as I say, no point in raking up the sorrows of the past.'

'You seem to have a lot of food in the fridge,' Miranda said, wondering if such a lot of mouldy food was a health risk.

'Ah, yes,' said Mrs Cartwright, 'did I say how kind your Rupert was, bringing me food? I'm sure he only charged me half of what it cost him. Dear boy.'

Miranda decided to try a long shot.

'Do you know how Rupert came to be living in here? Was the flat advertised?'

'I don't know, dear. He was brought here by his nice friend. She was always so kind and drove him about. I don't think he had a car.'

'Do you know the friend's name?'

Mrs Cartwright leant back against the sofa cushions and rubbed her hands across her temples. 'I think it might have been Tina ... or Mina ... That sort of name. Nice girl. Probably Tina,' she continued, getting out a handkerchief and wiping her nose. 'I used to have a sister called Mina. She was very pretty. She and I used to climb mountains together when we were young and then one day someone followed us. We were so scared. We waited and hid behind a rock. When he came past we jumped out and beat him to death with our high heels. Then we ran away!'

Mrs Cartwright smiled at her, as though she was telling a story about meeting a friend in the mountains. Miranda began to revise her judgement of Mrs Cartwright's sanity again.

'Hello,' said the disembodied voice of Cat, 'anybody there?'

'Hi, Cat, I'm here,' yelled Miranda, 'on the sofa. Mrs Cartwright is very kindly nursing me.'

Cat stuck her head trepidatiously around the door.

The old woman smiled at Cat and waved her hanky. 'In

here, dear,' she said. 'Call me Lottie. Mrs Cartwright makes me think I'm off to make wheels.'

Cat came in through the still open door and wrinkled her nose. 'Would you like me to take your rubbish out?' she asked.

Lottie Cartwright looked surprised. 'Oh no, dear, the young man took it out ... last week? Or was it the week before? How long ago did he die? Time goes when you get older.'

Cat followed the source of the smell to the fridge thoughtlessly, as though it was her own kitchen. 'Wow, it's packed,' she said. She began opening the cupboards and looking inside. 'There is food everywhere. Don't you eat much?' she asked. 'Or do you eat out?'

Miranda cringed. Cat wasn't usually so blunt—she was usually the tactful one. What was she up to? Lottie, however, just smiled blandly at Cat. 'Such a nice boy,' she murmured. 'And he said he was going to bring his little girl to join us. That would have livened up the block,' she giggled, 'no doubt about that.'

Miranda noticed Cat frowning at Lottie and wondered if she was missing something. Then Cat said, 'Who takes out the rubbish from the upstairs flats? It must be difficult to get all those bags down here.'

Both Miranda and Lottie stared at Cat as though she had reverted to Spanish. Miranda waited. Cat was clearly up to something.

'I had a fall,' said Lottie suddenly, 'nasty fall on my head.' She sighed. 'Since then I forget things. Have you ever had a fall? Very nasty.'

'Poor you,' said Miranda. 'Where did you fall? Was it here? In the flat?'

'No,' said Lottie, and she started singing. 'I fell down a

well. Pussy's in the well. Did she go up as well? Boom, boom. You're dead.'

Cat turned and looked at the fridge. 'Shall I take out the mouldy food?' she asked. 'If you tell me where to take it, I can put it in the dustbin.'

Lottie smiled at her. 'There's a chute,' she said, 'goes outside. The men come and pick it up on Tuesdays ... or is it Thursdays? Very noisy cart. Always comes very early in the morning. But I wake up early. Always have.'

Cat filled two bags of putrid rubbish and walked out the front door. The road descended deeply to the back and the back of the house was considerably lower than the front. Here there was a wide brick entrance leading to a small square with a row of garage doors. They had probably once been stables for the grand house and had been converted. On the opposite side of the square was a mountain of black bags and behind it the exit for the chute. She added her black bags and looked up the chute, wondering if she could see right up to the roof. It was dark and all she could see was black.

Cat frowned. This was a terrible system, benefiting only the laziest tenants. Presumably, Mr Cartwright had been a better caretaker, although Cat had winced when Diego said that Mr Cartwright liked young women and 'I told my wife no open the door unless I am here'. She was glad he was never going to meet Leggy.

CHAPTER 23

CHAMELEONS HAVE EXISTED FOR AT LEAST 100 MILLION YEARS

When Cat got back up to Mrs Cartwright's flat, Miranda's ankle was bandaged, and she was ready to go.

'Will you be all right?' asked the old woman, her fingers patting her cheeks. 'Did you have a car? Is it far away?'

'Oh yes,' said Miranda, 'not far at all. I'll be OK using Cat's arm to walk that far.'

Mrs Cartwright smiled and said she wouldn't get up. 'I'm afraid I get very tired these days,' she said, 'ever since the bump on the head.'

As they hobbled into the street, Cat dropped Miranda's arm and raised an eyebrow.

'Which car should we take, do you think? Can you see one here you fancy breaking in to?'

Miranda gave an angelic smile. 'I didn't want her worrying about me,' she said.

'Ha! So how is your ankle?'

'Miraculously,' said Miranda with a twinkle, 'it seems to have mended. Must be Lottie's medication. I feel top hole.'

'Good,' said Cat, 'then you'll be happy to walk over to

Eltham and see the Black Scabbard pub, which is where Anthony met Rupert and most likely where the old man who brought Rupert home came from. I'll tell you about it as we walk over.'

Miranda made a face. She hated walking in London, but Cat seemed to enjoy it.

'Ooh, I think I've got a twinge again,' she said, hopping on one leg.

'Ha, ha. Actually, I was joking. It's too far to walk. In fact, it is so far to the pub I'm amazed Rupert used it. Why Eltham, do you think?'

Miranda frowned. 'Probably because he'd been thrown out of all the closer ones. I know you don't visit pubs a lot, but I do, and they've changed since you were young. Not many allow rowdy behaviour—especially in smart King's Cross.'

'OK, point taken. Let's walk to the station.'

'OK,' Miranda said, following Cat lethargically down the street to the station.

The Black Scabbard sign was a thin, angry fish with aggressive eyes. It swung slowly above the narrow black door, giving off a screeching sound. As they searched for the well-camouflaged door handle, Cat noticed the only window this side had been painted, so it was impossible to look in.

Walking through the heavy door, their vision was blocked by a thick black curtain. Miranda pushed it aside and then stopped dead. Cat just avoided cannoning into her. The pub was crammed with people, all men and all white. Two or three had mastiffs and the dogs' heads rose in unison as the women entered.

'Nice dogs,' said Miranda loudly.

The pub went silent. Then a voice from one of the tables said, 'Why look, they sent in the strippers. How nice of you ladies to grace our pub, eh, boys?'

Cat looked at the speaker: a large man covered in tattoos. Both he and his dog gave her asymmetrical smiles.

'What's he talking about?' she whispered, turning back to Miranda.

'Nothing,' said Miranda. 'Ignore it ...'

Cat walked to the bar. Her legs felt stiff, but she tried to walk with a careless insouciance. Even Miranda had no more to say, although she looked lovingly at the dogs. The barman seemed to be having difficulty meeting their eyes. He stared over their heads, saying, 'Can I help you?' his voice almost a whisper.

'I'll have a glass of white wine and a tomato juice, please,' said Cat, her voice too loud for the silence.

A wild desperation filled his face. Perhaps he had hoped they were just asking for directions to another pub. He thrust open the bar flap.

'Come next door,' he said, waving them on with his free hand, his eyes fastened on the flap. 'There is another bar over the other side.'

Cat stood for a moment, bewildered, but Miranda pushed past her and headed for the back bar, so she followed. There was a chorus of catcalls from the previously silent room.

The other room was empty, with a pool table in one corner. 'Here,' said the barman, shaking slightly, 'you can have your drinks here and then you should go. This is not the place for women.'

'You're Polish,' said Miranda in an interested voice.

The barman finally managed to look at her. 'Yes. You too?'

'Yes. What's the problem here?'

The barman glanced over at the other room and moved further into this one. 'I'm not sure!' he whispered. 'Something is happening today. Since the Black guy was here, it has been strange.'

'Actually,' said Miranda, 'we wanted to ask you about that night. What happened?'

The barman looked even more nervous. 'You are police?'

'No,' said Cat, 'private detectives, working for the family.'

The barman grabbed a piece of paper and wrote his mobile number on it. 'Call me soon, not today. Now go. It is not safe for you here. Or me.'

He shoved the paper at Miranda and hurried back into the public bar.

'Odd,' said Cat as they let themselves out the lounge door. 'I suppose we do look rather strange together. I should probably have let you come here alone and no one would have noticed you.'

Miranda tilted her head. 'You think? Those men were up to something, and it wasn't dog training. Still, as long as'— she glanced at the note—'Piotr gave us the right number, we should still get some information.'

The two women headed for the station, leaving the eerie pub and its scratchy sign behind them.

CHAPTER 24

MOST CHAMELEONS EAT INSECTS AND PLANTS

As they emerged at Waterloo Station, Cat noticed she had a missed call from Caroline.

Miranda, her ankle now completely recovered, skipped over to the machine to get the tickets while Cat called her daughter back.

'Mum,' said Caroline, her voice full of desperate emotion, 'Anthony's been charged! I can't believe it. Charged! It's not right.'

Cat felt cold. She didn't know how to help. If anything, everything they had found so far seemed to add to the mystery surrounding Anthony.

'Did they find something else?'

'Yes, but it's rubbish, not true.' She paused and Cat heard the rustle of chocolate paper. 'They found some old blood on the floor. DNA testing shows initially that it is from Anthony's blood type ... Look, I don't really understand it, but the lawyer said it has some kind of genetic resemblance to Anthony's mtDNA, so it could be some relative of Anthony or Anthony himself.'

Cat pinched the end of her nose. 'Someone from Anthony's family? That's weird. Or was that police sarcasm?'

Her daughter made a noise. 'Apparently they need more tests. And they need to find members of his family.'

'Oh,' said Cat.

Would they go and ask George and Kaya for samples? Or Anthony's brother? Where was this going? She had a feeling she read something about mtDNA being the most reliable way to check heredity, but she didn't say anything about it to Caroline, who was quite anxious enough already.

'What happens next?' Cat asked.

'He goes in front of magistrates and the police ask for remand in custody. The lawyer is going to ask for bail, but he says they probably won't get it.'

Cat stared at the roof of the Tube station. 'What is the lawyer going to say? I mean, how is he trying to convince the magistrates they've got the wrong person and will be putting an innocent man on remand?'

There was more chocolate paper scuffling before Caroline's voice came back slightly stronger. 'Well, we know that Anthony was outside King's College when he talked to you. You are his alibi, but the lawyer says the police won't buy it. He says they say they only have Anthony's word for the fact that he was there. Oh Mum! If only you'd do WhatsApp video calls, you'd be a much better witness.'

Cat raised an eyebrow. Looks like it was all her fault. How did that happen?

'What about tracking records?' she asked. 'I thought that was the problem with phones; they always know where you are. Or CCTV?'

'Sure but! The lawyer is trying to get the information from Apple, but apparently they haven't been very forthcoming. If Anthony is found guilty, I'll never use an Apple phone again.'

Her mother said nothing. She wondered if the police had requested the CCTV from King's.

'And against him they have the gun, the silencer, the shooting certificate,' said Caroline, 'and—can you believe this—their DNA testing also found a match to one of the hairs in Rupert's flat. How can that be? It must be police incompetence like in that Foxy Knoxy case ... you know where the police accidentally got the boy's DNA on the bra. Tell me you remember?'

'I remember. But I don't think you'll get far with that one. Did anyone, apart from Anthony, go to Anthony's flat before they went to Rupert's? Unlikely, isn't it?'

'Thanks. You're a great help. Well, the only good thing is that when he's on remand I'll be able to visit him. Oh my God, poor Anthony. What will happen to him in prison?'

She put down the phone and Cat felt a wave of sympathy so strong she could hardly move. How could she help Caroline or Anthony when everything seemed to point to his guilt? You could hardly blame the police.

But they were the SeeMs Detective Agency, who see behind what seems to be true, and absolutely everything so far seemed to be against him. She needed to ask him some questions, which meant visiting him in prison, and they needed to find the old man who had last seen Rupert alive. Had the police found him yet? Or were they even looking?

CHAPTER 25
PRISONER C. 3-3

When Anthony received the visiting request from Caroline, he felt like Saint Hippolytus pulled apart by wild horses. On the one hand, as her friend he would love to see her, but on the other, as her therapist, he hated the idea of submitting someone as highly strung as Caroline to the virtual ravaging of the prison inmates and he did wonder if a visit from such a beautiful white woman might make his time in prison even harder. In the end his desire to see her overcame his caution, and he agreed.

When Caroline received the email informing her she could visit Anthony in HM Pentonville Prison, she screamed.

'Pentonville!' she said to her sister, who she was on the phone to at the time. 'How can Anthony be in Pentonville? It's the one with all the riots and disasters and ... and ... that's where Oscar Wilde was and ...'

Vanessa blew down the phone. 'Wait! Listen! OK, yes, it is known as the Vile Prison but ...'

'It is?' Caroline started to cry.

'Wait! But he will be in G Wing, and he will have enhanced privileges. He'll be able to go to the library, the education centre ... Knowing Anthony, he'll probably be teaching other prisoners to read by now ... He'll already have a support group. He'll be OK.'

Caroline didn't believe her for one moment, but she held on to the possibility.

'Only,' continued her sister, 'when you visit, don't go dressed like a day at the races, OK? And not wearing that scent that follows you around.'

'Oh shut up! Who do you think I am, an idiot? Of course I won't.'

When Caroline arrived at the Caledonian Road Tube station, to start the short walk to the prison, she was already getting sideways glances from the other visitors. Trying to disguise her supermodel appearance, she had worn an ankle-length black skirt, with black boots and a baggy black top and jacket, and she swept her hair into such a tight bun that she thought she looked like an old-fashioned school teacher. However, as she joined the queue, gently ambling forward into the security office, she felt the eyes of the guards on her, and even though she kept her eyes modestly down as she gave in her mobile and showed her passport and invitation letter, she felt a frisson of deep fear.

As they passed into the prison, Caroline's fear doubled. Firstly, there was the smell, a scent of disinfectant mixed with testosterone, as though the men's anger at being incarcerated led to them leaking hormones. Then there were the background noises. Noises which beat against her tense senses like a threat of torture: keys rattling, the irredeemable clank of closing gates. And, laced through it all, an eerie unhappy moaning from prisoners who were unable to quell their misery. In comparison to all this, the guard's lewd looks seemed no more than condensation dripping down a rough wall.

Caroline entered the interview room and walked towards Anthony's table. It seemed to her that the room shook with a physical tremor, as though a pulse of electricity had swept through the walls. She breathed deeply. This, she told herself, pinching her thumb hard, is much less awful than fighting a persistent wasp. The only important thing was Anthony and that he had a small bruise under his left eye.

She sat down. 'Tant. Are you OK?'

'I'm fine, Caroline.' His eyes smiled, and her spirits lifted. He was pleased to see her. Her body shook with relief. She had thought he might not want to see her, that her presence might be an annoyance. She felt her whole body relax.

'Now,' said Anthony, his voice like the touch of silk, 'here is something that will amuse you. Did you know Oscar Wilde was in this prison for a while before he moved on to Reading?'

Caroline gave a twisted smile. 'Yes. And so, do you have walks under a little tent of blue?'

They looked softly at each other. She wanted to reach out and touch his hands, which lay on the table in front of him, but wasn't sure if she was allowed. She kept her hands in her lap.

'We do,' he said. 'I think the exercise yard might be something he would recognise.'

For a moment she felt so emotional she couldn't speak. Why wasn't she allowed to bring in chocolate? She steeled herself.

'Miranda called me yesterday. They are trying to find proof you were outside King's when Mum rang you.'

'Yes. Your mother has requested a visit. I've agreed. I'm only allowed three visits a week, but my parents decided not to come. They said they'd come next week if I'm still here. I think they thought her visit was more important than theirs at this stage.'

He gave what was clearly trying to be an amused laugh. 'They are already organising the party at home for when I get out.'

Caroline tried to reflect his laugh, but her emotions stuck in her ribcage and the best she could manage was a grimace.

'Leggy sendss you her love. She wanted me to give you her latest drawing to hang in your cell, but I told her to keep it to give you when you come out. I wasn't sure it would be … appropriate here.'

Her voice stumbled and he glanced at her, his face understanding, before a shadow crossed through his eyes. Caroline looked around. Another prisoner had looked their way and she caught his lascivious leer.

She turned back and looked into Anthony's bright blue eyes, hoping to reassure him that she was fine, but what she saw instead was Rupert sitting opposite her. She gasped and shut her eyes tightly. With some trepidation she opened them, but, to her relief, she saw it was Anthony.

Of course, they were in some way linked in her mind, she thought. When, as a fourteen year old, she escaped from her repressive boarding school and found her way to London, Anthony was her saviour. Her social worker. Her guide. And then, when she played truant from her next school and joined the hippies on the Newbury bypass, Rupert was trying his hand at farming.

Just as Anthony had helped her escape her home life, so Rupert had helped her escape from the camp which had become her next prison. So ironic. It was as though the two men, so different in every way, were intrinsically linked through her. They were always the ones setting her free. And yet in the end Rupert became her prison and now Anthony was in one.

She pinched her thumb.

Was it the look in Anthony's eyes that reminded her of Rupert? That look she used to see in the early days of marriage when Rupert would look at her with a sort of unfathomable pain, longing for her support, wanting to be looked after like a child. She had loved Rupert once. After the angry activists with their causes, Rupert's laughter at anything serious seemed wickedly exciting. It was such a relief not to be with worthy people. And he was totally smitten with her—in the beginning.

She tried to concentrate her mind on what was happening right now. She wanted to make Anthony feel better.

'What's the food like?' she asked. 'I remember in *Paddington* 2 when the bear improved the food with marmalade. I saw it with Leggy, and your mum came too. She enjoyed it as least as much as Leggy.'

Caroline's voice trailed off and she dropped her eyes to the table. When she looked up she again saw his inscrutable look. Her stomach gave a little jump. That look *did* say he needed her. That he wanted her to look after him just like his mother did, the way she did with Leggy. Unexpectedly she wanted to laugh. Here she was sitting opposite the man she loved in prison, living with the fear he might not get a fair trial and spend the rest of his life separated from her, and yet her heart was singing for joy. She was suddenly sure he loved her too. She could hardly control her desire to jump from her seat and cover him in kisses. Instead, she slipped her hand slightly forward so their fingers touched. For a moment, he let his hand stay then he stroked her nearest finger before withdrawing so imperceptibly only she could see the movements.

'You'll be out in time for Leggy's birthday,' she said, 'and you'll have to think what to give her as a present. She's longing to see you.'

He smiled. 'I'll make her something,' he said. 'I have access to the workshop. I'll have to think what sort of toy I can make, but there are lots of materials.'

They began to discuss the sort of toys Leggy liked. Animals were a favourite. She enjoyed chess and backgammon, so perhaps a knight she could use on the chess board.

The time passed too fast for Caroline, but as the prisoners streamed out, she again saw the man who had leered at her. He was looking at Anthony in such a way that she wanted to run to the guard and complain. But even as the thought crossed her mind, she knew it would only make things worse for him. *He's a big man*, she told herself, *and versed in the ways of defence. He'll be OK.*

The guard came over to escort him to his cell and she forced back her tears. She said in a formal voice, 'I'll come back next week, Tant, or if you're out by then, I'll ...'

'See you soon, Caro.'

Oh. He used my nickname. He cares. He'll be out soon. He'll be free. We'll be together. It will all be OK.

But she wasn't sure she even believed herself.

CHAPTER 26

JACKSON'S CHAMELEON IS ALSO KNOWN AS THE THREE-HORNED CHAMELEON

'What do we do first,' asked Miranda, 'visit Anthony or his flat?'

'Definitely his flat,' said Cat, 'and then I'd better visit him in prison alone. I don't think your brand of humour is going to go down well in prison. You might find yourself slapped up beside him. Besides, he'll only be allowed three sixty-minute visits a week and if we go together, that might count as two.'

'OK.'

Anthony's flat was in Maida Vale in a purpose-built block with a live-in caretaker. The door was open when the detectives arrived, and the caretaker was sitting in the hall at an IKEA-style desk. On his left breast he was wearing a badge which said:

You don't have to ask me. I AM a Rumanian.

Behind him was a wooden board with an assortment of keys on it. Each key had an attached card with a name and date. Across from the front door were a couple of steel lift doors.

'Hello,' he said without looking up. 'Can I help?'

'Yes,' said Cat, flashing her card before Miranda could jump in with some joke about making badges in Rumania.

The man looked up now and frowned slightly. 'Have we met before?' he asked Cat. 'You look familiar.'

Cat examined him. Since she was six foot tall, people were more likely to remember her than she them. However, it was also a typical pick-up line. It wouldn't be the first time someone had wanted to know what it felt like to have sex with such a tall woman.

'I don't think so,' she said in a repressive voice. 'We are from the SeeMs Detective Agency, and we are working for the family of Anthony Dyer. Would it be possible for us to see his flat and perhaps just ask you a few questions?'

The man waggled his shoulders. 'Whatever. But for sure, I knew Anthony. Nice man. I couldn't believe he would murder, even for a lovely woman.'

Cat's shoulders sagged. Was that what they were saying on the streets, that her daughter caused a good man to go wrong?

'What hours are you here?' asked Miranda.

The man gave a twisted smile. 'All hours,' he said, flipping his hand sideways towards a door at the back of the stairway. 'I live here, eat here, work here. I'm a real on-site man. Sometimes I think the building grows out my head.' He laughed.

'Did you see Anthony on the evening of the 26th?' asked Miranda.

'No,' said the man, shaking his head sadly, 'not then, not now. He's not been here since the morning of the 23rd, but I was out doing the rubbish when he left for work. The police asked me that too. But no.' He shrugged. 'Sometimes he stays over at his office. He told me once he has a bed there in case he is working too hard to come home.' He gave his twisted smile again. 'That man works so hard he too could be a caretaker.'

He got up and indicated the steel doors. 'Come. You want to see his flat, what the police have left of it?'

The women followed him into the lift, and he punched a number into the keypad by the door. As they sped up to the fifth floor, Miranda asked, 'Won't it work without the number?'

He glanced at her. 'No, it's a security thing. Lots of flats have it now. If someone who doesn't live here wants to go up, I either must call the flat, and then let them in from the service button, or get the flat holder to tell them the number. If they have the number, they don't need me.'

'Hmm,' said Miranda. 'How often do you change it?'

He waggled his head. 'We are supposed to change it every month, but then the flat holders forget and put in the wrong number. Then they call me, even if it is three a.m.' He shrugged. 'So now we leave the same one all the time. Humans, eh! How different life will be when we're all AI!'

They arrived at the fifth floor and walked out of the lift onto a well-polished landing. The door of Anthony's flat was just ahead of them, its brass knocker covered with police fingerprint dust.

The man gave his twisted smile and opened the door.

'Anthony's lived here since long time,' he said. 'Some of the furniture and pictures he bought recently. He moved here after he split with his wife, and she keep most of the furniture.'

The women walked around a room which must have been clean and tidy before the police set to work stripping everything. The dedicated searchers had even ripped the stuffing out of the chairs. Cat pulled her ear. When Anthony was found innocent, she thought, would he get reparation for all this damage?

'The police took a lot away,' said the caretaker. 'Pictures, computers, huge boxes of things. And,' he indicated the police tape, now collapsing across the debris of the chairs, 'left behind their own form of decoration.'

In the bathroom, Cat noticed there was a space on the wall where a picture had been. Perhaps it was the gun certificate.

In the bedroom, where the mattress lay upended and slashed, exposing the bed springs, she saw a picture of Anthony with his parents—a young boy laughing at the camera and next to him a shorter, stockier lad. She smiled. He was tall, although skinny and lacking his present muscle, and he squinted at the camera, as though curious about what the future might hold. He would certainly never have envisaged this as his future.

'Handsome boy,' said Miranda, looking at the photograph. 'Is that his brother? His parents?'

'Yes.'

'Wow,' said Miranda. 'He's almost a foot taller than his older brother and his father.'

Cat shrugged. Although she was six foot like her father, her mother had been a much more average five foot six and all Cat's children were six foot or over. Sometimes genetics seemed to be playing tricks on its owners.

As the women walked through the other rooms, Cat asked the caretaker, 'Is there any other way into the flat? I mean like a fire escape or something.'

'Sure,' he said, leading the way into a small kitchen, 'there is this.'

At the back there was a fire door, openable only from this side, and outside a tight spiral staircase to the ground. At each level there was a little metal gate, and two floors below it had been propped open. The caretaker looked down the spiral, saying, 'Each gate is openable from this side only, but inevitably people go out and leave it open for an easy return. I tell them not to, but they do it anyway.'

Cat stared down at it. 'So, in fact, someone could come up from the street this way and into the flat.'

He spread his hands. 'Yes, but they would still have to open the kitchen door, and it only opens from inside, unless it too was propped open. Or the window was open,' he added, indicating a small window by the door latch. 'Anthony was more security conscious than most of the others, but yes, it could happen.'

'Do you know where the gun was found?' asked Miranda suddenly.

The cheeky, twisted smile returned. 'I do. I insisted on being with the police when they went round and it was found under the bed, slipped into the springs from beneath.'

'Hey, no kidding?' said Miranda. 'Weren't they worried you might tread on some evidence, or did they think you might give them some input as you went round?'

She grinned to show she was not being critical.

He shrugged. 'I guess they liked my face.'

Cat said nothing, but Miranda thought she'd push him a bit further. 'So, not like the movies then, when everything is sacrosanct?'

He laughed. 'No, not a bit like the movies. Interesting though.'

They went back into the bedroom and the caretaker showed them how the gun had been slipped into the springs, completely invisible from outside. 'They were lucky to find it,' he said. 'But then they were, as you can see, looking thoroughly.'

As they left the block, the caretaker said to Cat, 'Good to see you again,' and winked, giving his cheeky smile.

Cat laughed, but Miranda gave the caretaker her card. 'If you think of anything else, give me a call, eh? Thanks.'

The women walked out the door and Cat frowned. 'Why did you do that?'

Miranda looked at her. 'Face it, Cat. If he thinks he recognises you and you're sure you don't remember him, then the chances are he's thinking of Caroline. She's your image. Tell me she's never been here.'

Cat said nothing. She knew Caroline had been here at least once, but it certainly wasn't recent, and she doubted it was the same porter.

'All right,' she said, fighting the urge to ignore Miranda's idea. 'I'll go on. You go back. Ask him when he remembers seeing me or someone who looks like me.'

Cat went down the street. She sat on a bollard in front of a chained-off garden. Refusing to speculate what Miranda might learn from the porter, she looked up at the trees. Trees connect to each other, she reminded herself. The wood wide web! She smiled at the thought. Trees, fungi, plants all sharing nutrients through the soil, underground where we couldn't see it. Where humans couldn't interfere. Like the World Wide Web but less aggressive, less deleterious. Plants just wanted to help each other and allow their environment to continue. What did humans want? Nothing so simple, sadly.

It was almost ten minutes later before Miranda joined her.

'OK,' she said, slipping her arm over the seated girl's

shoulders and giving her a quick hug. 'Caroline was here. The night Rupert was murdered, she came here. As far as the caretaker knows, she didn't go into the flats, but he saw her outside, staring up at Anthony's flat. He noticed her because she was sitting on some kind of chair, half hidden amongst the parked cars, and he thought it was rather odd. When he looked half an hour or so later, she had gone.'

'How did he recognise her? Could he really see a like-ness to me from a woman sitting at a distance outside?'

Miranda twisted her mouth. 'Probably not, but appar-ently there was a picture of Caroline in Anthony's flat. It's gone now, but he remembers seeing it when he had a drink in Anthony's sitting room.'

Cat stared at the flowers, such delicate petals, so easily damaged. Anthony kept a picture of Caroline. Why? He was her therapist, not her boyfriend.

She looked up at the flats. 'What did he tell the police?'

'Well, obviously until we came along he didn't know who it was, but he told them a woman had been sitting, watching the flats. He told them it was the woman in the photograph.'

Cat frowned. 'How could he be sure? At that distance? Do they have CCTV in the flats?'

'They do, and the police looked at it, but it was put in years ago and the quality is pants. All they could see was a blonde woman sitting amongst the cars. And when the police found the photo of Caroline in Anthony's flat, he was the one that connected the woman outside with the photo inside. They took the photo with them.'

Cat bit her lip. 'I think we'd better go and have another chat with my daughter.'

CHAPTER 27

SOME CHAMELEONS EAT RODENTS AND SMALL BIRDS

While Cat when to visit Anthony, Miranda went to see Caroline. Cat couldn't face interviewing her daughter. 'She won't tell me anyway. You might as well do it. You're her friend. I'm only her mother.'

Miranda rolled her eyes. 'Don't try and make me feel sorry for you! I'll see what she says, OK?'

Miranda rejected the idea of interviewing Caroline at Spinners. Too many distractions. Instead, she dropped in on her in the house in Battersea.

'Hey, Miranda,' said Caroline, opening the door with a huge smile. 'Come in. Leggy's at school, and I've done quite enough cleaning today. Come and have a cup of coffee. These days I never see you without Mum hanging around. How's things? How are the kids?'

Chatting away with coffee and wishing she had a glass of wine instead, Miranda tried to ask Caroline questions without making it apparent she had Caroline on her potential suspect list.

'We went to Anthony's flat yesterday,' said Miranda.

'Nice place. I bet he was a tidy man before the police got in. They have devastated the place.'

'Have they? Poor Anthony. He is such a neat man, so different from Rupert, who threw his things everywhere as though he had a horde of servants to pick them up. With Anthony you really felt he cared about his flat and where his things were. When I went there, I thought I'd like to be one of his things, constantly being touched and caressed by him.'

She gave an emotional laugh. 'I know you lot think I'm an idiot about Anthony, but I've never met anyone like him. He's so cool. So relaxed and yet in control of himself. So ... oh, I don't know. Sometimes I feel as though he knows my every thought and forgives me for my weaknesses or even doesn't care about them.'

She shrugged. 'I know I shouldn't have gone there, but I couldn't help it. I was so obsessed with him I just wanted to see where he lived.'

Miranda went completely cold. Caroline was admitting it. She didn't say anything. What was there to say?

Caroline blew out noisily. 'And he was so nice about it. He agreed never to tell anyone.'

Miranda frowned. What was this? The caretaker had definitely said that Anthony was not at his flat on the 26th, now Caroline was saying he was. Caroline was still chatting on, as though saying things of no importance.

'I was such an idiot. He could have lost everything over that. In effect, you know, I stalked him, and he forgave me. But then ...' She shrugged and looked at Miranda. 'When we're younger we all do stupid things. Since Leggy's birth I've been more sensible. Though that's not to say I don't have bad moments. But I always tell myself *Leggy first* and pinch my thumb—Anthony told me to do that.' She glanced up at Miranda. 'Try and stay positive. You know, Miranda, I'm even learning to laugh at myself. And that is something.' Her laugh sounded a bit hysterical.

'So, when was this, that you visited Anthony's flat?'

'Must have been more than five years ago. Just a few days later I realised I was pregnant and Leggy's on her way to six now.'

'And you haven't been back to the flats since?'

'No,' said Caroline, almost laughing. 'How could I? I can't leave Leggy alone, can I?'

'No,' said Miranda, 'you can't. Do you have a regular sitter? I mean, for when you are at the club?'

For the first time Caroline looked shifty. 'Ah, well, sort of. You know. Friend's mum who helps out. Someone from the school. You know the sort of thing.'

Miranda nodded helpfully, although she definitely did not know. Phillip hated going out as much as she loved it and was always ready to do a night of baby-sitting (which meant falling asleep in front of the telly) when Miranda wanted to do a job.

* * *

'So,' said Cat as they drove back down to Owly Vale. 'Why was she outside Anthony's block the night Rupert died?'

'She wasn't. She says she didn't leave home at all that night. She and Leggy played chess until Leggy went to bed. Then she cleaned the house thoroughly and went to bed herself. No point in having a night off from a nightclub if you aren't going to spend it asleep, she said. And I believe her. But ...' said Miranda, moving the seat belt, which was feeling uncomfortable, 'there was something odd.'

'What?'

'Well, when I asked her something about who looks after Leggy when she needs a sitter, she didn't give me a straight answer. Said a friend's mum. She said someone from school, but I got the feeling if I pushed too hard, she would burst into tears. So I left it. But who do you think that might be?'

Cat shook her head. 'No idea. But leave her other anxiety problems aside for a moment. If she is telling the truth about the night Rupert died, then who was sitting outside Anthony's block for half an hour, and why?'

'And why did the caretaker say it was the woman in the photo if it wasn't?' said Miranda thoughtfully.

'Indeed. And why did Caroline's therapist have a photo of her in his flat?'

CHAPTER 28

CHAMELEONS CAN DIE OF STRESS IF LEFT WITHOUT SUFFICIENT COVER

When Caroline visited Anthony in the remand prison, her first thought was that he had lost weight and looked unwell. Cat, on the other hand, thought he looked pretty fit for a man of forty or fifty —she was not quite sure which—deprived of his liberty in a place that might not be particularly friendly.

Unlike her daughter, Cat had not dressed down for the visit and arrived in a black cat suit with Jimmy Choo leather boots. If there was any tension or strange looks, Cat did not notice them, concentrating fully on the job to be done.

'You OK?' she asked. 'I won't ask about the food. I doubt if I'd like it.'

Anthony smiled dourly. 'What do you want, Cat? I've had lots of sympathy from your daughter and my parents, but I'm sure you've come for another purpose.' He paused, perhaps thinking that sounded too cynical, and then continued in a lighter voice. 'Incidentally, I wanted to thank you. My parents are delighted you have taken on the case, and they have total faith in you. They are so sure I'll be cleared now that I don't think we need any evidence.'

Cat smiled at him, relieved that even with all the stress, he could still make jokes. 'Believe me, Anthony, the day you walk out of here a free man will be the happiest day of my life. But until then I'm afraid I must ask you some rather unpleasant questions. Can I apologise in advance?'

Anthony glanced at the warder, catching him just as he looked at his wrist. Cat followed his gaze and was amazed to see the warder wearing an Apple watch. Must be paid better than she thought. She looked back at Anthony, who raised his eyebrows.

'First of all can you tell me about the fight you had with Rupert on the night he died.'

Anthony shook his head. 'The police keep asking about that too, but there was no fight. An old man hit Rupert, but it wasn't me, and he didn't attack me either. Some eager young policeman seems to have got details of a fight in the Black Scabbard. I know witnesses are reputed to be imaginative, but that is odd. All that happened was Rupert moved my way. He was drunk. He was saying something rude, and the old man lashed out. I don't know why.'

'Can you remember what he said?'

'Just some abusive word. Nothing personal.'

'Tell me what happened.'

Anthony told her exactly what happened from the time he got Caroline's text to the moment he left the pub and bicycled back to Pimlico. Cat listened without interrupting.

'I stopped at King's on the way. I was looking in, hoping to see a porter I knew so I could stop in for a tea. But it was just some young guy who wouldn't have been there when I was there. Then you rang and I backed away. After that I biked on to my office and spent the night there. As you can see there was no fight at any time.'

'Did anyone see you at your office?'

'Nope. It was all shut up. But I have a key and a bed.'

'OK, now onto another subject.' She paused, not wanting to ask the next question, but knowing she must. 'Was Victoria ever your girlfriend?'

Anthony gasped and his eyes flared open. 'Victoria? No, hardly!'

He moved his arms in front of him and rested his chin on his hands.

'As you say,' he said more quietly, 'a frank and unexpected question. What made you ask?'

Cat dipped her head slightly. 'Yes, sorry. The police took a shooting certificate from the Acu Pistol and Rifle Club from your wall. So, Miranda and I went down there to see if you knew how to shoot. Your parents didn't think you ever had.'

Anthony gave a twisted smile and his head bounced slightly, but he didn't speak.

Cat looked at him and then continued. 'At the gun range we saw a picture of you. You were there with Victoria in 2016. I couldn't imagine any situation where you and a former patient would end up going shooting together, unless there was something between you.'

He snorted and for a moment gazed at the ceiling. He rubbed his arm and looked back at Cat. A couple of times he looked as though he was going to speak but didn't. The silenced lengthened.

Eventually he spoke, crossing his arms. 'Not a girlfriend. But we did have ... I guess you would call it a one-night stand.' He licked his lips. 'I knew it was a bad idea, but, well ...' He shrugged. 'The excitement of the moment. I told you before she was very persuasive and beautiful and she wasn't my patient anymore, so it didn't seem morally wrong.

But ...' He snorted and looked into the distance. 'Of course it was fatal.'

His eyes pleaded for her to understand, but Cat's shoulders sank. She had been hoping she was wrong. Hoping they were just friends who went shooting together. Although, a person like Victoria would never be just a friend. If she was there, then there was a purpose behind her action.

'But you knew what she was like,' Cat said, and she heard the desperation in her own voice. 'She had already blackmailed you once.'

Anthony spread his hands and seemed to fall into himself. 'You are right, Cat. I was tempted and I failed. My parents would be shocked and disappointed too. Caroline ...'

He put his right hand over his mouth and for a moment sat and stared at the table. Then he said, 'As you said, it was in 2016, so before I realised the extent of her ... her abilities. Not that that makes any difference. I shouldn't have done it.'

He looked at the ceiling again, back at Cat and eventually at the table, continuing. 'Victoria hadn't been in contact for years. She rang me one weekend when I had, unusually, taken some time off. She seemed to know I was free. Of course, there was no way she could know, so it must have been coincidence. But, anyway, I answered the call, and she was so happy to hear from me. Said things were going so well. The nightclub was a great success, and she said it was all down to my help and that she felt so grateful to me. I guess my vanity was awakened. I felt I had been clever with my treatment and achieved success. That itself is rare enough, and to be thanked ... well, that never happens.

'She said she'd like to take me to a shooting range south of

London as a gift. She said it would be fun for her, because she used to shoot as a girl and she'd like to practise again, and she'd love to show me what fun the sport was. I suppose I was flattered, intrigued and all those things. Anyway, I let my guard down. I went and picked her up from Clerkenwell and we drove down to the shooting club. We spent the day there. Pistols on the range. It was tremendous fun. I learnt a lot. I'd never done it before and haven't since.' He gave a great snort. 'I could hardly think that it was going to add to the evidence against me in a murder case. It wouldn't have crossed my mind.'

'No,' said Cat, 'nor anyone else's, except Victoria.'

He glanced up at her. 'So, she said she'd like to take me out to dinner, to make the day perfect, and she'd made reservations at a restaurant in Maida Vale. It is a fabulous place, near my flat and highly sought after. It's almost impossible to get a booking. I'd never been there and, of course, I was delighted to accept. Afterwards, she came back to my flat for a nightcap before she took a taxi home. She said she'd order one from my flat.

'She sat on the sofa while I got the drinks. I made mistake after mistake. I even laughed at her jokes. I gave her a whisky and I sat beside her on the sofa. We chatted ... Well ...' He snorted and traced a stain on the table with his finger. 'I'm sure I don't have to spell it out.'

'And while she was there she took a lock of your hair, enough to leave some at the scene of the crime,' said Cat, 'and she took an imprint of your door key.'

'You think? Could she really have been planning something so far ahead of time? You think so? Really?'

'No,' said Cat, 'not for one moment, but like the blackmail and everything else, it was insurance for the future. We totally underestimated Victoria last time; we mustn't do it again. She is one for whom Prior Planning Prevents Piss-Ups should be rewritten as Prior Planning Promotes Plans Perfectly.'

Anthony rubbed his chin.

'So, now I'm in here and she is somewhere ... You think she is still alive? That she, amazingly, could escape unhurt after a fall from an aeroplane?'

Cat shook her head. 'We know she's alive. We had contact with her after the fall, but I didn't want to tell you or Caroline. I didn't want to frighten you. I have another client who wants to find Victoria. I'm looking for her, but I think Victoria is going to find us, rather than vice versa. I don't think she's forgiven Stevie for refusing to be blackmailed.'

Anthony blinked but didn't speak.

'We visited your flat,' said Cat. 'The caretaker seemed nice.'

'Mihai,' said Anthony. 'His name means God-like and yes, he works hard, long hours. I doubt he's paid much. We had a drink occasionally.'

'In your flat?'

Anthony looked surprised at the question but answered anyway. 'Sometimes, or we went to the local pub. Despite all the hours he worked, he did get two hours off a day, which isn't very much in a seven-day week.' He tilted his head and smiled. 'He does like to drink, though. It was amazing what he could put back in two hours. I wondered if it would get him into trouble one day. But he's fine and I'm the one in trouble. Life and its ironies, eh?'

Cat sucked her cheeks and steeled herself to ask the question. 'Anthony, do you have a picture of Caroline in your flat?'

Anthony frowned. 'No. Why would I? Ours is a professional relationship. Even if I had wanted more, I knew that would not be right. Do you understand, Cat?'

He spoke emphatically, and she nodded.

'Yes, I understand. But the caretaker—you said his name was Mihai—said he saw a picture of Caroline in the flat.'

Anthony traced lines on the table and watched his fingers. They remained quiet so long Cat feared she was wasting time, but before she had to break the silence, he said, 'I'm thinking and thinking, Cat, but as far as I can remember, I only have one photograph in my flat, the picture of me with my family. Have the police left it there?'

'Yes, we saw it. But that is strange. Why would Mihai recognise me and say it was Caroline sitting outside if he hadn't seen her photo?'

'Caroline sitting outside? When?'

'On the night Rupert was murdered.'

Anthony frowned. 'She was sitting outside my flat on the night Rupert was murdered?' he repeated. 'Really?'

'Well, maybe not,' said Cat, chewing her lower lip. 'Miranda asked Caroline and she said she wasn't. But Mihai said she was.'

Anthony moved in his chair. 'I cannot imagine why either Caroline would be there and deny it, or why Mihai would say she was. Has he ever met her?'

'Not that we know.'

'OK. Let me think about it. Perhaps something will pop into my brain—in the night, when I can't sleep and go downstairs to get a cup of tea,' he said and smiled sadly at his own joke.

'How long has Mihai been the caretaker?' Cat asked. 'Was he there the night Caroline visited you before Leggy was born?'

'No, definitely not. He only came over eighteen months ago when the last chap left. He told me he used to do bar work before, but, although bar work was more social and he made friends there, this was a much better paid job, even if the hours were even worse.'

OK,' said Cat thoughtfully, 'let's return to how someone would get into your flat and leave the gun there. What happened if people wanted to get up to the flats when Mihai was out?'

Anthony rubbed his chin. 'Visitors, you mean. Well, if they didn't have the number for the punch pad, they would ring him. Otherwise, I guess some friends just climbed up the backstairs—you saw them?' He laughed. 'They might have had to jump the gates, but it wouldn't be impossible.'

'Unless you were in a wheelchair,' said Cat.

Anthony looked at her sharply. 'I'm following you, but Victoria hasn't been anywhere near me since that awful night.'

'Was it awful?'

He shrugged. 'What do you want from me, Cat? It was only awful in the consequences and, as you know, we all rewrite our history from the present. I am sorry, Cat, and I will tell Caroline about it.'

Cat said nothing. Odd that his thoughts yet again returned to Caroline, who, as he had pointed out earlier, was only a client.

She let her mind dwell on her daughter. Caroline's ex-husband had been murdered. Her therapist was the major suspect and she'd been publicly threatened and humiliated. Her mother was employed by Anthony's family to find out who killed her husband. Her own baby daughter somehow seemed to be important, although they had no idea why. Caroline was going to have to rethink her life big time after this. Her therapist's past one-night stand might not be the hardest thing that Caroline would have to deal with.

'But let's just suppose that Victoria is involved,' said

Anthony. 'What would her motive be? Why would Victoria shoot Rupert? Had she ever even met him?'

'I don't know,' said Cat. 'Did you give her the number for the keypad?'

'Well, we went up in the lift to my flat together. I would have punched it in, and obviously she has a memory like a spy, so yes, I expect she did remember. She could have waited until Mihai was on his break, gone in, up to my flat, used the key she copied. But although that is possible, the number has changed. When you get a new porter, there is always a new number.'

'Oh, OK. On another point, did you know you were sleeping on the gun?'

Anthony twisted his nose. 'Is that where they found it? In the bed?'

'Yes.'

'Ah. I suppose I'll need another new one now. Is it ripped into shreds?'

'Yes. I hope you get reparation when they find you are innocent,' said Cat.

Anthony looked at her a moment then, with a gentle voice, said, 'Why do you believe in me, Cat?' He moved on his seat, and she wondered if it was uncomfortable for such a big man. 'Caroline I know has complete faith in my inno-cence, as do my parents and brother, but you are not emotionally involved with me. Why do you believe in me?'

Cat was tempted to say, unhelpfully, that she wondered the same thing. Eventually she said, 'Character. You are too rational to kill Rupert. I'm not saying you wouldn't kill at all. There are circumstances in which we all could kill, even me, in hot blood, with our loved ones threatened, but this killer did not kill in defence or even in high emotion. To get up to Rupert's flat, he or she would have to have climbed up six flights, acquired a gun, known how to shoot, and thought out an escape plan so they didn't get caught after the deed. That requires prior planning.'

She paused for a while then asked, 'Do you know Rupert's address?'

'Yes,' said Anthony. 'Mansionetta Flats in King's Cross.'

Cat blinked. 'How come?'

'The police told me.'

'What? Why? When?'

'I can't answer why, but they suggested that when I said I biked from the Black Scabbard pub to Pimlico that I actually diverted past Mansionetta Flats in King's Cross, saw Rupert getting out of a car and followed him up the stairs to his flat where I shot him dead. I said as far as I knew, I'd never been there and certainly didn't know Rupert lived there. All my words engendered some disbelief. And they returned to the fact that Caroline was, in their opinion, my girlfriend.'

Cat frowned. She wondered if Caroline's outburst on hearing Anthony was in the custody suite had made things worse for him.

'Did you tell your lawyer this? It sounds odd to me and makes no sense. Why would they ask the question in that way?'

Anthony shrugged. 'My lawyer was there.'

'What else did the police ask you?'

Anthony frowned. 'About my relationship with Caroline, over and over again. Had I ever slept with her—the answer is no, by the way—had I ever slept with any of my clients— the answer to that was also no, although, as you know, Victoria was an ex-client. They asked me about Lagertha, about you, about how well I knew Rupert.'

'How well did you know Rupert?'

'Hardly at all. I could recognise him because he once picked up Caroline after a therapy session. But, as you know, we have a policy in our company that we do not mix our private and public lives. Caroline was an exception because, as I told you, she once visited my flat.'

Cat bit her lip. She took a deep breath. 'But Caroline also knew your parents,' she said. 'She rang them to suggest that they employ me to find Rupert's real killer.'

Anthony rubbed his finger along his jaw bone. Again he looked at the table before replying. 'OK, Cat. I am sorry. I should have told you everything straight away. I think some-times patient confidentiality gets in the way of truth.' He pinched the end of his nose. 'When I was her social worker, when she ran away from school and joined the squat in Peckham, which you know all about because you came there to collect her and to take her away ...'

'Yes.'

'The day before you were due to arrive, I told her you were coming, and you were going to take her home. She said she wouldn't go, and if I forced her to, she would run away from me and hide somewhere I'd never find her. I was really worried for her safety. She was fourteen and had no more street smarts than a puppy. I was at my wits' end. I couldn't find any way to convince her that you weren't going to take her back to that school. Then my mother suggested she came and visited them. They were only a few streets away and it was the only chance I had. I felt I had to let her do it.' He rubbed his finger down the opposite jaw bone. 'In fact it did the trick. She talked to Caroline in her soft, gentle, sensible way. She told her a lot about our lives. I was married in those days, although it didn't work and later I got divorced, and my mother told Caroline about her hopes for grandchildren and all those sort of things. Somehow she got through to Caroline and made her realise what it must be like for you, her mother.'

'Thank you. Having met your parents I can see it must have done Caroline so much good to see a family who gelled, who weren't all competing and fighting. Unlike her own.' She shook her head. 'No wonder she agreed to come home. She must have felt she could always escape back to your mother.' Cat laughed. 'Luckily we didn't try and make her go back to school, and she went locally, or your poor mother might have found herself with another child!'

He smiled. 'She'd have been delighted.'

He seemed to have finished speaking, but Cat felt more was coming and didn't say anything.

He looked at her steadily, rubbed his nose a few times and glanced at his watch. Then he seemed to force himself to continue. 'Since that time, Caroline has visited them often. They became like part of her family, and they've met Lagertha, and they sometimes look after her. I tried to stay away when Caroline was there because I didn't want to compromise our therapy, but inevitably there were times when we were both in the house.'

'Ah,' said Cat, wishing she had known about this before. What was the point of employing a detective if you don't tell them the whole story? she thought in irritation. 'So, it is your mother who sometimes looks after Leggy—the sitter Caroline called a "friend's mum"?'

'Most probably.'

'And, perhaps not so surprisingly, the police consider that suspicious.'

Anthony's head dipped in contrition. 'They do. It is one more thing against me. It seems impossible for them to believe that Caroline and I have never so much as kissed. If anything, we were like brother and sister.'

Cat said nothing, but she thought about her son Victor and how badly he got on with his sisters, even though he lived with one of them purely because he too loved her girl-friend. She thought about the love-hate relationship between her two daughters, and she wondered if Anthony knew what it was like to have a sister. They weren't the blissums someone with just a brother seemed to imagine.

As the first bell to end visiting clanged, Cat looked at Anthony. 'Is there anything else you haven't told me?'

Anthony rose to go. For a moment he looked as though he was going to say something, then the guard came over and he shook his head. 'Nothing relevant, Cat.'

He left and Cat was escorted back to the entrance by the prison guard with the Apple watch.

What, she wondered, was the irrelevant thing he might have said?

CHAPTER 29

CHAMELEONS HAVE ZYGODACTYL FEET—TOES FUSED INTO BUNDLES OF TWO AND THREE

W hen Cat got back to the office, Stevie was there doing something on the computer, ignoring Miranda's questions about South America.

'It's easier to do things on the big computer,' she was saying to Miranda. 'My laptop is brilliant for everything, but somehow I find the screen on the desk computer more relaxing. Especially now I've got an SSD hard drive and the start-up is so much faster.'

The others smiled blankly and Cat went to make them all some tea.

'You know,' said Stevie, 'I've been going further with Rupert's DNA research, and it is fascinating.'

'Not least,' said Cat from the tea corner, 'that Rupert suddenly seemed so interested in his ancestors.'

'Hmm,' said Stevie, wiggling her nose, 'I don't think most of this research was done by Rupert.'

'What do you mean?' asked Miranda.

'Well, the thing is we all have a certain digital fingerprint, if you like, the way we use the computer, what we look at and so forth. It's comparatively easy for someone who has investigated these things to see whether the user is the same person or not. They use this in fraud departments of banks, although they have better software, but even with what I've got, I can tell some things—particularly with someone as naive on the internet as Rupert—and I'm sure he was *not* the one doing the research. I think it was someone far more computer savvy on his behalf.'

Cat continued making the tea.

'You mean an agency?' asked Miranda. 'Did he employ an agency to look on his behalf?'

'It's possible, but I don't think so. I think the girlfriend might have investigated, given what Jane Fletcher said to Cat about Rupert's sudden interest in his DNA.'

'Good point,' said Cat, 'especially if she really is or thought she might be Rupert's sister.'

'Hmm,' said Miranda, doing a little dance round the office, 'I'd've loved to be on their first date. "Hello, I'm Drina, gosh you are sexy. Can I see your ancestry chart?" Must be a killer pick-up line.'

'I don't know,' said Stevie, screwing up her face, 'but she must have had some background on Rupert's heredity to want to look. Anyway, let me tell you about what Rupert's DNA shows.'

She brought up another site.

'So here you can see Rupert's site picture. He shares fifty percent of his DNA with Leggy, as you'd expect, and as does Caroline. Caroline has fifty percent of your DNA, Cat, but then there are a couple of surprises. Firstly, Rupert has a sibling or at least someone with whom he shares twenty-five percent of his DNA.'

'Oh,' said Cat, 'so Drina Regis was telling the truth. She is his half-sister?'

Stevie spread her hands. 'Maybe, maybe not. There is all

sorts of potential for fraud and faking DNA here, so I wouldn't jump to any conclusion too soon. What I need from you lot is DNA that definitely does come from Drina. And, as a control experiment, I think it would be good to have DNA from everyone else involved in the case. We need someone about the right age—I'd say born around the 1970s.'

Miranda gave a muffled laugh. 'Well, that will help our suspect list. Anyone born around the 1970s, only a few million or so.'

Stevie gave her a long stare.

'As I was saying. In rare cases, there are examples of unrelated strangers with small amounts of shared DNA, but here it is twenty-five percent, which is far too much, and besides, in Rupert's case, the simple solution is the sibling mentioned by Jane Fletcher. However, we don't yet know if the sibling is male or female. Or indeed anything else about them. Cat, I think you need to ask Jane Fletcher if she can remember anything else about the other baby.'

'OK,' said Cat, 'I'll ring her tomorrow. Thinking about it, she might have something of Drina's herself. She said she met her, albeit briefly, but, on the other hand, she said Drina didn't get out of the car.'

'This whole DNA thing is mind-blowing,' said Miranda. 'What did they do before they knew about genetic links? You could accidentally marry your sister.'

'Not so odd,' said Cat. 'In some cultures they deliberately married their sisters and close relations, thinking it would keep the blood strong. Ancient Egypt for example.'

Miranda sneered. 'So, setting aside old clever clogs showing off, can you find anything else about the researcher, Stevie?'

'Well, the name he or she works under is Mr Berthalot. I'm assuming it is a sort of pen name, owing to its duality.'

'Ha, ha,' said Miranda.

Stevie frowned. 'What?'

'Missed a birth a lot. Sounds like either an absent father or a mother who didn't use contraception! Or perhaps someone trans as in Ms Bertha.'

'Eh,' said Stevie, 'what? That sounds like intuition!'

At the same time Cat said, 'Not so fast, young Miranda. Bertha is a male name in Germany and means "bright one".'

Miranda stuck her tongue out. 'There she goes again with more linguistic showing off. Concentrate, Cat!'

Stevie wrinkled her nose at them both and returned to the point in hand. 'If they use a pen name, then it isn't so easy to find the connections on the ancestral tree, but at the same time the algorithms seem to know who they are, so they give you what they call "hints" about their relationships. I got a hint this morning which suggested that Rupert might have a cousin as well, since there is someone with whom he shares thirteen percent of his DNA.'

Cat frowned. 'Hang on! If you've got a cousin looking for results, then aren't you likely to have a mother—a shared connection? What percentage would an aunt take? Or can you find a father?'

Stevie took a sip of water. 'Yes, you can. But the problem is you can only find things that are "out there". I mean, if someone hasn't put their DNA up, it doesn't magically appear. But you can get connections, and that's how the hints help. Are you following me?'

'Sort of.'

'The company gave me another hint, this time fifty percent, and has dates that go back to the 1950s but no name. So, I'm guessing that could be the missing birth mother. Didn't Jane say she was a teenager when Rupert was born? But it could also be the father. I need to look and see what type of DNA it is, and even then it isn't always straight-forward.'

'Wow,' said Miranda, 'this is complicated. So near and yet so far. How do we get more details?'

'I'm working on it,' said Stevie, 'but you need to get me lots of samples. Go out and get it, my children!'

'Yeah, right,' said Miranda. 'It's not as easy as playing with the internet, you know.'

Stevie raised an eyebrow and offered Miranda the mouse.

CHAPTER 30

CHAMELEONS HAVE ACRODONT DENTITION— THEIR TEETH ARE ATTACHED TO THE EDGE OF THEIR JAW

'You can't blame the police,' said Miranda as Cat drove them up to London in the shared company car bought after their successful first case. 'Everything stacks up against Anthony in such a perfect way. It is almost as though there was someone framing him, and that that person was themselves a detective and knew exactly what the police would be looking for.'

'Wow,' said Cat, 'assuming someone framed him is a big proposition.'

Miranda waggled her head and stroked the dog. 'But not impossible, is it?'

Cat's phone rang. She pressed a button on the steering wheel, marvelling at how cars had changed since she was a girl. Bluetooth as standard made life so much easier. In her day you had to stop at a phone box to make a call.

'Diego. *Dígame.*'

'*Mucho gusto*, Cat. My wife has remembered something about that night. About the night Mr Rupert was killed. We have been talking, my wife and me, about moving to another flat. As we listed the things we needed in a new place, I said, "no rats" and told my wife how you and I had gone onto the roof and seen all the rats scurrying between the black bags. And my wife, she goes cold and says, "Oh, I remember. The night Mr Rupert died, I woke in the night. I heard this noise of sliding. Something was moving on the roof. I was so scared. I thought it was rats and they were coming in and I put my head under the pillow and prayed. But then I heard the door to the roof closing—it makes a little click when it closes—and I thought it must be Rupert and I waited for him to start singing."

'Mr Rupert,' Diego explained, 'often liked to walk on the roof at night singing. He liked to pee over the edge of the parapet in case there were people below who thought it was about to rain. Then he would sing "Singin' in the Rain" and laugh a lot.

'But this night there was no singing and only silence and my wife went back to sleep and forgot all about it, until we had that conversation about the rats.'

'Thank you, Diego,' said Cat.

She turned to Miranda. 'I think this might mean that the man who took Rupert home did go back onto the roof,' she said.

'Go on?'

'Well, he would need a witness to the fact that he had left, so he could have made a noise outside Diego's door. Diego then comes out and they have the conversation. He pretends to go downstairs. Once Diego has gone in, he pops back upstairs and waits on the roof until Rupert falls asleep, having had a period of singing, goes in and shoots him, and either leaves by the chute down into the rubbish heap at the back or just walks down the stairs very quietly. Most people would be asleep by then, so they wouldn't hear him.'

Miranda twisted her nose. 'Except, how would he have

got the key to the roof? You said there was a door, and it was locked.'

'That's true,' said Cat, 'but there is a key hanging under the postal boxes. It's possible he took it up with him without Mrs Cartwright noticing. Or he could have hidden in the empty flat opposite.'

Miranda leant into the footwell and scratched the dog's back. 'And it's hard to know what his motivation was. Or do you think he too is related to Leggy?'

'Ha, ha,' said Cat.

'However,' said Miranda, 'whoever shot Rupert had to already have Anthony's hair—remember Caroline said the police found a hair at the scene. How could he get that?'

'Well, that could be possible,' said Cat, keeping her eyes glued to the road, 'if he was in the Black Scabbard pub with Rupert and Anthony. OK, Anthony said they didn't fight but that Rupert did swing his glass into Anthony's face, and at that moment everyone would be looking at Rupert. So the bald man could just reach up and pull out a hair without anyone noticing.'

Miranda made a face. 'Maybe. Not easy though. And he's still got to go on to Anthony's flat and put the gun there. How would he have done that?'

Cat shrugged and accidentally put on the brakes, causing a heap of hooting from behind.

'However,' said Miranda, 'what about if he and Dotty Lottie were working together?'

'Bit of a leap,' said Cat. 'Why should a man in a pub in Eltham have anything to do with the caretaker of the flats?'

She moved to the slow lane where she could think in peace. 'That is a difficult connection to make, and we have no real motivation for either of them. Unless you are still thinking she was getting her revenge on Rupert for stealing from her.'

'That isn't impossible,' said Miranda stubbornly. 'We need to find this old man and discover why he was in the Black Scabbard. It might be something perfectly innocent or he might have a connection to Anthony, or Rupert. One drunken evening could hardly be cause enough to shoot a man or most men would be dead already and me too.' She grinned, but Cat was keeping her eyes glued to the road.

'Yes, you are right, we do need to find out more about the man in the pub. Which reminds me, we haven't heard anything from the barman at the Black Scabbard. Have you still got the piece of paper with his number?'

'Yes,' said Miranda, digging in her pocket and upsetting the dog, who jumped onto her lap. 'I'll call him.'

'OK, but let's leave the dog with your mother before we agree to meet him in some dingy backstreet where it can only cause trouble.'

'He,' said the dog's owner. 'He is not an it.'

* * *

The barman at the Black Scabbard had a night off, so they arranged to meet at Spinners at eight p.m., before the night-club got too busy.

'So,' said Miranda closing the phone, 'I can't go to Spinners like this. We'd better drop the dog off at my mother's and go shopping.'

Cat laughed. 'Sure. Why not! I need another pair of Louboutin heels.'

Miranda coughed theatrically. 'Need, eh? On expenses then?'

After a massive shopping session, and leaving the dog

with Miranda's mother, the women went on to the club. They parked in the basement and made their way up the stairs into the club.

'Caroline's here,' said Miranda, noticing her car with its child seat.

'Oh dear,' said Cat, 'I should have warned her we were coming. I hope she doesn't come down and make a scene. She is terribly on edge right now. And you know how she can go off half-cocked when she's stressed.'

As they got into the club, they were approached by a beautiful tall woman.

'Well! If it isn't the gorgeous Miranda and the purring Cat. I have missed you so much. Come and join Trixie and me at our table. Your daughter, my darling Cat, is a hoot. All the boys want to date her now! Husband killer. Lover in jail. The amateur sleuths are out in force. Life is so exciting. No wonder the place is rammed.'

Cat and Miranda could see that was true, even though it was still before eight p.m. Spinners had never been so busy and the cash tills behind the bar chattered with constant action. Cat glanced up at the two-way mirror, wondering if Caroline was watching them. However, if she was, she stayed put.

'Jenny,' said Miranda, 'my favourite pilot.'

She kissed her gently, making sure to avoid the carefully created makeup.

'We were immune to COVID,' said Jenny. 'We never did any of that dreadful lipstick sharing the rest of you girls get up to. Now what brings you here to Spinners? You must be in search of action. Cat has had plenty of opportunity to watch the kitten and has obviously come here for a quite different reason. But now, that's a thought. Since mother and daughter are both here, who is looking after the lovely

Leggy? Don't tell me she is having an introduction to night-club life.'

Cat shook her head. 'If I told you, you wouldn't believe me.'

'Oh,' said Jenny, 'you are such a spoilsport. Now, if I get little Miranda a negroni or two, I shall soon find the truth. And what can I get you? Please don't say tomato juice.'

'Tomato juice.'

'Ho! You'd better come over to the bar and help me. I won't be responsible for asking for such embarrassing drinks. We'll go over to my favourite barman, and we'll be liperty quick. Check out the muscles on him and the sexy scar!'

As they walked to the bar, Jenny said quietly, 'Amy asked me to tell you she doesn't want you to go on attempting to find Victoria. As far as she's concerned, the whole thing is over. She was humiliated, but she doesn't want any more publicity and, with all the things going on around Caroline, she can see how easy it is to get unwanted publicity. She just wants to forget the whole thing. I'll send the last payment. But if you do find Victoria, let me know. I'm curious to know how she can hide in *plane sight*.'

Jenny laughed, but Cat bit her lip. She liked having two cases on the go and Graham and Amy's money had been useful. Now it seemed there was no sponsor for examining Victoria's doings. The police certainly appeared to have relegated Neil's murder to their cold cases file. They were not even searching for the woman and apparently accepted that Victoria was dead.

'Oscar, darling!' said Jenny as they approached the bar. 'Of course you know my adorable friend Cat. But you probably don't realise she is everything from a cougar to a Rumpleteazer!'

Oscar gave a great belly laugh and asked them what they would like to drink. Cat watched him, wondering why Caroline employed him as a barman and not a bouncer. Was he one of the staff Victoria left behind? She must ask Caroline.

She walked back to the table in a thoughtful mood. They had been joined by a tall woman with a nervous face. Cat saw that Miranda was trying to practise her fledgling Polish while flirting with her hands and smiled.

'Hello,' she said, 'I'm Cat.'

The woman smiled. 'Piotr,' she said in a curiously gruff voice which made Miranda giggle and Jenny smile in deep appreciation.

'Cool,' said Miranda. 'Shouldn't that be Petra?' She giggled again, flashing her eyes, and Cat shook her head. What was in that negroni? She sat next to Piotr and dropped her voice.

'Thank you for talking to us,' she said. 'You like this place?'

Piotr smiled. 'This is one place where no one from the Black Scabbard would ever come,' she said. 'When I was young I saw pictures of what English men are *really* like, or rather what they really like to *wear*. After that I always wanted to come to the UK. Even since I was so high.' She put her hand on the chair.

Cat gave a spurt of laughter, trying to imagine her staid late husband Charlie trying on her clothes. But perhaps, she reflected, you never know what people really like underneath a conservative front. Forcing herself back to the crime, she asked, 'What was happening in the Black Scabbard that day, something that made it so necessary for us to leave?'

'It was a C18 meeting.'

'Combat 18, the right-wing militants? Part of the British National Party? Aren't they banned?'

Piotr shrugged. 'I don't know, maybe they don't care. In Black Scabbard they have regular meetings and don't encourage strangers to frequent the pub.'

'But Rupert? He wasn't a member, was he?'

Piotr shook his head. 'I never see him before. He was already what you say POA when he arrived.'

'POA?'

'Pissed on arrival,' said Piotr, smiling proudly. 'I know much English slang.'

'And the old man who carried Rupert away? Was he a member?'

Again Piotr shook his head. 'He too was stranger, but he had slight Irish accent. I hear C18 did once have an Irish paramilitary connection. So maybe.'

Cat frowned. Piotr seemed even more observant and knowledgeable than most barmen: the drunks' favourite psychoanalysts. 'And how come they didn't mind you being there? Didn't they notice your accent?'

'I told them I am from Liverpool,' said Piotr, grinning. 'They probably thought I was Irish too.'

Cat shook her head, but she wasn't surprised. The BNP had once used a Spitfire with Polish markings on their leaflets, purporting to support their desire for a pure Anglo-Saxon race. Clearly doing research was not one of their priorities.

'I do know his name,' said Piotr. 'He passed me a credit card for his beer, before changing his mind and using cash. I noticed his name was Charles FitzRoy. When I was learning English at school, they told us that meant "bastard of the King". Of course, I remember a name that heralds its owner as an illegal child.' Piotr roared with laughter.

CHAPTER 31

CHAMELEONS DON'T SO MUCH CHANGE COLOUR AS USE SMART MIRRORS!

As they drove home discussing whether Stevie would be able to find Charles FitzRoy on the internet, Cat's phone rang. She saw it was Piotr but didn't know how to say 'hello' in Polish.

'Cat,' he said.

'Yes. We're here. Driving home but we're not far away. Has something happened?'

'Not happened exactly,' he said, 'but ... I went to buy Jenny a drink. She said to use her favourite barman, and when I went up there, it was the old man. You know, him from the Black Scabbard. The guy I told you took Rupert home. I recognised him.'

Cat swallowed. This was bad news. The guy worked in her daughter's club. Why?

'Did he recognise you?'

'I don't think so. He works at Spinners, so he's used to seeing men in drag, but can he see through it? I doubt it. He didn't show any sign of recognition.'

'Did you get his name?'

'Eventually! I asked Jenny and it took a while of her obfuscation and accusing me of flirting with her favourite, but eventually she came clean. His name is Oscar.'

'Thanks,' said Cat. Just as she was ending the call, Piotr added, 'Oh, I tried Miranda's phone first, but no one answered, then I got your number from Jenny.'

'Thanks,' said Cat again, wondering why Miranda wouldn't answer her phone. She glanced over and saw Miranda had fallen asleep. She really ought to stay off the booze; she was getting as bad as Rupert.

However, that was something of less importance, something to think about later. Now she had to think over the problem of one of Caroline's most trusted barmen being the old man they were looking for. Why was he in the Black Scabbard? And why was he there on the night that Rupert died? She didn't believe it could be a coincidence. Was he there to protect Anthony? Or to incriminate him? They needed to be careful how they interviewed him. She glanced over at Miranda, but she was still asleep.

As they drove into Cat's drive, Miranda woke up.

'We here? Cool. I'll be off before I have to watch you and Frank having a luscious reunion.'

Cat laughed, but she hadn't even collected her things together before Miranda was back.

'Did I leave my phone in your car? I can't see a thing in this dark village. When do you think they'll get street lights?'

Cat laughed. 'Never. And even if you don't care about light pollution, I wouldn't let Caroline hear you suggesting more lights. But you're welcome to search my car.'

Miranda, who was doing just that, waggled her fingers in Cat's direction. 'I must have left it in the club.'

'OK,' said Cat slowly. 'Any idea where you left it?'

'No.'

'I'll let Caroline know. You'd better borrow a torch.'

CHAPTER 32

CHAMELEONS CHANGE COLOUR BY REARRANGING TINY CRYSTALS IN THEIR SKIN

After three attempts of calling Jane Fletcher's number, Cat decided she must be away. That Jane had neither an answerphone nor a mobile number, nor any email, didn't surprise Cat. Jane struck her as someone who preferred to live in the past, probably an idealised fantasy form of the past, but nonetheless not the present.

Cat rang Jane's daughter Angela instead, hoping that one of her enormous brood of children wouldn't answer the phone.

'Cat,' said Angela, 'so nice to hear from you. So terrible about Rupert, but who would have ever thought we weren't related? I must say it did change things totally for me when I realised he wasn't even my brother. We hadn't been getting on well for a while anyway, and I did wonder how one's own blood could be such a mean drunk, but then all was revealed and, I must say, I was much relieved.'

Like mother like daughter, thought Cat drily, but she simply said, 'I wonder, Angela, did your mother ever talk about the other child Charlotte had? Did she ever think of adopting ... was the baby a boy or a girl?'

'Oh ... hang on ...' said Angela. There was a scuffling noise at her end of the phone, and she was clearly rebuking one child for hitting another. Eventually, she gave Cat her attention again. 'I'm sorry, Cat, I've really no idea. All Mum said to me was that once she'd got one of her own, she didn't want another one. I hope you understand. You know, blood is thicker than water and all that.'

'Thanks,' said Cat. 'Do you know where your mother is? I'd quite like a chat.'

'Oh, they've gone off hiking,' said Angela. 'Dad loves walking, and he said it was about time Mum gave him some attention. The police have kept the body, so we can't have a funeral, and it seemed like the perfect time to have a holiday, so they've gone off somewhere for three weeks. They did tell me where, but I've completely forgotten. If she rings me, I'll tell her to give you a call. Sorry we can't help any more. Must go, the kids are so demanding. Love you! Bye.'

She rang off and Cat felt a rush of sympathy for Rupert. There is always, she thought bitterly, another story behind the one you know. People are so complex.

As Cat put down the phone, she got a call from Caroline. Caroline was clearly in a hurry and talking fast and breathily.

'Hi, Mum, thanks for the text. Why don't you use Whats-App? Much safer and cheaper. But yes, Oscar found Miranda's phone. She'd dropped it by Jenny's table. We call it that because that's where she and Trixie usually sit.'

'Thanks, darling, can you get into it?'

'Whaaa? Of course not. You don't think I go nosing around in other people's phones, do you?'

'No,' said her mother, 'but if you open the cover, are there any missed calls there?'

She heard a click.

'OK. Hang on. I'm only doing this because I'm assuming this will help free Anthony as you are his detective-buddy.'

She scrabbled around and came back quickly. 'No, no missed calls or anything on the front, so she probably didn't miss anything. I'll give it to Agata when she comes round for a drink tonight, and she can give it back to Miranda tomorrow. OK?'

'Fine,' said Cat, closing her own phone.

Although Cat wasn't very internet savvy, she was observant and she knew that as Piotr had tried to call Miranda last night, there should have been a missed call notification on the phone. The fact it wasn't there meant that Oscar must have opened the phone before he gave it to Caroline and got rid of it. Which presumably meant he had Miranda's password. How did he get that? But still more worrying: Miranda would almost certainly have put Piotr's name with the number into her contacts, so Oscar would have seen the name and known that Piotr and Miranda were in contact. If Oscar had killed Rupert, then Piotr might well be in danger. She felt very cold, and the worst thing was that it was Miranda's fault he was in danger. She was about to pick up her phone when she thought she'd prefer to use a completely anonymous one and borrow Frank's, which he had, as usual, forgotten about and left on the table.

However, when Cat tried to call Piotr, there was no reply. At least this would be just a number, she thought. If someone else saw Piotr's phone, there would be nothing recognisable. She called Miranda on her landline.

Miranda, when the problem was explained to her, grew serious for a moment. Then she said, 'OK, we need to warn him. No reply to your call may not mean anything; he might be working in the Black Scabbard and can't get to the phone. I'll get hold of my sister Agata and ask her to go over. OK with you?'

Cat nodded and then, realising Miranda couldn't see her, said, 'Yes, fine, but don't put Agata in danger as well.'

Miranda laughed. 'She's in the police! They have protection.'

'Oh yeah,' said Cat, closing her phone.

CHAPTER 33

CHAMELEON SKIN CELLS CONTAIN GUANINE—A DNA BASE

The next day, even before her colleagues were in the office, Stevie drove up to London in her Triumph Spitfire. She had rebuilt the car herself from a wreck and she loved driving it, but she wasn't keen on driving into London. However, since no one else seemed able to get her the DNA she needed, she had decided to get it herself.

The first place to go, she reckoned, was Rupert's flat. Although she didn't doubt the mysterious DNA agent, Mr Berthalot, had used Rupert's real DNA, it was worth double-checking.

After that she would go to Anthony's flat. Since the police seemed to think the blood found in Rupert's flat was either Anthony's blood or a close relative, she needed to check that out too. After that she was going to try and get DNA from Drina Regis, the potential sister and aunt.

She would also have to find time to visit Anthony's parents and get their DNA for a potential match. Honestly, she thought, this DNA search was getting out of hand. She had warned Kaya Dyer she was coming to see her but hadn't told her why. She thought it would be better to explain in person.

She needed to go to Spinners, where she hoped to find some of Victoria's DNA, left over from the time when she owned the club.

Victoria was clearly involved. Both the name—Mister Birth A Lot, so much Victoria's humour—and the digital pattern in Mr Berthalot's research showed her hand. And then there was her inexplicable obsession with Caroline, which had led to her giving Caroline the club in her will. Why did she do that?

Stevie was not usually a person who dwelt on the past. She preferred to focus on now, to work with facts, but even thinking about Victoria caused a deep pain in her body. She had been entranced by her. Excited by her. Even loved her. But Victoria was willing to kill her. Stevie hadn't yet said anything to Cat and Miranda about Victoria being involved. She didn't want to alarm them. She knew how Victoria worked, how her mind functioned. She could handle her.

Once in King's Cross, Stevie slipped quietly into Rupert's block and silently climbed the stairs. There was no sign of Mrs Cartwright, who presumably was dozing in her flat, nor of Diego, who was probably at work.

The flat itself remained as Cat and Miranda described it: a horrible example of destitution and destruction. No one, it seemed, had bothered to look for clues in the tiny bathroom, which the designer had squeezed into an inconvenient corner. There was an elderly toothbrush with bent-out bristles sitting covered in toothpaste on the side of the sink. As there were no others, it was most likely Rupert's. Stevie took it. She also took a scraping of the dried blood, although she doubted it would yield any results.

In Anthony's block, the caretaker, Mihai, was there, and

happy to let her in to Anthony's flat, so his toothbrush too was collected with ease. Mihai came up to the flat with her and chatted with her as she went round. On a whim, she showed the caretaker a picture of Victoria.

'Have you ever seen this woman here?'

He looked at her and smiled. 'Beautiful woman,' he said. 'But no.'

Stevie showed her a picture of Caroline.

'How about this woman? Do you recognise her?'

He smiled again. 'For sure. That is Anthony's girlfriend. There was a picture of her here.'

'Where?' asked Stevie, looking around the flat.

'Here,' said Mihai, pointing at the photograph of Anthony's family. 'Beside this one, but the police took it when I told them she was the one outside.'

'I see. So, you hadn't met her before?'

'No. I thought she must have been a new friend because the picture wasn't here the first time I had a drink with Anthony.'

'And the second?'

'No. We went to the pub.'

'Ah, I see. So, when did you see the photo for the first time?'

Mihai wrinkled his nose. 'I think ... maybe when I went around with the police, when they were looking and searching.'

Stevie nodded, watching him closely. 'And then you remembered you saw her outside and recognised her.'

'Yes,' said Mihai, but his voice sounded suddenly diffident.

Stevie said nothing.

As they were leaving the flat, Stevie put her hand to her pocket.

'Oh, bother. I must have left my phone somewhere. Mihai, could you ring it and I'll try and find it?'

'For sure.'

Mihai rang her number and Stevie's phone was located under Anthony's destroyed bed. She shook her head.

'Silly me! I must have dropped it when I was taking photos. Thanks, Mihai.'

'Anytime.'

As they waited for the lift, Stevie said, 'I had a Rumanian friend, like you.' She tilted her head at his *Don't ask. I AM Rumanian* badge. He was a pilot like me.'

'You are pilot? That's nice. I would have like to be pilot.'

Stevie moued. 'We used to fly into Europe together on the small twins. The job was hard work, but fun for me because I was learning, but for him, well, he was an experienced pilot and a good one. I was surprised he wasn't with some well-paying airline. One day I asked him why.'

The lift came. They got in and Stevie continued her story as they descended.

'He said no airline would employ him because he had a criminal record. I was amazed. I'd been flying with him for months by then and he was so honest he wouldn't even cheat over the hotel bill on his accounts. That was unusual.' She smiled at Mihai. 'But then he told me. He said: "I was accused of stealing from the company I worked for. I didn't do what they said I did. I didn't steal. The problem was, the only witness the night the money disappeared was the night watchman, and he said he heard someone talking on the phone and he had a Rumanian accent. Well, I was the only man in the company with both keys to the office and a Rumanian accent. So, I got the blame."'

They arrived at the ground floor.

'But later,' said Stevie, 'he overheard the night watchman

admitting to a friend he hadn't been at his post when the money was stolen. He'd gone out for half an hour, but he didn't dare admit it or he'd lose his job.' She sighed. 'Terrible when an innocent person is blamed for a crime they didn't commit.'

Stevie walked out of the lift, but Mihai stood still, silent, his hand holding the lift door open.

She turned around and looked questioningly at him.

He avoided her gaze.

She waited.

'OK, Stevie, you are true. I tell you.'

He went to his station near the keys and turned on the computer.

'Here,' he said, 'you see the CCTV for that night, the night the woman was here.'

Stevie looked at the screen. They could just make out someone sitting between the cars. The image was very hazy and even Stevie, who knew Caroline well, could not have identified her. At a stretch, she would say that the hair was blonde. The person sat there for about five minutes and then, without warning, the screen went black. Stevie looked at Mihai.

'I should have been here,' he said, 'that night. But Charles, an old friend from my life as a barman, dropped by and we went out for a drink. I was only away for half an hour ...' He glanced at Stevie. 'Maybe three quarters. But when I came back the CCTV had gone off. I looked back at when it was working, and I saw the blonde-haired person. I realised she must have been here when I was away and it was even possible she went up in the lift, although we have punch pad security. But, I thought, if she knew someone in the block, then she would know the code.

'At the time, I just wondered why. But then later, when

the police came, we went up to Anthony's flat. I saw the photograph of the blonde woman and I thought that must be her. Both women were blonde and here. Seemed certain she was the one. Honestly, I didn't think I would implicate her in a murder case. I just thought my boss would sack me if he knew I'd gone to the pub when I should be here.'

Stevie didn't comment. The longer she lived, the more she saw how people ignored the things they didn't want to see, preferring to focus on the things they did, whatever the outcome.

'But you, and the other women, you care about her. You don't want her to suffer, eh?'

'Yes,' said Stevie, 'and we don't want Anthony to spend his life in prison. He's got too much to give to the world. Thank you.'

'What for?'

'For telling me the truth. It's hard to do, I know, when you've told a lie, and it comes back to haunt you. You are very brave. I hope your boss doesn't find out.'

She left the block and checked she had Mihai's number before getting back into the Spitfire. It was only after the murder of a schoolgirl and the massive press around her hacked phone that Stevie had discovered how easy it was to get into someone else's phone. Naturally, once she knew it was possible for the journalist from a cheap newspaper to do it, she wanted to do it herself. Mihai might have told her everything, but just in case he hadn't, she decided to check his messages.

CHAPTER 34

THE CHAMELEON SPECIES IS
AT LEAST 100 MILLION
YEARS OLD

The next collection was more challenging: Drina Regis. Stevie had thought long and hard about how to get a Drina Regis sample and thanks to Cat's unsuccessful sit-out, she was fully aware of the number of surveillance cameras in the street. She had discovered there was one blind spot around the house, oddly at the garage.

However, when Stevie drove past the back of the house and saw a large sign announcing the garage door was alarmed, she understood. No need for a camera there because the alarm would alert the household to anyone going in. She drove on past and then stopped. Just down the road from Drina's house was a hairdresser and next to that a theatrical costumier. An odd juxtaposition of shops, Stevie thought wryly. Still, it was not impossible that Drina might go into the hairdresser to have her hair cut. It looked expensive and inviting for someone of Drina's avowed temperament.

As she walked towards the door, a young girl with metallic-red hair pushed past her and jumped on a bike, pedalling off down the road as though her life depended on it. Her overall had *Apprentice* on the back. Stevie jumped back into her car and followed her. Luckily there was a twenty-mph speed limit, so she was unlikely to be arrested for kerb crawling.

After a few streets, the girl stopped, threw down the bike and leapt towards a café. Suddenly she stopped, shot around, hoicked off her overall, threw it into the bicycle basket and dashed into the café. Inside Stevie could see her greeting a young man with such passion it seemed unlikely she would be back at work anytime soon.

Stevie stopped next to the bicycle. Glad she had the top of the Spitfire down, she leant over the low door and quickly slipped a nail from her repair box through the girl's back tyre. She grabbed the overall out of the basket, muttering: 'I'll take it back home for you.' *Sorry*, she thought as she drove off, *but needs must in a detective's day.*

Once outside the theatrical costumier, Stevie parked in a disabled bay. Looking around guiltily, she brought out a disabled badge. Yes, it was naughty, but on the other hand there were no special bays for amateur on-call detectives.

Half an hour later, Stevie, now with metallic-red hair and wearing the overall, entered the hairdressers, hoping to blend in and quickly mix with the other apprentices.

She was surprised by the first words of the receptionist.

'Oh, there you are! We've got a full afternoon, and you suddenly disappear. Where the heck have you been?'

Stevie said nothing and shuffled her feet.

'Oh, never mind, just get in here and do some sweeping up. There's a whole new set of customers coming in at two.'

She threw Stevie a broom and tilted her head in towards the salon. 'Do Mark first—he's the one who's really pissed off—then you can do Delila's. Go.'

Luckily, there was only one male cutter, and his chair was indeed surrounded by hair, so Stevie headed over there and started sweeping. He gave her an evil look but didn't say anything. By the time she finished, she'd heard someone use Delila's name and knew where to sweep next.

Drina Regis, however, did not appear. Stevie clicked her tongue. It had been a vain hope and not at all well thought out. In fact, she had behaved rather like Miranda, far too spontaneous. She shivered as she remembered that once before acting without planning had got her into trouble. She needed to think again.

As she dawdled near the basins, her lack of useful action was spotted by the eagle-eyed receptionist.

'Oi. You. Work-experience girl. Over here!'

Guessing that must be her, Stevie approached the reception slowly, shuffling her feet and sucking her lower lip.

'You!' said the receptionist. 'I saw you slacking around the corner, checking your phone. Well, I need to pop out for a while, so you can make yourself useful. You can mind the reception for a few moments. Don't say anything rude to the clients. Try not to be funny. Or sleaze up to them. Or anything really. Just say please, thank you and sir and madam. Don't make any decisions or offer to cut anyone's hair. OK? Got that? Good. I'll be about twenty minutes.'

Stevie looked deferential. It wasn't much different from being a first officer at BA.

Once the receptionist had gone, Stevie thumbed through today's appointment list, which, surprisingly, was on paper. No Drina Regis. Perhaps she used a different outfit. Perhaps she'd already had her hair cut. It had been a silly idea, but at least she had tried, she thought, trying to pump herself up.

The phone rang. She looked around her. No one sprang

up in response. While she stared at the ringing phone, hoping that someone else would take the call, a hoarse voice from the salon yelled, 'Hurry up and answer that! Second ring, I said! Every time! Not just when you bloody well feel like it!'

Stevie gulped and, putting herself into official-sounding mode, lifted the receiver.

'Hello. Glam Glam Hairdressers, Phyla speaking, can I help?'

'Hello, Phyla, Drina Regis here. Bit short notice, I know, but I wondered if I could come in for a haircut. I usually have Mark but given the short notice I'll take Delila if she's available.'

Stevie looked at the list and found that, amazingly, Mark did have a cancellation at three o'clock. There was a long waiting list for other favoured clients, one of whom, no doubt, should be slotted in first, but Stevie bypassed them.

'Yes, you are lucky. Mark has a cancellation at three o'clock. Would that suit you?'

'Perfect. Aren't I the lucky one?'

She rang off and Stevie, feeling a frisson of nerves, put Drina's name in the vacant slot. She hoped she wouldn't get a rocket from the receptionist for ignoring the waiting list.

Her hope was unfounded.

'Jesus Christ!' said the receptionist on her return. 'Can't you do anything right? Didn't you see that waiting list? It's right by his name. Now we'll have to take that silly cow. She's a right biscuit. Mean as hell. Never tips and gives everyone the holier-than-thou treatment. Bitch. All right, you go back to sweeping and leave the thinking part to me. Idiot.'

As Stevie walked back into the salon, Mark came out and she could hear the receptionist smoothing his feathers.

'Darling Mark, something wonderful has happened. Just as your client cancelled, a new one called and was desperate for a haircut. What could I do but let the dear girl in?'

Mark made a sort of harrumphing noise. 'Just so long as it's not the bitch in the wheelchair! Oh my God! It is. Well, we'll have to hope she behaves like a normal person for once. The old cow.'

Stevie was surprised the receptionist hadn't mentioned that it was all the work-experience girl's fault, but it could be that the receptionist was not supposed to leave her post. Certainly, no yelling came her way from Mark.

At three o'clock, Drina Regis arrived, and Stevie understood why they were all in awe of her. She threw open the doors with a flourish, pulled her chair in and sat, staring at them as though expecting them to run up and curtsy.

'I see you still haven't got DDA compliant doors here,' were her first words. 'That is breaking the law.'

The receptionist started to explain about exemptions for listed buildings, but Drina was not interested.

'Here, you, take my coat. Careful how you hang it. It costs more than you make in a year. Where is Mark? I hope he's not dawdling over another less important client. Ah, there you are. Good.'

Stevie watched her performance with interest. *Reminds me of someone*, she thought, *someone who looks different but ...* She did her job quietly and in due course helped herself to a selection of Drina's hairs, making sure they still had the root attached. Carefully secreting them in a plastic bag in her pocket, she continued to work until the end of the day. As she was leaving, she saw the young girl with metallic-red hair coming back. She was running and clearly rather upset. She cannoned into Stevie, apparently oblivious to the fact Stevie was a mirror image of herself.

'Oh! I'm so sorry. It's just I'm in a hurry. My bike ... my overall ... Martha is evil if you miss ...' She suddenly stopped and stared at Stevie. 'Who are you?'

Stevie grinned. 'It's OK. I just did your afternoon job for you. Go back tomorrow and she'll never notice.'

Stevie walked away and the girl, frowning at her departure, went on into the salon. As the door shut, Stevie could hear Martha saying, 'What? You forgot something. Get out. We don't need you back until tomorrow morning and don't be late this time or upset the clients. Fool.'

Stevie climbed into her car and drove on to Spinners.

At Spinners she went straight upstairs. No one was in the office, and she assumed Caroline was probably fetching Leggy from school and taking her home. She walked into the bathroom. As she expected, the bathroom was spotless. Caroline could not live in an environment with dirt; it was an anathema to her that anybody would not clean their house, office and everything else from top to toe every day.

Stevie looked in the bathroom cabinet. Fortunately, Caroline's cleaning had not continued inside and there were two toothbrushes in a mug, both dusty and pushed to the back of the cabinet. There was a good possibility at least one was Victoria's. Stevie took both.

Smiling, Stevie drove on to her final appointment in London. One that she felt might hold the final clue to why Rupert was shot.

CHAPTER 35
CHAMELEONS' BONES GLOW
IN THE DARK

A few days later, when Caroline arrived at the club, she decided to go straight up to the office. She checked the cars and saw Tom and Oscar were here, but even so she decided not to go into the club. Most days she did go straight onto the club floor, but today she felt tired. This constant fear was wearing her down. She didn't feel like listening to the endless rumours that were now circulating the club, the innuendo, the overall belief that she had killed Rupert and framed Anthony. Oddly, Anthony had emerged from this as the hero, and somehow she had become the villain. She didn't understand it. However, she and the rumour-mongers appeared to have the same goal: Anthony's freedom.

She opened the door of the office and stopped dead. To her surprise Drina Regis was sitting in her chair.

'Hello?' Caroline said, forcing her voice to sound normal. 'Can I help you?'

'Probably you can,' said Drina, 'but not nearly as much as I can help you. Despite your reluctance, I have come to offer my services and my money to your daughter. Again.'

Caroline moved quietly towards the chocolate cupboard. This was a situation and she needed reinforcements.

'Ah,' said Drina, 'the chocolate queen. I heard you are an addict. Can't do without your daily drug. I wonder what family law feels about addicted mothers.'

Caroline stopped and looked at the woman. Although she was seeing Drina Regis, there was something familiar in the voice. Not the voice itself but the method of speaking.

She shook her head, but inspiration would not come. However, she thought to herself, *I need DNA from this woman —perhaps I can get her to have a glass of something with me or borrow my hairbrush.* Or, she thought even more desperately, *if I start a fight with her, I could pull a hair out of her head.*

'Would you like a drink?' she asked in what she hoped was a measured, polite voice. 'My predecessor had a fine bar up here and I don't drink, so it's untouched.'

Drina laughed. 'No, thank you, but most kind. Where is your daughter? I was sure you'd bring her to the club. Rupert told me she was already a fine drinker.'

Caroline's lip curled. She pinched her thumb, but she refused to be riled. Drina noticed the pinched thumb.

'Oh! So that hit home. So, you do give her a little drinkie from time to time. Perhaps to help her sleep, or when you want to go out and visit the boyfriend. How is the lovely Anthony? Enjoying the comfortable prison he's made his home? He might as well enjoy it. I expect he'll get ... what, say ... thirty years ... perhaps a little reprieve on good behaviour because that man knows how to wind people round his little finger, doesn't he, darling.'

'Shut up,' said Caroline, feeling palpitations. 'Stop lying.'

'OOH, how rude. You'd better help yourself to some yummy chocolate. At least it might improve your temper.'

'I don't need chocolate, thanks. Seeing you has made me

lose my appetite.' Caroline pinched her thumb painfully, breathing hard but refusing to let herself shout. She spoke in a quiet voice. 'What do you want?'

'Leggy,' said the woman, smiling so her features appeared vulpine.

Caroline felt a wave of nausea surge through her body. Why did everybody suddenly want to have Leggy? Had the girl come into millions or something? Her daughter was a lovely, sweet child but not exactly Helen of Troy. What was going on?

'Why?'

Drina simpered nicely. 'I'm her auntie, and I have no children of my own, so naturally I want to spend some time with a little version of me.'

Caroline tasted sick in her mouth. She breathed deeply and walked towards a chair. She looked back at Drina and, to her surprise, saw Drina's features were transforming, although the woman hadn't moved.

'What's happening?' she said reflexively. 'What?'

She moved forward and the woman now had an odd leer on her face, then moving backwards returned her face to normal.

'You're ... you're ... you're a dummy!' she screamed and ran up to the apparition in her chair, hitting it fiercely. It fell on the floor, its legs waving in a curiously helpless manner.

'No need to be rude,' said the voice, but it too was now moving and appeared to be on the other side of her. 'Hello,' it said, 'I'm over here.'

And now the face was on the wall over the planning table.

Caroline headed for the chocolate cupboard. Then stopped. What if Drina had booby trapped it? *I must change all the locks tomorrow*, she thought. What if she was hiding somewhere? She stared at the cupboard. The doors were tall, but the space was small. If Drina was in a chair, she couldn't hide there, but what if the alleged birth injury and the bunions were all lies? She could have put a punch bag in there like Victoria did with Neil. On the other hand, Caroline thought feverishly, she needed her chocolate. Couldn't think without it. Perhaps if she opened the cupboard slowly and from a low position ...

Crouching down, she stretched up and opened the cupboard. It swung open but nothing came out, no one was hiding there, and the chocolate was still on the third shelf. She sighed. She was letting this whole thing get to her. She stood up, but, turning, she lost her footing and stumbled back. She grasped at the shelf and immediately the punchbag zipped out of the cupboard, missing her arm by inches. She heard Drina's voice laughing.

'OOH, only just missed you!'

Caroline stared at the bag bobbling on its spring. It was so low tech, and yet the hologram or whatever was so high tech. Caroline's blood zipped up and down her body. She felt numb and yet she knew her body was shaking.

She breathed deeply. No! She would not let Drina send her mad.

'Enough of your rubbish, Drina. You are a burglar and I'm calling the police.'

She pulled out her phone and started dialling.

'I wouldn't do that if I were you,' said Drina, her voice softly soothing. 'I don't mind, but you'll look an awful fool. Hysterical even. And then there's all those years of therapy. You aren't looking like a very suitable mother, are you?'

Caroline stared at the faceless dummy lying on the floor by the two-way mirror as the phone connected. Was Drina trying to make her crazy so she could steal Leggy?

She must be calm. What was she doing? She had nothing to report.

'Emergency services,' came a voice from the phone, 'how can I help?'

'Sorry,' said Caroline, cancelling the phone, 'wrong number.'

She could hear the frustrated murmur before the call ended.

'Where are you, Drina?' Caroline asked, her voice under control. Just.

'Look behind you,' said Drina and as Caroline spun around there was her disembodied face, smiling like a Cheshire Cat.

'Yes, indeed, my little mother. I'm watching you.'

Caroline pinched her thumb savagely. 'No!' she shouted, failing to keep herself under control. 'This is not magic; this is just some silly trick. Go away, Drina.'

I can do this, she told herself. *I will not let Drina win.*

'I know what you've done,' she yelled at the empty room. 'You've wired the place. I'm not falling for your tricks.'

Silence.

Could she have done all this by hacking her computer? Caroline kicked herself. Why hadn't she paid more attention to Stevie's computer lessons?

However, one thing was certain. Someone had put a camera in her room and was watching every move she made. She leapt for the door and hurried down the spiral staircase. Then stopped. She had thought to get Oscar to come up and look at the office, see if they could find the camera and anything else Drina was using, but was that such a good idea? She had used Oscar to go see Drina Regis, and he had found a website which showed she owned the house she was in. That expensive pile in Chelsea. But was it true? Drina might not be related to Leggy. It might be a plant. Oscar was one of the barmen she inherited from Victoria. She had thought she could trust him completely. But could she?

Caroline stood uncertainly on the stairs. She really hated her family, but, at a moment like this, they were the only ones she could trust. Which one of them would know how to dismantle a camera and find some bugs? Not her mother. Her sister, Vanessa, would be too busy. *'Don't you know some of us have to work for a living.'* Gloria, Vanessa and Victor's wife, was too surrounded by children to be free, and anyway, she was a doctor, not an engineer. Anthony was still in jail. There was only one other person she could really trust. She dialled a number.

'Hello, Caroline.'

'Victor! I need you.'

'Well, my darling little sister, what's the problem?'

'Do you know anything about engineering?'

Victor gave a hollow laugh. 'Well, I did a degree in it at Cambridge, but you're probably right, I don't know much about it.'

Caroline ground her teeth. This was why she hated her family. Both Vanessa and Victor loved to remind her that they got degrees at prestigious universities while she just scraped one A level in art at a crammer. It made her sick. If she didn't need Victor's help, she'd probably have rung off.

'I need help,' she said in a melodramatic voice that she hoped would stimulate her brother's interest. 'Someone is trying to send me mad.'

Victor laughed unsympathetically. 'Too late for that, my darling. What's happened?'

Caroline explained briefly and he laughed again. 'Hey

hey, so you are joining the Hobby Agency. What fun. I wish I had time for that.'

Caroline stamped her foot in frustration. They had all happily called the SeeMs Detective Agency Mum's hobby, but now she needed it, she resented Victor's mocking.

'Look! Drina's got a camera in my office, and a listening bug, I think, and some kind of hologram projector which she can direct all around the office. It's weird.'

An odd noise came from Victor at the other end of the phone. 'Now you've caught my interest. OK, I'll be over. Have you told Mum yet? She might want to rush over and make an arrest.'

'Ha, ha! I'll wait for you in the club. I'll be talking to a girl called Jenny. She's tall and she's a friend of Mum's, so she's OK.'

'Not the incomparable Jenny? Love of my life! Second only to Gloria.'

He put down the phone and Caroline sighed again. Honestly, her family! There couldn't be another one like it in all the universes. Vanessa and Victor both lived with and loved Gloria but didn't speak to each other. Victor fathered the children, but Vanessa considered herself the father and Gloria's husband. And, somehow, Gloria managed them both. What a wonder woman she was.

She walked into the bar, curious to find out how Jenny knew Victor.

CHAPTER 36

CHAMELEONS LIVE IN A RANGE OF HABITATS FROM DESERTS TO RAINFORESTS AND SAVANNAHS

'Look, big sis,' said Agata when Miranda picked up the phone. 'I don't want to worry you, but Piotr has completely disappeared. I went to the Black Scabbard with a friend. We split outside and he walked in and had a pint and chatted to some of the guys while I went to meet the barman. It wasn't Piotr but another guy, English, and he didn't know anything useful. He just said the pub had called him yesterday and asked him to come in. He usually does odd days, when Piotr has time off, but now they've offered him a full-time position. He was told Piotr had left. The manager said Piotr had gone back to Poland.'

'Yeah, right!' said Miranda.

'Umm, anyway, I talked to the manager. He seemed OK, but you can't tell, of course. He gave me Piotr's address and I went round there.'

'And?'

'Gone. The landlady said he always paid his rent in advance, so it wasn't about money. But when I questioned her closely, she admitted he never came back last night and that someone had come in this morning and picked up all

Piotr's clothes and things. She described him. She said he was nice, short but muscular, bald and had a scar under his left eye. Mean anything to you?'

'Yes,' said Miranda, 'it does. And it means I may have got someone into a lot of trouble. How about your friend? Did he find any joy?'

'Not really. The guys he talked to said Piotr was a good guy, but he didn't talk much. Just minded the bar and occasionally gave them "free pour", so they liked him. Otherwise, they didn't have much to say.'

'Thanks, Aggie. See yer.'

Miranda felt terrible. If only she hadn't lost her phone. She shouldn't drink so many negronis. She desperately hoped Piotr was still alive.

CHAPTER 37
THERE ARE MORE THAN 200
SPECIES OF CHAMELEON

When Cat and Miranda arrived at Rupert's block of flats, this time accompanied by Stevie, they found the front door open as usual. Cat ran lightly up the many stairs to talk to Diego, Stevie went outside to look at the bottom of the chute and Miranda went down the hall to Mrs Cartwright's flat. The door was open, and Miranda peered inside, calling, 'Lottie, are you there?'

A young woman carrying piles of clothes came out. She looked at Miranda with interest. 'Hello,' she said, 'are you looking for Lottie Cartwright?'

'Yup, that's the lovely lady. We visited her last week and we thought she looked a bit lonely, so we decided to visit again, see if she was OK. Or if she needed anything.'

The young woman frowned. 'Last week? You mean you visited her in hospital? Oh dear. Are you good friends?'

'Sort of,' said Miranda.

The young woman put on an appropriately sad face. 'I'm afraid she died yesterday. She was my godmother,' she added, as though to explain her presence in the flat.

'Oh,' said Miranda, 'but ...'

Cat also arrived at the open door, somewhat breathless. 'Hello,' she said, flashing her card, 'I'm Cat. We are from the SeeMs Detective Agency. Has Mrs Cartwright moved? We visited her last week, and she was very helpful about a case we are investigating.'

'Gilly,' said the young woman in a quiet voice, reaching around the clothes to give Cat her hand. 'But no, sadly she died yesterday. But I'm a little confused. Your colleague said you visited her last week. Do you mean in hospital?'

'No,' said Cat, 'here.'

'But she's been in a home for about three months, maybe a bit more,' said Gilly. 'She got ill and was sent from there to hospital and, as I told your colleague here, died yesterday.'

'Oh,' said Cat, frowning, 'how sad. Where was the hospital?'

'Ah,' said Gilly, suddenly looking embarrassed, 'I'm not ... that is ... hang on, I have the address of the home here. They would know. I mean, I have young kids ... so busy ... I telephoned often. Indeed, the nurses told me her daughter visited regularly. I was a bit surprised because I didn't think she had any family. I thought they'd confused her with another patient. You know how things are in these places.'

'I understand,' Cat said, 'but if not a daughter, do you know anything else about her visitor?'

'Well, not really,' said Gilly. 'I asked my mum and she said there'd been a bit of scandal years ago, but she didn't know the details either.'

'But who took over the running of the block?' said Miranda. 'When we met her—or whoever it was—she was a sort of caretaker.'

'Yes,' said the young woman, 'she used to be. Her

husband too. They lived here for some twenty or thirty years, and when he died years ago, she carried on.'

She looked at them thoughtfully.

'But it started becoming too much for her. She had dementia. We decided that really she needed to move to a home.'

'So, there was no new caretaker? Didn't they need someone to run the block?'

Gilly shrugged. 'I guess not. The owners stopped paying her, of course. But they let her live here for only a peppercorn rent while she was sick. I suppose they didn't think a caretaker was necessary or perhaps they hoped she'd get better. They sent a man from time to time to put out the rubbish and so forth.'

'So, you are saying the person we met here was not Lottie Cartwright but an impersonator,' said Miranda. 'Someone pretending to be her.'

And because you were too busy and the tenants changed often, no one knew that the woman they met was not the person who had been here so long, thought Cat.

'I guess it must be,' said Gilly. 'Hard to imagine why anyone would want to impersonate the caretaker of a block, although, of course, I guess they are like barmen in that they get to hear all the news and they know who is going in and out. If she'd been here, she'd probably know who it was that killed that poor guy upstairs.'

'Rupert.'

'Yes,' said Gilly, putting down the bundle of clothes on a nearby surface. 'I read in the papers they had found the murderer. Isn't that correct?'

'No,' said Cat, at the same time as Miranda said, 'Yes.'

'Go on, Cat,' said Miranda.

'We are working for the family of the man who was

arrested,' said Cat. 'We don't think he's guilty. We are trying to discover who really killed Rupert, the man upstairs. Also,' she said slowly, 'he is my ex-son-in-law, and my daughter doesn't think they have the right man.'

Gilly looked at Cat, nodding thoughtfully. 'I see. Bit of a family affair. Well, in that case ... do you want to come in and sit down for a moment?'

They nodded in unison.

When they were sitting in Lottie Cartwright's small sitting room, Gilly continued. 'It's only a small thing, but when the police said I could go upstairs and clean the flat where the man—sorry, Rupert—died, I did. And I found Lottie had given Rupert loads of her old bits of silver. She was rather dotty at the end and there was a whole pile of them in his flat. Not worth anything much, but I did wonder why they were there. Seemed odd anyone outside the family would want such pieces of junk.' She shrugged. 'But anyway, I brought them downstairs from Rupert's flat if you think they'll give you any information.'

She tilted her head, and Cat and Miranda saw a pile of tarnished silver plate.

Gilly pointed a finger. 'She even had a child's christening spoon. Rather sad that. I expect she wanted children. I've no idea why they didn't have any.'

'Do you know what Lottie's maiden name was?' asked Miranda.

'Yes, I know she was a Miss Robertson because I just found her birth certificate.' She began rummaging in the pile in front of her. 'It was in one of the drawers I was turning out. They'll want a new caretaker in here, most probably, or else they'll let out the flat. Either way I need to take her things home.'

'Here,' said Stevie, coming in from the basement, where

she'd been examining the chute, and handing Gilly a bunch of keys. 'I found these on the floor outside.'

'Oh, thank you.' Gilly took them absent-mindedly and placed them on the pile with everything else.

'Did you find anything else with the birth certificate?'

'Well, only this old photo. It looks like it might have come from one of those old photo booths they used to have in stations. It says *20 Rand* on the back, so I guess it was taken in South Africa.'

Cat took it and made a small noise. Miranda looked over her shoulder. In the picture there were two young people laughing, their cheeks together, clearly happy and enjoying the fun of picture taking. The young woman was not pretty but had soft, kind features, and the man was Black.

Cat gasped. She flipped the photo over, but there was no date, just the handwritten *20 Rand*. 'Do you know when this was taken?'

'No idea. But it's long, long ago. Even when I was young, they had colour in photo booths. This is still black and white.'

Cat looked at Miranda, then back at Gilly.

'Your godmother, she was in South Africa in, what, the seventies or eighties?'

'Yes.'

'You know it was illegal then to fraternise—that was what apartheid was all about. Looks like she and her friend were breaking the law.'

Gilly looked at the photo, raising her eyebrows. 'Really? I had no idea. History was never my thing.'

Cat sucked her lip.

'I wonder. Could I keep this for a bit? I just want to show it to someone.'

'Sure, why not. I'd probably just chuck it out. It's yours.'

'Thanks.'

Miranda squeezed Cat's arm and murmured, 'It's just coincidence,' she said. 'Those booth photos, don't you remember how terrible they were, how ... confusing.'

Cat looked at her sharply. 'So, you noticed it too.'

Miranda shrugged. 'Maybe.'

'Do you know who owned the block?' asked Stevie, who hadn't noticed all the consternation over the old photograph and had been examining the elderly kitchen equipment.

'Yes, actually, I do,' said Gilly. 'It is owned by the Bella Chantry Trust. I corresponded with someone from there called Drina. She was the one who let me know about the poor boy upstairs. But I imagine she's just an employee.'

'Oh,' said all three detectives together.

'Do you have any contact details?' asked Stevie. 'And her surname?'

'Yes, absolutely,' said Gilly, 'there is an email address, and a couple of days ago, Drina sent me an address in the UK, in case I needed to send over anything physically. They are an unusually communicative company.'

She went into the back and found her handbag, coming back with it open and rummaging around inside. 'Here it is. You need Drina Regis, and this is the address in Chelsea. Oh, and here is the address of the home Lottie was in.'

'Let me know if you find out who was impersonating my godmother,' she said as the detectives got up to leave. 'I'd like to know.'

'Drina,' said Cat as they walked to the Tube station. 'Here she is again. Drina, working for the Bella Chantry Trust Fund. That was Victoria's former name and the company that sold Caroline Spinners. She must work for Victoria.

She is probably neither in a wheelchair nor has a bunion problem but simply was told to give us false clues.'

'I examined the rubbish chute,' said Stevie.

Her colleagues looked at her curiously. With anyone else such a change of subject would mean they weren't listening, but Stevie was different.

'There's a box, Cat. Didn't you notice the wires?'

Cat shook her head. 'It just looked all dark,' she said, mouing apologetically.

'A box to take something up to that little room on the roof. Presumably you can take the box out of the lift and then use the chute for rubbish, but when it's in place it is a perfect lift to the roof. That means anyone could go up to the roof.'

'Provided they had the key,' said Cat.

'Indeed. A key that sat under the letterboxes,' said Miranda.

'Hang on,' said Cat, 'that's only the key to the roof door. What about the key to the doors in the chute?'

Stevie raised a finger. 'In Mrs C's bunch. They were hanging just inside the door. I borrowed them to try, and one key fitted the chute lock perfectly.'

'Oh!'

'But I don't buy that,' said Miranda. 'Even if you could get a wheelchair up to the roof, you'd still have to get across the roof, down those little stairs Cat talked about and then back up again after shooting Rupert. So, if it was Drina Regis, then she is not in a wheelchair.'

'OK,' said Stevie, 'let's go and see Miss Drina Regis and find out what she has to say.'

CHAPTER 38

SEVENTY-SIX CHAMELEON SPECIES ARE FOUND IN MADAGASCAR

Stevie looked at Drina Regis's house in admiration. 'Imagine having a house of this size in Chelsea. Drina must be very wealthy and that cannot be the result of working for Victoria.'

'Beautiful,' said Miranda, 'lovely wide front, set back from the street for privacy and step free. Lovely. Good for growing old in. And lots of lovely protective CCTV. Good for protection from burgling detectives.'

'Ha, ha,' said Cat, rolling her eyes and ringing the bell.

There was the sound of barking inside the house, but it was a while before anyone answered. Eventually, a woman in her thirties with long blonde hair and designer jeans opened the door. She smiled at them.

'Hello,' she said, 'can I help?'

'Yes,' said Cat, 'we are from the SeeMs Detective Agency.' She flashed her card, which the woman looked at with surprised eyes. 'We are looking for a Drina Regis. She was living here a few weeks ago ...'

Cat was starting to say 'my daughter met her,' but the woman's reaction stopped her. She was gawping at them, her hands flapping in the air as though she could not breathe.

Cat wondered if she was about to have a heart attack. 'Are you OK?'

'Eh?' gasped the woman. 'Drina Regis? Really? Here?'

And then she slammed the door in their faces.

'What?' said Miranda. 'What the hell was that?'

Cat shook her head and was about to knock on the door again when Stevie put a hand on her arm.

'Wait,' she said, 'she'll be back.'

'Hmm,' said Miranda, crossing her arms, 'she'd better be.'

After a few minutes the woman returned. She looked at them in an enigmatic way and Cat wondered if she'd hoped they would just have faded away like a dream.

'Sorry,' she said, squeezing her hands together. 'I was just letting my friend know what was happening. He said ... sorry ... Who are you? ... I didn't think ... before ... my friend ... well ... he said I should listen.'

Cat got out her agency card again.

'We are detectives working for the family of Anthony Dyer, who has been arrested for murdering Rupert Fletcher. Drina Regis was Rupert's girlfriend.'

The woman shook her head and took a deep breath. '*This is amazing*,' she said. 'You'd better come in.'

She led the way down a long hallway with a lot of shut doors. One door at the far end of the passage was open and they saw a man chopping vegetables on a granite-covered island. He smiled and dipped his head politely.

On one side of the hallway, the woman opened a closed door, ushering them into what turned out to be an ornate drawing room.

'I think this must have been the room Caroline came to,'

said Cat, partly to her herself. 'She talked about the amazing antiques you have here.'

The woman looked around her as though seeing them for the first time. 'Yes. Yes. Er, my parents bought them all years ago. They lived all over the world and had things sent here.'

She looked at them again, but Cat got the feeling she wasn't seeing them at all. Dragging a pouf over, she collapsed onto it. She put her elbows on her knees and leant her chin on her hands.

'Sorry,' she said. 'Would you like anything to drink? I've got elderflower handy.'

They all said no. She ran her hands up and down her jeans, then started picking at the seams. No one spoke.

'Right,' she said so suddenly the word seemed to echo round the room, 'I'm sorry. I'm sorry. I'm so nonplussed. So you say you met Drina Regis here a couple of weeks ago? Here?'

Cat nodded. 'Yes. Perhaps I should explain further. There are two connections here. One is my daughter, who came here to visit a woman who said her name was Drina Regis and that this was her house. The other is a Lottie Cartwright. We went to visit Lottie and discovered she had passed away, but her goddaughter, who was in her flat, confirmed that she had been corresponding with a Drina Regis and gave this address. Does the name mean something to you?'

The woman made a noise like a fountain starting. 'Well. I can tell you about Charlotte Cartwright.'

She stared at the ceiling, rubbing her chin.

'So, I am Emily Regis. My parents died last year. They were in their eighties and had been through so much together; it was a blessing they both died within days of each other. This would have thrown them off beam, for sure.'

She shook herself and put her hands on her knees again, leaning forward. 'Anyway, I inherited this house, which perhaps makes up for the loss of my parents.' She gave a little smile.

'As I am an only child, I inherited this house last year or, sorry, I should be more accurate as you are detectives.' She smiled. 'My parents put this house in my name when I was born thirty years ago. It was to do with death duties and stuff—basically they paid me rent for living here for the rest of their lives.' She gave a partly embarrassed shrug. 'But anyway, after they died I came to live here full time. I did it up, modernised it and then thought *What now?* so I decided to go travelling with my friend.' She inclined her head towards the kitchen. 'I thought of renting out the house, but I have various animals—cats, lizards and so forth—and I wasn't sure what to do with them. So I applied online for a house-sitter. A woman called Charlotte Cartwright answered my advertisement. She explained that she and her husband had been looking after some flats in King's Cross as caretakers, but that he had died. So, she decided to allow someone else to take over the job and get house-sitting jobs while she decided what to do next. She came for an interview, and I was rather surprised to discover she was a middle-aged woman in a wheelchair. However, we do have a lift in the house, which was super useful when my dad ...'

'A wheelchair?' interrupted Miranda. 'Mrs Cartwright was a middle-aged woman in a wheelchair?'

'Yes,' said Emily, glancing at Miranda. 'A woman about fiftyish in a wheelchair. I did wonder if she'd be able to do her duties, but then she explained it was only temporary, that she'd just had her bunions done and in a few weeks she'd be running around again like a youngster. So, anyway, I thought lucky we have the lift until she gets better.'

'But do bunions mean you need to be in a chair?' said Cat. 'Surely not?'

Emily raised her eyebrows. 'Oh, serious? I had no idea, but I wasn't going to question her. If she said she could manage, then I was happy, and she had fantastic references.'

'References?' echoed Cat. 'She had references?'

'Yes, and super good ones over many years. She seemed exactly what I needed and, anyway, no one else applied.'

Stevie frowned and moved on her seat, but she didn't say anything.

'So what happened?' asked Miranda. 'How long did she stay for and how was the service?'

'Good, very good. She sent me messages about the animals at least once a week, gave the place a very good clean before she left and was an excellent house-sitter. I'd use her again.'

'Just one question,' said Stevie. 'You have cameras here. Did you ever watch her? See what she was up to?'

Emily tilted her head. 'Funny you should say that. I told her about the cameras. You have to. It's all to do with personal protection. I offered to turn them off, but she said no ... leave them ... she'd wave at me from time to time.

'Anyway, I checked them about once a week—thing is we were often in places without Wi-Fi—but when I did check them, they all seemed fine. However, when I returned I realised the internal cameras had all malfunctioned and were still showing the same pictures as they had when I left. It does happen occasionally if the internet goes down or we have a power cut. So I wasn't really surprised.'

'And the external cameras?' asked Stevie.

'Oh, I haven't checked them yet. They seemed OK. But I

daresay it will be the same problem. But since nothing happened I didn't worry about it.'

'Hmm,' muttered Stevie.

'When did Charlotte Cartwright leave?' asked Cat.

'Yesterday morning. I got back at midday, so I said it would be fine. You know with these sitters they are often in a hurry to get on to the next place.'

'Do you have a picture of Charlotte Cartwright?' asked Stevie.

'Yes,' said Emily, 'I do. It may seem oversuspicious, but I always do a Zoom call and ask for a mugshot before they arrive. It's another form of security.' She paused. 'Like the noise of the dog barking when you ring the bell. I don't really have a dog.' She giggled.

Emily got out her phone and handed it to them. A fifty-ish-year-old woman posed on a log, smiling, her hand up as though she was waving to the camera.

Cat and Miranda stared. 'Never seen her before.'

'I have,' said Stevie. 'That's Drina Regis. I saw her having a haircut at Glam Glam Hairdressers.'

'Glam Glam,' said Emily. 'Did you go there? I avoid them. That receptionist makes me queasy. I often hear her bawling at the young ones and they sometimes come out in tears. I don't want to support a place like that. But that is Charlotte Cartwright. Did she say her name was Drina Regis?'

Stevie looked at Emily, making thoughtful circles on her cheek. 'Do you have car parking here? Did Charlotte bring a car?'

Emily nodded. 'Yes, absolutely. Charlotte had a Yaris, which I said she could park here. Everyone loves having a garage in London—parking is such a pain. I wondered how she could drive when she was using a wheelchair, but she said she borrowed it from her sister. Apparently, her sister had been in a car accident years ago and was paralysed.'

Stevie frowned. 'Ah. Did she tell you her sister's name?'

'Um, I think she did ... maybe Findus or something.'

'Finlater?' asked Stevie. 'Rebecca Finlater?'

'Yeah, that's it. Mean something to you?'

'Yes,' said Stevie, 'I once knew a girl whose sister was called Finlater, but her name was different.'

Emily smiled vaguely.

'I wonder,' said Cat, 'did she give you a forwarding address? In case anything came in that needed to be sent on?'

'Why yes,' said Emily, 'she did. I remember it because it sounded so romantic.' She tapped on her phone and produced the address. 'Here it is: The Manor, Owly Vale, West Sussex. Sounds lovely, doesn't it, Owly Vale?'

'It does indeed,' said Stevie, a glacial smile fixed on her face at hearing her own address being given out.

As they got up to leave, Emily suddenly said, 'Oh, um, it may not be relevant, but there was once a Corinna Regis. It was a long time ago and if she was still alive, I would be super excited. I'm sorry ... it's just the shock ... I should have ...'

She spread her hands and the detectives sat down again.

'Tell us,' they said.

CHAPTER 39
CHAMELEONS RELY ON VIBRATIONS TO WARN THEM OF APPROACHING PREDATORS

'How are you doing finding Victoria?' Stevie asked as they left Emily Regis's house. Picking up her phone, she fiddled with something on the screen.

Cat frowned, realising she hadn't told Stevie that Amy was no longer interested in prosecuting Victoria for kidnap. Perhaps Stevie wasn't the only one forgetting to share information.

'What makes you think of her right now? She isn't the only person who could fake an identity or disguise themselves as someone else.'

'Yes,' said Stevie, 'but they don't turn up in a converted Toyota Yaris claiming it belongs to her sister and they don't give my address as their own. This is Victoria all right, and she is sending us clues, proving how much cleverer she is than us. Last time we underestimated Victoria. We mustn't do it again. She is the CEO of a large, successful company. She is a mastermind, an expert in disguise, and the fact that she is in a wheelchair is totally irrelevant. But we still don't know where she is.'

'Maybe she's back in Owly Vale, in your house,' said Miranda.

'No,' said Stevie, 'I just checked the cameras. We put them in to protect my mother. There's no car anywhere near the house, and inside you can see my mother and the carer pottering around. They are both fine.'

'Are you sure about this carer?' asked Miranda. 'Given Victoria's ability to disguise herself and reappear, she could have become your new carer.'

'Not this time,' said Stevie. 'This time I'm ahead of her. Have a look for yourself.'

Miranda and Cat looked overly intrigued. There on the camera were Kaya and Leggy, playing a game of spillikins with Blinkey.

'George is doing the DIY,' said Stevie. 'Heaven knows there's plenty to keep him active.'

Miranda looked slightly shocked. 'Is it a good idea to put all Victoria's potential targets in one basket, as you might say? Especially when she's just given your address as her next sitting post.'

'Yes,' said Stevie, 'it is. Apart from the fact the safest place in the world is a small village where all your neighbours know everything that is happening all the time, I also have Frank on watch.'

'Frank?' said Cat, annoyed. 'What? You told my boyfriend about something you didn't tell me?'

Stevie put out her hands pacifically. 'Sorry. I just thought he'd be useful, and you must admit he has helped us quite a bit in the past. He loves being a detective's muse.'

Cat laughed. 'OK, doesn't matter. I'm sure he'll be over there by now telling them jokes. Poor Kaya!'

Miranda glanced at her watch. 'Since we're up here, I

might just go and see my mother. After that I could meet you both at Spinners.'

'OK,' said Stevie, 'I'm going to pop in to the library. I just want to do a bit more research.'

The others exchanged glances and Miranda yawned. 'Or is it just time to make love to Terry Terminal? Any particular reason?'

Stevie grinned. 'Yup. I want to get the results of some DNA I collected. Not my own! And I want to check a couple of facts the library is searching for me.'

'Mysterious,' said Miranda. 'I'm aching to hear the results.'

'OK,' said Cat, 'but I'm going to pop over to the care home where the real Charlotte Cartwright lived. It may give us some clues.'

CHAPTER 40
CHAMELEON DON'T
HAVE EARS

At the same time as Cat was heading for the care home, Jenny was climbing up the stairs from the car park to the club. A couple of hours ago, Amy had sprung it on her that she was having a lunch party for school friends.

'They think I have a *respectable* husband, darling. I just can't be bothered to do all that explaining, so make yourself scarce. Go to the office or something.'

Jenny most definitely did not want to go to the office, where the CAA were doing one of their interminable, nitpicking inspections, so where else was there to go but Spinners? A home from home where you were welcome anytime.

She was still muttering about selfish wives as she sat down at her usual table. When she saw Caroline approaching her table, she leapt up joyously.

'Oh, my little pet, want me to order something for you? Chocolate? Tomato juice? Anything else in the family store.'

Caroline shook her head and sank down into one of the chairs. 'No, I've rather gone off chocolate recently.'

Caroline looked around the club. It was almost empty, she thought. Perhaps the scandal no longer had the same allure. She looked at her watch and realised it was still the afternoon. So much seemed to have happened since she arrived that she thought it was around midnight.

'You are here very early, Jenny.'

'Indeed. My delightful spouse is having a lunch at our house, apparently a school reunion, and I found myself a little de trop, so I decided to come to my home of homes instead.'

'Fair enough. I want to ask you about Victor.'

'The charming and delightful Victor Victoria?' asked Jenny. But when Caroline's eyes started to shoot around nervously, Jenny continued, unwilling to cause one of Caroline's episodes. 'Who wouldn't like a night with Julie Andrews or even Burt Reynolds?'

Caroline bit her lip, then suddenly remembered that lip-biting was a habit of her mother's and felt sick. Was she turning into her mother already? 'Victor my brother,' she spurted out. 'How do you know him?'

'Alas, I don't, at least not in the way I would like to. No, he was merely a client in one of my other guises. Amy, my darling wife, enjoyed flying him around the world. Your brother is a real big spender, isn't he!'

'Ah,' said Caroline, annoyed. Why did her family always have to muscle in on her life? Couldn't she have one friend that wasn't already known to her siblings?

'Well, he's planning a visit this evening. I need a little DIY in my office. When I've finished with him, I'll let him out to play.'

Jenny batted her eyelashes flirtatiously. 'Always delighted to entertain any relative of the hostess,' she murmured. 'Incidentally, where is my favourite barman today? He doesn't appear to be here. Is he going to break my heart by being off tonight?'

Caroline looked over at the bar. 'Oscar? Isn't he? How odd. It's not his night off. And I saw his car in the car park. I'll go and ask Tom.'

But Tom, it seemed, was as nonplussed as the rest of them. 'He's on tonight,' he said, 'and he's never late. We're shorthanded as it is with all the interest you generated.'

He gave a boyish grin and Caroline frowned at him. 'I saw his car,' she said.

'Oh, then I don't know. He did work very late last night. I left before him, and he said he'd clean up and lock up. One of the clients was still here and they were chatting ... maybe he went in her car. Left his here.'

'Any idea which client?'

'No. I've not seen her before. I thought she was a friend of his.'

Caroline nodded. 'OK. Do you want to come and watch while I check whether his things are still here? I've got a key to his locker.'

Tom obediently followed her down to the lockers and Caroline opened Oscar's. She was glad to have a witness. The way things were going right now, she almost expected Drina Regis to pop out of the locker. However, when the door swung open, Oscar's bar clothes filled the small space, clean and neatly stacked. No strange notes or automatic talking machines and nothing hidden beneath. But, as she moved his clothes, she saw there was a wallet underneath.

'Tom?'

'Yes.'

'Did Oscar say anything about finding someone's wallet?'

'No.'

'Hmm, there's no money in it, just credit cards in the name of Charles FitzRoy. Mean anything to you?'

'No.'

'OK, well, I guess Charles FitzRoy dropped it in the bar and Oscar decided to keep it until he returned.'

She closed the locker.

'Did he say anything to you about not being here tonight?'

'No,' said Tom, 'nothing. When I left last night, he just said the usual "see you tomorrow" thing and nothing else.'

They returned to the club and Tom went back to serving customers. Caroline sat down by Jenny and waited for Victor to arrive.

Caroline's phone pinged. She pulled it out of her pocket and gasped.

'What?' said Jenny, always ready for intrigue. 'Is it my gorgeous Oscar?'

'Actually, it is.' Caroline opened the WhatsApp. *I saw Drina Regis leaving the club as I was arriving*, said the message. *She looked suspicious, so I followed her. She's now at your house and is trying the bell. I'm worried because she has a child seat in her car. Could she be going to kidnap Leggy? You'd better hurry round ASAP.*

Caroline read it. She nibbled her lip. Stopped. And laughed. 'Well, well,' she said. 'Talk about letting the cat out of the bag. And not my mother this time! Unbelievable!'

'What?' asked Jenny, leaning forward with curiosity. 'Tell me about that naughty, naughty boy. What's he done?'

Caroline looked at her. 'Do you know what, Jenny, I think I will. I trust you. I remember you were involved in the Victoria Affair and came up roses.'

'Darling,' said Jenny, 'roses? I so much prefer jasmine. What's afoot?'

Caroline leant back in her chair. 'Stevie came to see me at home yesterday. We all thought she was a bit of a pants detective and only really good for computer work, but how wrong we were! She has the whole thing figured out, and because she understood what was happening, she thought Leggy might be in danger. So, she has taken her somewhere Drina will never find her.'

'Where? Tell me, where?'

Caroline smirked. 'Don't worry, Stevie will be back soon, and she'll tell you all about it. Meanwhile, I can see Victor arriving, so I think he and I are going to do some redecorating in my office.' She winked at Jenny. 'We'll be back soon. I'm certainly not prepared to miss all the fun.'

Jenny twisted her head in an exasperated fashion. 'Aren't you going to at least give me a clue?'

Caroline smiled. 'OK,' she said, 'right at this moment Drina Regis is performing some house-breaking, admirably assisted by the devoted Oscar, and they are about to get a taste of their own medicine.' She grinned. 'Don't worry. They'll be here soon too.'

She got up and walked towards her stairs, waving. 'Catch yer later.'

'Well,' said Jenny to Trixie, who had just arrived, 'something has made our friend Caroline happy, and I think we should have a little bet on it, what do you say?'

Trixie cocked her head. 'A swift negroni?'

'Why not? Beats Mars Bars.'

CHAPTER 41
THE BROOKESIA CHAMELEON VIBRATES TO WARN OFF PREDATORS

The care home car park was full. There were a few spaces left for blue badge drivers but nothing else. Cat bit her lip, wondering whether to risk parking in a restricted bay or go for a yellow line. As she was debating, she saw the rounded cap of a traffic warden coming her way. Perhaps if she let her pass and then parked. How long before a warden came back to the same spot?

'You can't park there!' said the warden too loudly.

Cat jumped guiltily. Even her naughty thoughts were read by the warden. She looked at the woman under the hat.

'Agata? But ...'

Agata snarled. 'Yes, quite. Agata the superstar. Agata climbing fast through the police ranks. Agata the demoted. Blame my stupid, phone-losing sister. The idiot!'

Cat stared at her, baffled. 'Er ...?'

'And what's worse,' said Agata, 'is she involved me in it. Honestly, I'm not sure I want to help you lot again.'

'What? What happened?'

'Piotr,' said Agata wrathfully. 'Our lovely helpful barman.'

'What?'

Agata snarled and dished out a few angry tickets before continuing. 'Miranda asked me to go over and check on Piotr. Well, if he wasn't looking suspicious before I got there, that certainly made him more so.'

Cat was still confused. 'Is Piotr still alive then?'

'Yes, of course he is. He was an undercover cop, sent in to find out all about the Combat 18 meetings in the Black Scabbard. Then along comes the SeeMs Detective Agency and asks for information. At first he was absolutely fine. No one took much notice of the dicky girls.' She gave a slightly wobbly grin. 'That's what they call you at the station. But then he went off to Spinners and recognised Oscar and blew his cover.'

'I still don't understand.'

'Oscar used to be an undercover cop. His real name is Charles FitzRoy, but he went rogue. The police were trying to follow his movements and discover who was responsible for him now. But when Oscar saw Piotr, he became suspicious, and when he found Miranda's phone, with a message from Piotr, he realised his cover was blown and thought it was time to split. So they lost Oscar.'

'And Piotr?'

'Well, he wasn't sure what side Oscar was on, so he decided to split too. So now the police no longer have any information about Combat 18. And because Miranda is my sister and I was involved with checking on Piotr, I got put on the beat. I'm helping out here because it's more interesting than walking the streets.'

Cat felt a terrible urge to laugh, but she swallowed it seeing that Agata was truly angry. 'Oh dear. Sorry, Agata. Still, I'm sure it won't be long before you are forgiven. You are clearly an asset to the police. But I thought it was Oscar who came and cleared out Piotr's room—you told us that. Are they working together?'

'From the description it sounds like him, but I doubt they knew each other. Piotr was a recent recruit, and Oscar had been there for years. The guys who used to run him for the SDS—Special Demonstration Squad—were sure he was working for someone else and trying to find out who.'

'Whom,' said Cat vaguely.

'Humph,' Agata replied and went to give out some more parking tickets.

'I don't suppose you'd mind watching my car, would you?' Cat asked.

Agata blew out hard. 'Don't push your luck, Cat.'

Cat double parked and left a note on the window. It used to work—perhaps it still would.

She walked through the front door, impressed, like Drina a few weeks earlier, by the modern aspect of the care home. Ahead of her was a desk with a big poster welcoming relatives. Unfortunately, there was only the poster to welcome her as the desk was empty. She was about to push the bell when a couple of people came out of a side room.

'I was afraid I would be too late,' said the taller of the two women, who was wearing a mask.

The other woman, wearing a plastic apron, was nodding fast and sympathetically, pulling off the apron as she walked. 'Yes, yes, such a shame. But you mustn't feel guilty. She was well looked after in her last days, and she did have a lovely regular visitor ...'

They came to a stop by the desk and automatically turned towards Cat. The tall woman pulled off her mask. Cat gasped and took a few paces back.

'Victoria?' she said. But this woman was walking, she was on Cat's eye-level, and her features seemed younger.

Both women looked startled, but 'Victoria' laughed. 'Ah,' she said, 'I see you have met my twin sister, Bella. I believe she does call herself Victoria these days. I haven't seen her for many years.'

'Twins?' said Cat. 'But I thought ...'

The woman looked at her steadily. 'What? She used to describe me as *Rebecca, my much older sister who flies with farmers' hands.* Is that what you heard?'

'Yes.'

Rebecca snorted, but one word had connected with Cat. 'Rebecca? Rebecca with Victoria ... Do you have a car?'

The woman raised her eyebrows. 'Do I have a car? Er, yes ...'

'Oh, sorry, I mean, are you Rebecca Finlater?'

This time the woman laughed. 'Yes, I'm Rebecca Finlater.' She put out her hand. 'And the relevance of the car ...?'

Cat made an embarrassed gesture and shook the woman's outstretched hand. She noted absently what a firm handshake Rebecca had.

'Yes, sorry. I'm Cat Harrington. I work for the SeeMs Detective Agency. We have been looking for a Victoria Bell who drives a Toyota Yaris registered in the name Rebecca Finlater. I must have sounded mad.'

Rebecca shrugged. 'That is often the way with people caught in Bella's fantasy world. Sorry, I know you said Victoria, but to me she will always be Bella, no matter how often she changes her name cand appearance.'

She glanced out of the window and back at Cat. 'So she's registered her car in my name. Why not? Since we are identical—or were when I last saw her—it will be easy to pass herself off as me. After all she is dead, isn't she!'

'I'll see you later, dear,' broke in the woman holding the

plastic apron. 'Sorry, dear,' she addressed Cat, 'but we are rather busy.'

'Yes, yes,' said Cat, 'do you have a coffee shop?'

Rebecca looked kindly at Cat and took her arm in the manner of a niece guiding an elderly relative. 'I'll show her,' she said to the retreating woman's back.

Rebecca bought Cat a coffee but a mug of hot water for herself. 'I've had their coffee before,' she said, raising an eyebrow. 'So, tell me, have you had many dealings with my sister? Is that why meeting me gave you such a shock?'

Cat drank her coffee.

'I think so,' she said. 'I thought for a mad moment the whole thing was a performance. That she'd never been hurt in that car accident which had such terrible results.'

Rebecca sighed. 'If only. But yes, sadly that car accident in which Bella was so badly hurt did happen. Her career was completely ruined, and she became the vindictive revenge seeker she is now. My life is so different I never see her at all.'

'Oh?'

'Yes. I live in Hong Kong. I'm an airline pilot. I have three children. Perhaps I lead the life Bella craved. I have no idea. I cannot imagine how she thinks, nor can anyone else in my family.'

She took a sip of water and added, 'After Bella's accident and the way she behaved, my whole family cut her off, left and went to Australia. My mother ... well ... enough to say she did not like any kind of deviancy—as she saw it.'

'Ah,' said Cat. 'Is she still alive?'

'My mother?'

'Yes.'

'No. Sadly her sister outlived her, but not by long. That's why I'm here. I had a trip to Heathrow and while I was here

I wanted to come and visit my aunt. She was in this care home, but they rushed her to hospital a few nights ago and she died there.'

Cat nodded. 'I'm sorry,' she murmured.

Rebecca made a dismissive gesture. 'Oh. It wasn't a great heartbreak. We had no contact with my aunt at all. If I say my mother also cut her off, you will think my mother is cold and unkind ...' The woman stopped. 'Sorry, I don't know why I'm telling you this ... it must be the sudden mention of Bella, who I haven't thought about for years. It cannot be of interest to you.'

'On the contrary,' said Cat, 'I think you might be explaining a great deal of things. I've been looking for Bella/Victoria for months. She seemed to have totally disappeared ... but if there is an aunt involved ... well, this is a possible option. Can you tell me more? Did the aunt have a house? Might Victoria have stayed there?'

'Yes, I can tell you if you like, but why are you looking for my sister?'

Cat moued. She wasn't sure how much she should tell Rebecca, but then a lot of this was already in public circulation.

'She's involved in a murder case. She tried to blackmail one of my colleagues and then tried to kill her. She faked her own death again and disappeared, but then reappeared and kidnapped and humiliated another female pilot. We were looking for her, but just recently we have reason to believe she has another plot against us.'

'Wow!' said Rebecca. 'That is a lot of Bella. How did she try and fake her death?'

'She pretended to fall out of a Tiger Moth,' said Cat, 'but was carrying a parachute.'

Rebecca gave a half-laugh. 'Very Bella. She always loved

tail-draggers.' Then, seeing Cat's confused face, she added, 'A type of aircraft. With tail wheels or skids instead of nose wheels. It doesn't matter. Pilots ... well, we focus on different things. Sorry.'

'Whatever.'

'But, if you are looking for Bella, I can tell you she has been here too, visiting my aunt. I had no idea of that either, until the carers told me my aunt had a regular visitor. I thought it must be her goddaughter. But then the nurse told me the visitor was in a wheelchair, so I asked the inevitable question.'

Cat frowned. 'Which is?'

'Did she look like me?'

'But did she?' asked Cat. 'She is a master of disguise.'

'Yes, true. However, I have seen many disguises in the past, and I rather thought the same ones might come out. Anyway, you are right, they said no, not at all, she was short. Ha! She's in a wheelchair—they tend to be short. And she was dark haired. Why does everyone focus on the hair? However, she had left a card with the flowers for my aunt, and even though there was a palpable lie in it, I recognised the handwriting.'

'You should be a detective,' said Cat drily.

Rebecca shrugged. 'I'm observant, that's all. I have children, which tends to give you a sort of people focus, even when your daily work is machines. I'm sure you know what I mean.'

Cat nodded. 'You certainly have a calmness that Victoria lacks.'

'Yes, that was always the case. She took terrible risks. Thrived on excitement. She would have been much better as a fighter pilot than an airline pilot, but she was born in the wrong era for that. Women didn't start flying in the forces until the 1990s. By then, even if she hadn't been in a wheel-chair, she'd have been too old.'

'Hmm,' said Cat, her mind buzzing, 'is it OK if I ask a few more questions about Bella?'

Rebecca glanced at her watch. 'Sure. I'm on a night flight out of here and I like to get to the airport well in advance, but I've got plenty of time. I just need to visit one other person while I'm here and since she's a child I'll have to wait until schools finish.'

Cat nodded. Presumably this was a grandchild.

'You said you and Bella were both visiting an aunt here. Can you tell me her name?'

'I can, but I will have to ask you to be a little discreet. As a detective you are probably used to that anyway, but fami-lies hold secrets which, in general, they do not want broad-cast to the world.'

She drank some water and stared for a while at the table.

'My mother fell out with her sister many years ago and did not speak to any of her family again. We, the younger generation, did not know my mother had a younger sister until Bella's accident. Bella needed a blood transfusion and none of us had suitable blood. Bella has that sort of blood that few people can donate to.'

'But you are identical twins,' said Cat. 'Surely ...'

Rebecca made a gesture with her hands. 'Yeah, I know, you'd think, but rather suitably, she is a chimera, which means she has a different blood type from me. You'd expect Bella to be difficult. And she was.' Rebecca looked at Cat. 'Do you know what a chimera is?'

Cat shook her head. 'I thought it was some Greek beast with the head of a lion and the body of a goat.'

Rebecca laughed. 'Probably. But in medical terms it is to

do with the mother and children. The mother carries two types of blood and gives one to each twin. It is incredibly rare. The result was that we—Bella and I—have different blood types. I'm not a scientist, so I don't know how it works, but I do know Charlotte, my mother's sister, had the right blood type for Bella.'

Rebecca looked at Cat and snorted. 'I can't overstate what a difficult time that was for us. First Bella's accident, and then discovering we had an unknown aunt. I still remember how shocked we all were. But, you know, life goes on.' She shrugged. 'Survival of the fittest and all that.'

Cat drank her coffee and Rebecca drank her water.

'Why did your mother cut her sister off?' asked Cat.

Rebecca rubbed her hands and Cat thought that was the first time she'd seen any unease in the other woman. When Rebecca started talking it was slower than before.

'You'll probably think us strange. Harsh. But there were other issues involved. You need to understand my mother was born during the Second World War. Morality was different then, people thought in ways we would now consider unnecessary, even cruel.'

Cat thought back to her conversation with Jane Fletcher, Rupert's adopted mother. 'Do you mean like eugenics and things?'

Rebecca looked at her carefully. 'Not precisely, but almost, yes. But perhaps there was an instinctive understanding of how genetics worked even before we had the genome trail.'

Here we go on DNA and genetics again, thought Cat. *Odd how things like that dominate our thinking these days.*

'Go on,' she said.

Rebecca said slowly, 'Look. I mentioned survival of the fittest just now. Well, that was my mother's belief. She told us when we were little that if we were seriously hurt, she would end our lives. That was kinder, she said, kinder than allowing us to be "half people". That belief, of course, resurrected when Bella was injured.'

She stared at the ceiling and took a drink of water. 'Perhaps it was also relevant that there was a fifteen-year gap between my mother and her sister.'

She shook her head.

'My grandparents seemed to have been lovely people, enjoyed a party, lots of friends. They were also imbued with the innocence of their time.'

Cat made a gesture to show she was still listening sympathetically.

'My grandmother had two daughters, my mother, Mina, and her sister, Charlotte. As I said, my mother was considerably older than her sister, and her parents were amazed to have a child at their old age.'

She paused and, realising she had finished her water, jumped up and offered Cat another coffee. Cat had drunk hers despite the bitter taste.

Sitting down with the new drinks, Rebecca continued.

'My mother had trained as a doctor, married, and was working when her sister was just a teenager and, of course, she had left home and had a very busy life as we were born in 1967. My grandparents doted on their young daughter, but they also, in the way of older parents, slightly left her to her own devices. I think you could say she was lonely.'

She stopped for a moment and drank some more water.

'Then my grandfather had a heart attack and died. It left my grandmother a young widow of fifty-nine with a sixteen-year-old daughter, and she didn't know how to entertain her, so she took her on a cruise.'

She looked at Cat, half shrugging. 'We wouldn't think

that was the way to do it now, but those were different times. When my children were teenagers, they were in school and working hard.' She moved lightly in her seat. 'And the results show that was the right thing to do.'

Cat said nothing, but she could see the injured Victoria might find the assured Rebecca a rather annoying twin sister.

'My grandmother ... well ... she loved life. She came from the generation who partied. She loved being admired, and she really wasn't that fussed about restraining the young girl with her. I think she thought my aunt was still a child—my mother's friends said she certainly dressed her as one. So I suspect that the cruise was for her, and she forgot about the girl.' She glanced at Cat. 'You got daughters?'

'I have.'

'Well, then you know what they are like when the hormones start bubbling. I have two sons and a daughter, and the sons were never any trouble compared to the girl. I had to watch her like a hawk. I can't tell you how pleased I was when she got married and started having children of her own.' She snorted. 'But I'm digressing. The point is the inevitable happened. Charlotte got pregnant.'

'Charlotte?' said Cat.

'My aunt, the one I was visiting.'

'Oh!' said Cat. She felt cold but kept listening, hugging her body.

'My grandmother—she was called Margaret, but everyone knew her as Maggy—looked around for someone to adopt the baby. She wanted it to be in-house, as you might call it. My mother was furious. She said they should get the child adopted through an agency, and not try to both hold on to it, and let it go.'

Rebecca shrugged. 'But my grandmother did what she

thought was right. Her friend Jane was desperate for a child, so they set it all up, and soon Jane had a baby, and Charlotte had none!'

'Ah,' said Cat. 'Do you know her friend Jane's surname?'

'No. I only know she is Jane because my mother used to refer to her as Dreadful Jane.'

'I wonder ...' said Cat, 'could it be Jane Fletcher?'

This sounded all too similar to Rupert's adoption story, which would mean Leggy was related to Victoria/Bella. Cat did not like the sound of that. It was bad enough having Drina Regis claiming to be a relative.

'Might be.'

'OK. Leave that for a moment. What happened to Charlotte?'

'She was sent off to relatives in South Africa. They had a private hospital and my grandmother, who by then realised Charlotte needed work, asked them to train her as a nurse. Which they did. However ...'

She looked at Cat, who said nothing.

'Well, she got pregnant again. And this time Jane wouldn't take it. Sorry, I should say him.'

'Him? Then not Drina Regis?'

'Who?'

'Someone who was claiming to be Rupert's half-sister.'

'Sorry, who is Rupert?'

Cat sighed. 'My son-in-law. I'm pretty sure from what you are saying that Charlotte's first child must be Rupert. He was married to my daughter, but he is now dead. The police say murdered.'

'Oh,' Rebecca said, 'let's come back to that in a moment.'

Cat was surprised at the lack of shock or pain on hearing that her aunt's son was dead. In fact, she hardly seemed interested.

'But as I was saying,' said Rebecca, 'Jane refused to take the second boy.'

'Why not?'

'Well, she'd already had another child, and I think the idea of three was too much. So this time my grandmother did what my mother had suggested in the first place and had him adopted formally.'

'Any idea where?'

'No. My grandmother got remarried to an American and they moved to America, taking Charlotte with them. Bad luck for Charlotte since that's where they met Cartwright.'

'Oh! Cartwright? Hang on ... were you visiting Charlotte Cartwright here?'

'Yes.'

'That was the person I was coming to find out about.'

Rebecca's brows drew together. 'What a coincidence.'

Cat snorted. 'You think? When Victoria is involved, there is no coincidence.'

'Hmm,' replied Rebecca, clearly wanting to get back to her story. 'So, Charlotte needed to be married, and they chose Cartwright because he was English. I think my grand-mother thought they would have some lovely legitimate grandchildren.'

'And?'

'Nothing doing. It appears Cartwright, who was older and a rogue, had had VD and it left him infertile. They went back to England. He went in and out of jobs until eventually finding himself a place as a caretaker in a block of flats in King's Cross. That was a pretty shady area in those days, and the company didn't mind his history.'

'Oh,' said Cat again, and this time Rebecca did stop her narrative and look at the detective.

'This all seems to mean something to you.'

Cat reached into her handbag and found the picture of Lottie Cartwright with the man in Africa.

'Is this your aunt?'

Rebecca glanced. Then investigated the picture more deeply. 'Probably,' she said eventually. 'When we found out about her, my mother did show us some pictures of her as a child. Looks like the same girl, although photos can distort. Who is the man?'

'We don't know,' said Cat.

Rebecca looked up at Cat and stared at her for a long time, her hand encasing her chin. 'The SeeMs Detective Agency, you said. Is that right?'

'Yes.'

'So Stevie is one of your colleagues?'

'Stevie? Yes, but ...'

'I think you need to talk to her.'

'Why?'

Cat felt a sudden shaft of annoyance. Did Stevie already know this and hadn't been telling her colleagues? Not good. She'd have to have words about this. Ever since Victoria had been around, the SeeMs detectives had been divided.

'Look,' said Rebecca, apparently aware Cat was irritated. 'Stevie's a pilot. I understand how she thinks. We like to process information, not jump to conclusions. It can be important when you are flying.'

She glanced at Cat and then continued. 'Stevie contacted me through another pilot. I met her in a nightclub last time I was in London. Thanks to her I made an unusual visit while I was here this time and found a new relation in a place where I never would have thought to find one. I guess she'll tell you about it soon.' She looked at her watch. 'I'd better go. Schools will be finished, and I need to go and see someone before I fly home.' She smiled at Cat. 'Another interesting visit.'

'Oh,' said Cat, now wondering how much more she didn't know, 'anything to do with what you've been telling me?'

'Yes, actually.'

'Go on.'

'Well, I don't want to say too much until I've talked to the girl's mother, but I've got something for the little girl.'

'What's her name?'

'Lagertha Katherine Fletcher. Now I come to think about it, didn't you ask if Jane's surname was Fletcher? I think it must be.'

'My granddaughter,' said Cat.

There was a silence. Rebecca stared at the ceiling. Cat wondered if she wished she hadn't been put in this clearly rather uncomfortable situation. However, Cat wanted to know what was going on and she wasn't going to wait and find out from Caroline. 'Jane Fletcher said your grandparents were extremely rich. They had cut off your mother and didn't speak to her, but they were in touch with Charlotte. Does that mean that Charlotte received a lot of money? Is that what this is about? Does Leggy now inherit it?'

Rebecca made a face. 'Sadly not. Yes, my grandparents were extremely rich, but was my grandmother worldly? I think you can see already she was not. When she remarried, her new husband spent it all. Then Cartwright blackmailed her and eventually she died penniless in a home far less comfortable than this one.

Cartwright approached my mother for money too, but she just laughed in his face. However, it did mean she had her sister's contact details, which was useful after Bella's accident.'

She gave a spurt of laughter. 'Always a silver lining in every cloud.'

So, thought Cat, *so much for the idea that Leggy is an heiress and that is why everybody wants to have a piece of her. What a mystery.* But that also made her wonder about this home.

'If her mother died penniless, how come Charlotte was in such a comfortable home?'

'Good question. Until today I did not know the answer, but I asked the accounts staff here and they told me her stay was paid for through the Bella Chantry Trust.'

Cat bit her lip. She should have realised. This was, of course, all returning to Victoria.

'When would you like to visit my daughter? I'm afraid I can't come with you now, but I should be free in a few hours.'

Rebecca looked at her watch. 'I'll be flying home by then. But if you ring her, you could tell her I'm on my way to Spinners.'

Cat frowned. 'You know Bella used to own Spinners. That she sold it to my daughter for a peppercorn and gave her a lot of debt.'

'Yes, Stevie told me.'

Ha, thought Cat, *what happened to that SeeMs* onc for all, all for one *motto?* Ever since Victoria had been involved, Stevie had been going solo. She tapped her feet on the floor and pulled out her phone.

'I'll ring Caroline and tell her you are coming,' she said.

Rebecca smiled. Perhaps she saw this as an attempt by Cat to regain control.

'Hey, Mum,' said Caroline, 'we are having such fun here. You will not believe what has happened, but anyway, Victor's here and being brilliant. Yes, of course Victoria's twin sister can come over. She's going to have a ball, I can tell you. And you'd better come over when you can. We have a discovery for you that you are going to love.'

Cat stared at her phone and told Rebecca she could visit. She'd never heard Caroline so happy.

CHAPTER 42

THE LABORD'S CHAMELEON IS ONE OF THE SHORTEST LIVING ANIMALS ON THE PLANET

'OK,' said Cat to Miranda as she picked her up from her mother's house. 'OK, if we go to Spinners via King's? I want to talk to someone there. How about you drop me off and then drive the car onto the Embankment? If you stay in the car, you shouldn't get a parking ticket.'

'Great,' said Miranda, 'I get the fun job then. I just hope Agata isn't the traffic warden, or I'll get an earbashing as well as the ticket.'

She got into the driving seat and turned the car towards King's.

When Cat walked into the porter's office at King's, there was a young man sitting there playing *Genshin Impact* on his phone. He jumped up when he saw her entering the lobby and started sorting papers. Looking up vaguely, as though just disturbed, he said, 'Hello, can I help at all?'

'Yes, thank you.' Cat placed her detective card on the desk. 'I'm working for the family of Anthony Dyer, who is involved in a murder case, and I wondered if I could find out which porter was on duty on the night of the 26th of October. Is it possible to find out?'

'The big Black guy?'

Cat frowned. 'Are you asking me if Anthony is a big Black guy or saying there was a big Black guy on the desk that night?'

'No,' he said, 'I was on the desk. I do most of the night duty. It suits me. I'm studying to be an actor and I like working nights. Yeah, I was on duty, and I saw him looking in, then his phone rang, and he disappeared. I didn't think much more of it, until I saw his picture in the papers. Made me laugh when I looked into it. I saw he was being charged for killing a guy in King's Cross and I thought he must be a high-class runner to have been here at eleven p.m. and killing the guy at the same time. Honestly!'

Cat's eyes flared. 'So, you didn't think of calling the police and saying you saw him?'

'Nah,' said the lad, 'why should I? Let the rozzers work it out themselves. I don't go near 'em unless I must. Why would I?'

Cat pulled a face which the man misunderstood.

'Oh, you're OK,' he said. 'I don't mind the private dicks. In fact I watch a lot of true crime. It's good stuff. I'd like to play Sherlock Holmes or one of those guys.'

'Ah!' said Cat, mentally rolling her eyes. 'So, you won't mind if I take down a few details and pass them on to Anthony's lawyer.'

'No problem. I love that Jenny Seagrove; she's the best. Did you see her in *Judge John Deed*? She was super good.'

'Thanks,' said Cat, wondering how long it would take to get his statement. Miranda might get a parking ticket after all.

.   .   .

As they drove the rest of the way to Spinners, Cat's phone rang, and she saw it was George Dyer. She listened to what he had to say, closed the phone and turned to Miranda.

'Do you know what?' she said.

'Yes,' said Miranda, 'I'm a mind reader, but sadly you didn't have your speakerphone on, so no, I clearly don't, although I did hear him say he was sorry he hadn't told you before, but he didn't think it was relevant.'

'Yes,' Cat said, baring her teeth. 'I wish clients would let me decide what is relevant and not make their own decisions. If he'd told me everything at the beginning, I'd have had a much clearer picture.'

Miranda laughed and the car wobbled across the road. 'Still, whatever he said is making you very happy.'

Cat grinned at her. 'And not just me. I have some news and it is going to make everyone very happy indeed, including Caroline.'

Miranda looked at her, causing Cat to blanch. 'Keep your eyes on the road.'

'OK. Go on then. Make me happy too.'

'OK. Well, as you drive to Spinners, I'm going to give you twenty questions and see if you can guess what George Dyer told me.'

'Oh, great.'

Cat laughed. 'Go on then. What's the first question?'

'Does it involve Agata getting cross with me?'

'No! Next.'

CHAPTER 43

A CHAMELEON'S TONGUE
CAN MOVE AT 8,500 FEET PER
SECOND

When Rebecca arrived at Spinners, Caroline was waiting for her. It was still only eight o'clock and the only people sitting at the table with Caroline were her brother, Victor, and Jenny. Jenny was listening with delight to Victor's story of finding the cameras and listening bugs secreted in the most unexpected places.

'There was even one,' he told her, 'in the replica of a Tiger Moth on the wall. She'd only put the camera in the centre of the spinner! Clever, eh? In the spinner at Spinners! I want to meet this Victoria bird. She sounds like someone with a cracking sense of humour.'

Rebecca accepted a cup of tea from Caroline, and they moved away from the others.

'To be honest,' Rebecca said, 'I never thought you could get jasmine tea in a nightclub.'

Caroline laughed. 'You can get hot chocolate too, either with or without brandy. So, Rebecca, my mother said you had something for Leggy. I'm almost afraid to ask what it is since it's clearly causing her a lot of trouble. First Rupert wanted charge of her, then that lunatic Drina Regis takes Oscar to try and kidnap her.'

Rebecca stifled a yawn. Since she didn't know who Oscar and Drina Regis were, she had no interest in them.

'Well, you know already about Rupert's birth and adoption, so you presumably also know my mother had cut any connection with her family. But after Bella's accident, when she perforce met her sister again, she heard all the horrors of life with Cartwright, and she felt sorry for her. But that was it. My mother was a woman of unshakeable morals and Cartwright was still alive, so she didn't want to get too close to Charlotte. Bella, on the other hand, reconnected with her aunt, and when she cut off me and the rest of her family, she allied herself with Charlotte.'

Rebecca sipped her tea.

'Unfortunately, that put her in contact with Cartwright. He was an evil man. I think we were all glad when we heard he was dead. But, after Cartwright died, although my mother still didn't want to contact her sister, she did start understanding the pain she must have given her mother and sister by her unrelenting stance.

'So, the upshot was she decided to start a trust fund for any children of Charlotte's children who could be found. She never managed to contact Charlotte's other child, so she has no idea if he has children, but, of course, it was easy to contact Jane Fletcher and she did so.

'There is only one condition to the trust and that is that the child had to be born within matrimony. Luckily, in your case, or rather the case of your daughter, that is so.'

Caroline raised her eyes to the roof. Everyone wanted to give Leggy gifts but with their own conditions. That was not a gift. It was control. She shook her head. Leggy did not need any restrictions on her life.

Almost as though she read Caroline's mind, Rebecca shrugged. 'Yes, I know! My mother had certain mores. You can hardly expect her to change them while doing a good deed. Anyway, the point is, she started this trust with a very small amount of money in 1988. Obviously, since the money has been well invested, it has accumulated a lot since then and so Leggy will come into a fair amount. I'm happy to transfer the guardianship of it to you when and wherever.'

'No!' said Caroline.

'What? No?'

'No, I don't want my daughter to be given lots of money. Look what having money as a child did for Rupert. I'm not having my daughter corrupted that way.'

Rebecca shrugged. 'Well, you can use it for her education then. I'm told everybody goes to university these days, although neither Bella nor I did, and that it is expensive. Perhaps you want to send her to a fee-paying school.'

'No way,' said Caroline. 'I hated my boarding school. I'd never put her through that. And look what a fee-paying school did for Rupert! No way. Keep your money. Give it to charity.'

'I can't,' said Rebecca, 'it's your daughter's. You are to manage it until she comes of age. My mother made that twenty-one in this case, and then it is hers. You can read it in the terms and conditions!' She laughed. Caroline didn't.

'Is this what Victoria wanted, Leggy's trust fund? Why? She has plenty of money of her own, more probably.'

Rebecca sipped her tea. 'Maybe Bella only wanted it because she couldn't have it.'

Caroline shook her head. 'I can't accept money from you just because you don't want your sister to have it. Give it to her.'

Rebecca raised an eyebrow. 'On another subject, do you know someone called Stevie?'

'Stevie ... what ... yes, I mean, we grew up in the same village ... She's a regular here and a friend. Do you know Stevie?'

'She rang me a few weeks ago. I met her here on my last flight over. She told me all about Victoria/Bella and said she rather thought the reason Bella kept targeting pilots for her schemes was all to do with her desire to take revenge on me for being far more successful than her. A sort of madly extreme sibling rivalry. And, of course, her fury at my mother for having deserted her.'

Caroline frowned. 'And ... so?'

'Well, she had a friend in Cathay look up my schedule—bit naughty of her really, but leaving that aside—and she knew when I was next in the UK, and she asked me to visit a friend of yours in prison.'

'Anthony?' Caroline gasped. 'Stevie asked you to visit Anthony in prison. Why?'

'He wanted to tell me something. I have to say I was amazed, but having talked to your mother, I see it must be true.'

'What? What?'

Rebecca pouted. 'Sorry. I promised I'd let him tell you himself, but it's just I wanted you to know I know too. And now ...' She looked at her watch. 'I'd better go. You can tell me what you want me to do with Leggy's trust when you are ready. It's not going anywhere.'

Caroline shook her head. 'Burn it,' she said. 'I'll get my sister on to the rules and see how we can get rid of it.'

Rebecca waved her hands indifferently. 'Talk to Anthony. Let me know. But until then, it's nice to know I have some new relations. Welcome to our family.' She smiled.

Caroline shook her head and reached for the chocolate. 'Oh God, and I hate all the relations I already have and now I must add you!'

Rebecca looked vaguely amused. 'Really? Well, at least you'll have plenty to chat about with Bella.'

She looked at her watch again. 'OK. I'm off. The skies call. I'll drop in when I'm next back. Won't be for a few weeks. See you.'

After she left, Caroline continued to sit, blankly staring at the table. Why had she ever thought it would be OK to marry Rupert? She simply doubled the number of dreadful people in her life. Now she was related to the mad Bella. No! She wouldn't believe it. It wasn't true. How could it be true? Did anyone else in the world have such a list of awful relationships?

The door from the car park opened automatically and Drina rolled in.

CHAPTER 44

THE VOELTZKOW'S CHAMELEON, EXTINCT FOR 100 YEARS, FOUND ALIVE IN MADAGASCAR!

By the time Stevie arrived at the club, Drina was sitting on one of the small, round tables with a special cut-out for wheelchairs. Stevie got herself a tomato juice and went and sat on the woman's table, opposite her.

'Hello, Victoria,' Stevie said. 'Long time. Must be nearly six months since we met. How do you like the way the new owner is running your nightclub? Pretty successful.'

Drina inclined her head politely, a half-smile indicating her amusement. 'I'm so sorry, young lady, you must have confused me with someone else. My name is Drina Regis and now, if you don't mind, I have come here for some space. To quote someone more famous but less interesting than me, "I want to be alone."'

Stevie smiled. 'Yes, indeed, alone in the space of the sky, to quote that Victoria you don't know. Now, since you don't know me, you won't know that I'm a pilot. If you had been a pilot too, you would know that many of us must build hours in order to get enough time to qualify for a commercial licence and then start the long and merry path onto the airlines.'

Drina tapped on the table. 'Interesting, no doubt, but, as I said, I wish to be alone.'

'And so you shall but not yet. When I was hour-building I had many jobs flying to the Isle of Wight. Many of my clients wanted to see Osborne House, which, as you know, was Queen Victoria's favourite haunt and where she was known by her nickname, Drina.'

Drina sneered. 'Victoria equals Drina. Very clever, not! But so? I have a queen's nickname; however, my name is Corinna, which also shortens to Drina.'

'Indeed it does,' said Stevie. 'We went to visit Emily Regis at the house she owns and which you claimed belonged to you, and she told us all about you.'

Drina sneered. 'Indeed, dear lady? I don't think I've had the pleasure of meeting Emily Regis, probably an imposter if she's claiming my house is hers.'

Stevie continued. 'Corinna Regis was a beautiful baby, born in 1970 in Uganda.'

Drina shrugged. 'So, I was in born in Uganda. No law against that, is there?'

Stevie raised an eyebrow and continued. 'Indeed. However, Emily was born fifteen years after her sister. She has a house in Chelsea and needed a sitter while she went travelling to look after the accumulation of birds, lizards, cats and insects. She advertised and was contacted by a Charlotte Cartwright, who could move in as soon as Emily required.'

Stevie glanced at Drina and saw she was listening.

'Emily went to see the world, and Charlotte came to live in her house, the only odd thing being that Charlotte Cartwright also lived in King's Cross.'

Drina raised a lip. 'Lots of people have two addresses.'

'Yes. Except you invited Caroline to your house in Chelsea, where Charlotte Cartwright was house-sitting, and told her your name was Drina Regis. Why was that? Could it be that Drina Regis was a fictitious name, but a name that could be identified with the spacious, attractive house and lots of wealth?'

'Fictitious?' Drina said, moving in her chair. 'Here I am, flesh and blood.'

'Apparently! Then Drina Regis claimed to be Rupert's half-sister.'

'Claimed? I have the DNA to prove it,' said Drina, pulling up her phone and producing Rupert's DNA chart. 'Here, see for yourself.'

Stevie ignored the proffered phone. 'Until I met you and recognised your digital fingerprint, it never occurred to me it was possible to manipulate DNA and genealogy charts, but I'm learning every day.'

Stevie finished her tomato juice. 'Who would benefit from being Drina Regis, and who would benefit from being the sibling of a drunk, a divorcee and someone without any money or prospects? And why only claim to be his sister after his death? Why not while he was still alive? Then there was your interest in Leggy. Was Leggy coming into an inheritance? If so, where from?'

She looked at Drina.

'So, I realised we had to look much further back. Back to Bella Chantry, the woman who faked her own death not once but twice. First in a car crash, and then by falling out of a Tiger Moth. Bella Chantry who was reborn as Victoria Bell, the owner of Spinners Nightclub. Obviously, Bella/Victoria was still alive and on the run. We knew that because you kidnapped Amy, but what we didn't know was where you were now.'

'Golly,' said Drina, 'what an immensely clever person I am, so many disguises. A chameleon amongst women.' She giggled. 'However, you know, truth is often very simple.'

Stevie raised her eyebrows. 'Not with you. Then I remembered Victoria told me her mother had cut off her sister years ago. Your mother's surname was now Chantry, like her husband, but her maiden name was Robertson. She was Mina Robertson. Charlotte Cartwright had a sister called Mina.

'I was able to get a friend to look at your hospital records and I discovered Bella Chantry had a blood transfusion from Charlotte Robertson. Was she your missing aunt? But to be sure I decided to contact your sister. This wasn't hard as your sister has something in common with me.'

'Oh,' said Drina, 'are you farmer-fisted too? Fly the plane as though it is a tractor, do you? Poor passengers.'

'Very funny, not,' said Stevie. 'So I contacted Rebecca, pilot to pilot, and she came and met me here.'

Drina frowned, but Stevie continued. 'Neither you nor Rebecca had been told about Charlotte by your mother, let alone that she'd had two illegitimate children. All hushed up in a nice middle-class way. But Bella is in a car crash and nearly dies. She needs a blood transfusion, and guess who had the only blood that would fit? Aunt Charlotte. So your mother was forced to contact her sister.'

Drina frowned. 'Lots of your actions sound illegal to me. My hospital records—or rather those of Bella Chantry— should be known to me and my medics alone.'

Stevie continued. 'Charlotte, like yourself, badly treated by your mother. I imagine at this point you started to see a perfect way of taking revenge on your family for going off to

Australia and leaving you to cope on your own. Your mother couldn't stand weakness, could she? And you were now the weakest member of the family.'

Drina yawned. 'Are you hoping to write a film? If so, it needs a bit more sex appeal.'

Stevie sneered. 'You think? We haven't got to the good bits yet. Having established a connection with the real Charlotte Cartwright, you got to know her. And she was the one who told you about the two children her family had forced her to adopt. You decided to take revenge on her behalf as well as your own.

'You set about finding Charlotte's birth children. I imagine it was a long search. If you started in the 1990s, there was no DNA available in the public domain, and much of your work would have to be done in libraries. But then someone—and we'll come to who in a moment—suggested you change your name to Victoria and start a nightclub.'

Drina moved her shoulders restlessly. 'Anthony, my therapist, suggested I start a nightclub. Shame he's now in jail for murder.'

'Did he? Is he? That's what you told me, but I think someone else suggested it as a perfect place to snoop on people who were not necessarily conforming to society's norms.'

Drina looked at her watch. 'Snoop? I would say intellectual research.'

Stevie smiled. 'So, now you had two ways of researching. Firstly, the nightclub, where you were being heavily subsidised for the useful information you were passing on. And secondly, you were able to use the network of the subsidising party to get information on Charlotte's adopted children.'

Drina waggled her shoulders dismissively. 'You are confusing me! What is this "subsidising party", something where you bring your own booze? Oh, sorry, silly me, - you don't do jokes, do you?'

Stevie continued without smiling. 'It wasn't hard for you to find Rupert. Charlotte knew the name of the woman who adopted him, Jane Fletcher. Jane only had two children and one was a girl. But the second child was much harder. Charlotte didn't even know if it was a boy or a girl.'

'Boring!' interrupted Drina. 'Now if you don't mind, I have reserved all the seats at this table for a game of bridge.'

Stevie shook her head. 'Trying to deflect me, darling!'

Drina smoothed her hands over the surface of the table.

Stevie continued. 'Then I had a moment of weakness. Perhaps Drina Regis was a real person who had nothing to do with Victoria or Bella Chantry. So, I checked the DNA I took from the hairdresser and discovered that Drina Regis shared thirteen percent of her DNA with Rupert Fletcher.'

'What?' yelled Drina, startling the nearby drinkers. 'You stole my hair and checked my DNA? That's illegal.'

She breathed deeply and continued calmly. 'Besides, this is no surprise. I've already told Caroline that I am Rupert's long-lost sister and now so happy to take a large part in her life as aunt to the lovely Leggy.'

'But you aren't, are you? If you were his half-sister, you would share twenty-five percent of his DNA.'

Drina shrugged. 'Look at his chart—it says he shares twenty-five percent with me.'

Stevie smiled cynically. 'However, you had forgotten about that elusive thing, the Y chromosome. You didn't have it and Rupert's real sibling did. So, you definitely were not Rupert's sibling—that was a boy.'

'Oh,' said Drina, 'so you've discovered my secret. I was

born a boy, but had to have a sex change ... My mother insisted ...'

'Oh, please!' said Stevie. 'Lie and deny? I think not! You were an identical twin with another girl. Either you were both boys or both girls. But when I checked your DNA, I found out something else. You shared one hundred percent of Bella Chantry's DNA. So, Drina Regis was Victoria Bell, who, as we have already seen, was Bella Chantry.'

Drina sneered. 'Boring.'

'But then I asked myself if you weren't Rupert's sibling, who was?'

She looked at Drina, who was silent.

As Stevie was about to continue, there was a kerfuffle at the other end of the bar, near the entrance, followed by cheers and clapping. Both women looked over.

Caroline ran past, arms stretched out, yelling as she got to their table. 'It's Anthony. He's been released.'

The Anthony who walked into the club seemed a shadow of the previous buoyant man who took a positive stance on every issue. Caroline had stopped in the middle of the room. For a moment he too paused, then walked on to her and took her hands. Everyone in the bar stopped and watched them.

'I know "thank you" is inadequate but even so ... Thank you, both for your complete faith in me and for my freedom. Without your mother and her friends, I would undoubtably have been in prison for much longer, if not forever.' He paused, then he said, 'But I have something else to tell you. Something you need to know.'

'What?'

'I am ... Rupert's half-brother. Charlotte Cartwright was my birth mother.'

Caroline's hand flew to her mouth. 'What? You are my brother-in-law?'

'Yes.'

'But ...'

'I didn't know until Stevie told my parents the results of the DNA tests.'

He smiled at her, but to Caroline it made no sense. All she knew was a pain was creeping through her body and her mind was asking: *Is it legal to marry your former husband's brother?*

She watched him as he walked over to where Drina and Stevie were sitting at the bridge table.

'Well, Bella,' he said, 'perhaps I should thank you. You certainly have changed my life, my outlook, and my family knowledge. If you hadn't done DNA tests, I wouldn't know who I was.' He swallowed. 'I think you will now be bene-fiting yourself from some of this useful knowledge. Enjoy your stay in Life's University.'

Drina said nothing, and he moved away to thank others in the club.

'Huh!' said Drina. 'More guilty people outside prison than in it,' she said.

'Luckily,' said Stevie, 'you are going to change that by a statistic of one.'

'What are you actually accusing me of?' asked Drina.

'Murder. Identify theft. Even burglary ...'

'Of whom? I have papers to prove I am Drina Regis.'

'Forged. Drina Regis died in 1973 of congenital heart failure.'

'You'll never prove it. And who am I supposed to have murdered?'

'Rupert.'

Drina laughed. 'And how do you suggest I did that when Rupert was shot on the sixth floor in a building with no lift?'

'Simple,' said Stevie. 'And it explains why you needed to become Charlotte Cartwright in that block of flats.'

Drina rolled her eyes.

'Mrs Cartwright had the keys, not only to the attic but to the dumbwaiter. You only had to sit in the box and press the buttons for the roof to be transported to the floor above Rupert's. You then came out of the lift in your chair and moved over to the door. Since you can walk a little, you then went down the short stairway and shot Rupert as he lay helpless, inert. Full of the whisky your helper Oscar had given him.

You then left one of Anthony's hairs where it could be found by the police and went back to the lift and down to the car park, where you had left your car. Oddly, the blood stain on the floor, Rupert's blood, which you either didn't notice or thought would help your case, worked against you since it got me wondering.'

Drina frowned.

'You drove over to Anthony's flat. You sat outside between the cars, waiting for Oscar to go in and take the caretaker Mihai out for a drink. They had worked bars together in the past and Mihai knew him as Charles FitzRoy, as I saw from the messages on Mihai's phone. Oscar got the lift code out of Mihai, which he sent to you. Then, while they drank and drank, you went up in the lift and placed the now clean gun under the bed and the broken-up silencer around the room. You placed a picture of Caroline next to Anthony's picture of his family, in a place where Mihai would see it. You went back down to Mihai's station, wiped the CCTV from the place where you were seen between the cars, hoping that he would make the connection between Caroline's photo and the woman sitting watching the house. Perhaps Oscar talked about Anthony's girlfriend, put suspicion into Mihai's mind.

'Then you went back to your house in Chelsea to become Drina Regis once again, apparently completely unaware of Rupert's murder. You must have thought you had both Anthony and Caroline marked as villains.'

'Speculation,' said Drina. 'You'll never prove it.'

'But the police will. And before then we have you for identity theft and breaking and entering at Caroline's house. We have you on camera.'

'What possible motive could I have for killing Rupert? My friend. My colleague. My helper.' She ostentatiously pulled out a large handkerchief and wiped away a tear.

'Yes, I wondered about that too. And then I realised. Rupert knew about the Y chromosome. He knew he had a brother, not a sister. And he told you so. He wanted money. Perhaps you didn't mind the loss of money, but you have always hated losing control. Especially to Rupert, the leaky vessel. He might let out the information at any time. So, you killed him and then played the devastated sister.'

Drina lifted a bored shoulder. 'You'll never get a conviction.'

Stevie looked at her. Slowly she said, 'And why do you say that? Is it because you know something about the police system I don't?'

Drina was silent, but she watched Stevie closely.

'You know,' said Stevie, 'for ages I could not fathom how Victoria survived jumping from an aircraft. Yes, you had a parachute when you jumped out of the Tiger Moth, but you really cannot walk much, and your car was still back in your hideaway.'

Drina made a noise. 'So again Victoria was too clever for you.'

Stevie tilted her head. 'For a while I was wondering if you were right. But then I got thinking. First, there was the dead homeless man with all the clues leading to you and no interest from the police until the SeeMs Detective Agency highlighted the connection. Then, there was the fall out of the Tiger Moth when nobody could find the body. Then, you reappeared, kidnapped Amy and disappeared again, but nobody bothered to look for you except the SeeMs Detective Agency. Why?

'And then we get onto all the DNA and the fact that Rupert, or rather you as his manager, was able to do the DNA not only of himself and his daughter but his wife, his mother-in-law and even his half-brother. Something that most companies simply don't allow. Well, it all seemed to be leading somewhere, but where?'

Drina shrugged. 'A dead end most likely.'

'No. I no longer thought that, but I knew my thinking was almost crazy and it would seem ridiculous, but then I came across a newspaper article by Jacqui about her under-cover policeman boyfriend and the father of her baby. You still following me?'

Drina sneered. 'All sounds irrelevant to me. I don't have a baby.'

'Well, it made me think I probably wasn't mad. There were so many things pointing that way. First, your nightclub actively recruited people who would not be welcome in other nightclubs. And it made a huge profit, despite having all the best brands of everything and sometimes not a lot of clients. Could there be an expense account behind you?

'Then, there was the old man in the Black Scabbard, oddly called Charles FitzRoy—bastard of the King. Roy and

Regis both relate to king, something for your humour. Anthony said he looked like a boxer, and when I looked up Charles FitzRoy, he was indeed. More than that, he had been police champion four years in a row.'

'So you found a man called Charles FitzRoy who was a champion boxer,' said Drina. 'Do you want a medal?'

'Then, we have the barman at the Black Scabbard. When he met us here at Spinners, he recognised Oscar as the same man who came to the Black Scabbard. Oscar, a barman you trained, and Caroline inherited. A lovely man, trusted by Caroline. The same man who "proved" to Caroline that you really were Drina Regis. A man we know used to be an undercover policeman and went rogue. Who controlled him now?'

Drina laughed. 'That Caroline really isn't normal, is she? Anyone else faced with a rich auntie who wanted to leave her daughter all her money would have jumped at it, but that Caroline was off like a fox had got her tail. Jesuuusss!'

'I started researching the deep web and what did I discover?'

Drina shrugged.

'You were funded, although, of course not employed, by first the SDS and then, when they were discredited, by the NPOIU.'

Drina yawned. 'All sounds unprovable to me. SDS? NPOIU? What funny initials. Never heard of them.'

Anthony walked past their table, heading for Caroline, who was still standing in the middle of the room, staring into the distance.

'Your mother is outside,' he said, taking her hands. 'She's going to drive me down to Owly Vale so I can see my parents and Leggy. My niece, Leggy, will be the first person I have ever met who shares my blood. At least, the first person who

I know shares my blood, there may now be many others. I never thought I cared about it, but now I see I do.'

He looked at Caroline. 'They told me, you know. My parents. They told me I was adopted when I was fourteen. But I wasn't interested. I loved them too much to care about my birth parents. But ... now ...' He shrugged. 'Perhaps things look different when you are older.'

'What will you do now?' asked Caroline, grasping a chair, trying not to fall over.

'I don't know, Caro. I need time. Time to think. Stevie has asked my mother and father to stay on in her house with her mother, so I'll go there and spend some time getting to know your daughter. If that suits you?'

'Yes. Of course. I mean, yes, take your time, Anthony. But I might come down too—say, tomorrow.'

He took her hands and held them to his cheeks, the knuckles making little indentations in his skin. Then he gently placed them against her cheeks.

'See you tomorrow then.'

She watched him leave, holding her hands against her cheeks. Miranda walked over, put her arm around Caroline and hugged her. 'Chocolate?'

Caroline shook her head. 'No, thanks, Miranda. I learnt to live without therapy. I can learn to live without chocolate. Leggy will always be the most important thing in my life. What happens next will be a challenge, but I can cope. I can wait.'

'I wonder what Rupert would have been like if he had been brought up with Anthony?' said Miranda quietly.

Caroline looked at her. 'Yes. One brother a therapist. The other a drunk.'

* * *

'So,' said Drina, 'what now? You pull me, crying and screaming, out of your friend Caroline's nightclub? I don't think so. There's so much scandal here already I think I would find many are on my side.'

'The other barmen for example,' said Stevie.

Drina looked at the table.

'Yes, after we knew about Oscar, we looked at the others, and what did we find? Tom, aka Mr Two Salaries, one from you, one from Caroline. Caroline quickly realised that if she sacked Tom, he'd be useless to you. Tom's not your body-guard like Oscar. So she gave him a choice and he decided to switch loyalties. Wise man!'

Victoria shrugged. 'Rats, sinking ship. Pah. There'll be others. There always are. There are always people who can be bought. You may think you've won, Stevie, but I'll be back. And until then I'll dominate your dreams, your thoughts. You won't escape me!'

'This time you will not escape justice,' said Stevie. 'The police who will take you in are not interested in your under-cover history. All they want to know was who shot Rupert: you or Oscar.'

Oscar came over. 'They are waiting for you,' he said quietly. 'And me.'

'OK,' said Drina, 'let's go.'

He pushed her outside, where the police were waiting with a van.

Stevie joined Caroline staring at the exit. The door where Rupert left to die. Anthony left to find himself and Victoria left for prison. 'What will happen to Victoria?' asked Caroline. 'It can't be easy being in prison in a wheelchair.'

'No,' said Stevie, refusing to feel sympathy for her former girlfriend. 'They've got our information about how and why she killed Rupert. And they have her for breaking and entering into your house. And identity theft. This time she really won't be back.'

Caroline looked at Stevie. 'Victoria has used up a lot of her lives, but she still has seven left,' she said. 'How many more times can she fake her own death?'

The End

SNEAK PEAK INTO THE NEXT BOOK

Murder Under the All-Seeing Eye

Prologue: Singapore 1967

Slithering down the fire escape as fast as possible she stopped at the balcony outside her room; their room. The French windows were open, the curtains blowing in and out: she had closed both window and curtains when she left.

She stopped, teetering on the metal platform and, stupidly, unable to restrain her curiosity, peeked in. An unknown man was turning over the bed, ripping the sheets, pulling out the stuffing from the mattress. Looking for something? But what?

He pulled her Revelation suitcase from under the bed and his parang flashed in the lamp light as he brought it noiselessly down, slashing through the leather as though it was paper.

She gave an involuntary gasp and stumbled back. Her

heel caught in the wrought iron grid, her shoes making a clacking noise.

Inside the room, the man's head shot up. For a moment she saw his face. Young. Her own age perhaps. European. Then he turned, speaking to someone in the other room.

'What was that?' His accent was English.

'I didn't hear anything.' The second voice was too faint to analyse, but they were still speaking in English, not Cantonese.

She didn't wait for any more but slid down the rest of the fire escape and on to the gravel beneath.

Stepping away from the hotel she put out her hands instinctively, for a moment she had slipped into total darkness, before her night-vision returned. Here, in the Kampong, it was completely different from outside the Raffles Hotel where the glare of lights had blinded her. Here the night was black but not silent: the noise of the cicadas behind her competed with the endless insistence of the jammed traffic ahead. She ran across the gravel and dashed into the choking fumes of the crawling cars.

Now, backlit by the slow-moving headlights, the men saw her. She heard a cry behind her, low though it was. Almost a whisper. 'There she is!'

The men were out on the balcony. She heard the drumming of their feet as they started to descend in the semi-darkness.

She jumped into the road, weaving in and out of the virtually stationary traffic, oblivious to the hoots and the curses. On the opposite side were smaller streets, leading who knows where. She didn't care as long as it was away from the men. She skipped, half running, not wanting to arouse attention, moving quickly with long strides past stalls selling everything from satays to tee shirts. She had to weave her passage to avoid knocking into the drinkers, who were leaning back and enjoying their beers. She steadied her steps to prevent tripping over the rubbish those same drinkers threw onto the street behind them, but the smell of rotting vegetables made her pause even before she saw the dead dog. She swallowed and forced her legs over it and on.

Entering an alleyway, she began running again. This lane was too small for night stalls, although the houses probably still held the same numbers of occupants crowded into the three stories. Washing straddled across the narrow streets and balanced on bamboo poles from windows. Shirts. Vests. Trousers. Pyjamas. Cheongsams. Kebayas. Even sheets.

Despite her speedy passage she wondered how the householders knew how far to put out their washing poles before it tumbled into the streets. She giggled. How was it you could find laughter in the deepest pain?

Somewhere she could hear dogs; howling, barking, sniffing. Were they in the narrow houses or were they following her? With the men. Who were they? Would they have dogs? She reasoned 'no' as they had followed her from the hotel, down the fire escape and dogs could surely not do that.

The edges of the alley crowded together almost touching now, too narrow for anything more than a bicycle. In India they had horses to work in the meaner streets, did they use horses here? Donkeys? Definitely too narrow for elephants? But was it too hot for horses? These thoughts teemed through her brain in time with the reverberating pulse of her sore feet. She was still wearing her evening clothes, her elegant heels. Blisters began bursting out as she ran but it was better than exposing her bare feet to the mounds of rubbish underfoot. Broken glass? Very likely. Syringes. Extremely possible. Anything and everything went on here in the backstreets. A very different side of the town to the one she was used to seeing. Her Singapore had theatres, dances, racecourses, smart people. This was the opposite side of a strangely fetid coin.

An unexplainable clang sounded behind her, and the thought of what might happen forced her forward like a hurricane pushing on her back. She was not planning to escape the parang only to die of some banal infection here amongst the rubbish, the hanging washing, and the satay sticks. She had not fought out of a life of poverty to die in someone else's deprivation.

And then, just as her instinct told her she was approaching safer streets ahead, a blockage emerged from the darkness. This lane ended. Just like that. A house? A wall? Whatever it was, she was trapped.

She turned. Her pursuers had entered the top of the alley – two men lit up by the streetlights behind. One man still held the parang, which glittered in the lamplight. She was shrouded by the darkness. Slowly she edged along the darkest wall feeling its roughness. Could she rush them? It happened in films. But she was too slight. Too female. They'd catch her. Drag her somewhere and then... She was worth more dead than alive.

Something hard cut into her back. A door handle. She forced back the giggle that rose into her throat and pushed the door. She fell into a black space. Stumbling down some stone steps. As pushed herself back onto her feet, a hand shot out and grabbed her arm. Thin fingers like a claw gripped her flesh, hurting the bone. An oddly accented voice said, 'quick, here.'

The door clicked shut. Would the men hear it? Would they follow her? Was any she safer here? Her choices were limited.

Two claws grabbed her hands in the dark and put them on someone's waist. Uncertainly she clasped the body, feeling the protruding hip bones. A woman. Malnourished. Chinese or Malay, possibly Eurasian. Too narrow for European. She mirrored the woman's steps through the total darkness pairing the girl's slender thighs, being led to who knows where. Conjoined twins. A curiously close dance where she could no longer see, only feel.

Were the men behind her? They would see the door. Would they come through?

The journey through the blackness seemed endless. The smell almost overpowering. What was this place? A mixture of putrefaction. Of sweat. Of bodies. Of incense. Of opium. There were people here. Lying down. Smoking. Who were they? Occasionally she stepped on something that felt alive. Her foot rolled on an unresisting... what... arm? Leg? She gagged. Tripped. She held tighter to her guide. Leg to leg. Hip to hip. Keep going. Where there is life there is hope. Family motto. Not her family, but she took it over with the man.

And then the guide stopped. So quickly they almost fell. Her arms slipped around the thin body in a spooning embrace.

The girl opened a wooden door and pushed her into the light. She turned enough to see a lined face. Eurasian. Looked old. But was it really? The voice sounded old too, but hips and claws had been young, adolescent.

'Go,' said the woman brusquely, again speaking in accented English, 'see it?'

As she turned and looked down the street the door slammed behind her. She saw a flashing sign. Amber Mansions. She was in Orchard Road. Thank Heaven. She put her hand in her skirt pocket and felt the sharp outline. Her passport.

She sighed and accelerated into a sprint she had never achieved at school. Here she would be safe, at least for a while.

AFTERWORD

The title of this book The Killer Chameleon Mystery is a reference to the ability of the main character, Victoria, to hide in plain sight, just like a lizard melding in to its background. However, in researching about chameleons to ascertain whether this was a suitable title I came across so many other fascinating aspects of these clever little creatures that I couldn't resist using them as chapter headings. It may seem a little quirky to some readers but I hope that others will enjoy the facts.

ACKNOWLEDGMENTS

This book is dedicated to Andrew Healey, who died earlier this year. Many of the things I learnt about wheelchair usage came from his knowledge and the way he lived, which was amazing. Before his accident he was a successful Navy pilot where, amongst other things, he was awarded Queen's Commendations for Valuable Service in the Air for a challenging night rescue of the crew from the MV Melpol, which was ablaze and adrift in a storm. He then moved into the civilian world as a helicopter pilot. Here he was involved in a serious helicopter accident which changed his life but which he refused to allow to prevent him doing the things he loved.

He also edited a helicopter magazine for many years and wrote articles in several of the dailies highlighting the difficulties people in wheelchairs have in everyday life.

This short piece is from his wife, Linda Healey.

'He broke his back when he was 32 years old in 1985.

Not only did Andy take part in a London to Paris charity bike ride (on his handbike), he also completed the New York Marathon in a wheelchair to celebrate his 50th birthday.

He enjoyed being involved in local amateur dramatics and always managed to incorporate his walking sticks and wheelchair into his performances whether it was as the hungover man in Mr Banana or the alien in a panto!

He did love cowboy music and also cowboy films. We

even went on holiday to a 'dude ranch' in Arizona where they hauled him on to a horse (he hadn't ridden before) complete with a cowboy hat!

I would also like to thank Becky Stradwick for her editorial, Eleanor Smith for copy editing and Abbey Rutherford for proof reading. To my beta readers and to my family and friends for their many helpful comments and laughter!

ABOUT THE AUTHOR

This is Gina Cheyne's fourth crime novel and the fourth in the SeeMs Detective Agency series (the agency that looks beneath the apparent to the reality beneath). The first one, The Mystery of the Lost Husbands, came out in 2021.

The second, Murder in the Cards in 2022. The third, which is the forerunner to this book, The Mystery of the Homeless Man, came out earlier this year.

Gina worked as a helicopter pilot and instructor, including taking part in the UK team for the World Helicopter Games in Moscow in 1994, and in the USA in 1996.

She is also a keen Tiger Moth pilot and edited a helicopter lifestyle magazine called Helicopter Life.

She now lives in West Sussex with her husband and dogs. She has written under various names and for many years edited a lifestyle magazine and taught flying.

She was awarded the HAI Lightspeed Salute to Excellence in Communications Award 2022.

ALSO BY GINA CHEYNE

Book 1 The Mystery of the Lost Husbands

Book 2 Murder in the Cards

Book 3 The Mystery of the Homeless Man

Book 4 The Chameleon Killer Mystery

Biscuit and Oscar Learn to Fly

Under the name Georgina Hunter-Jones

Atlantic Warriors

Peckham Diamonds